The Fall

of Jordan

Rome

Greg Lawrence

Published by Christmas Lake Press 2025
www.christmaslakecreative.com
Copyright © 2025 by Greg Lawrence

ISBN 978-1-960865-32-8

Interior layout by Daiana Marchesi

DEDICATION

To those lives lost and irrevocably scarred on 9-11-2001

Preface

On September 11th, 2001, at just after 8:45 AM a Boeing 767 crashed into the North Tower of the World Trade Center. It would be the first of four plane crashes caused by terrorism that day. There would be another into the South Tower, one into the Pentagon, and one into a field Near Shanksville, western Pennsylvania.

A total of 2996 people were killed in the World Trade Center attacks. Forty percent of those individuals would never have their remains discovered. In addition, 3000 children were left as survivors of those lost. Countless publications have carefully documented these events that changed the world. Regardless, not all the stories have been told.

TABLE OF CONTENTS

PART I

JORDAN ROME AND JACKSON MARTIN

Bisbee, Arizona
1977: 24 Years Before

I THINK HE'S DEAD

"*MI BEBÉ... I THINK HE'S DEAD,*" my mother said without a trace of emotion. Standing inches from her motionless husband, her calm eyes had lost the look of terror from just sixty seconds before. There was no expression reflecting the surreal circumstance—just a blank stare from her black pupils and blended irises. She took no notice of the stream of blood running down her cheek from the top of her hairline, or the red and blue marks on her throat left by the massive hands of her attacker.

"Impossible," I said. "I didn't hit him hard enough to hurt him. Besides, the bastard is unkillable."

The man in question—my father—sat at the dining room table with his elbows on his knees and his head slumped from his shoulders. Even from this angle, I could see that his head looked almost deformed, blood pooling at his feet between his legs.

I was in my room when I heard her shout, "Where is my son?!"—followed by a crash of furniture and, finally, a scream of fear. Immediately, I knew he was on her again, as he had been so many times in the past.

But this time was different. The house had been a powder keg over the last couple of days.

I grabbed the baseball bat from the corner of my closet and ran to the kitchen, where he had straddled her, both hands around her neck. She saw me standing there, holding the bat, and our eyes locked. As always, her instruction was the same: she pushed her free hand toward me and mouthed—barely audible—"*Go away.*" She was more afraid of his wrath toward me than concerned for her own safety.

But this time, I did not—would not—yield.

"Get OFF her, or I swear I'll KILL you," I said, holding the bat as if I were at home plate.

He turned and looked at me with the same expression he always had when he was like this. "This" meant explosive—fully fueled with brown liquor. His eyes were wild, his face reddened and glistening with sweat.

He screamed something incomprehensible. Though the words were unclear, the message was unmistakable: back off.

I cursed him again.

This time, he didn't turn to acknowledge me. He only tightened his grip on his wife, my mother, his lifelong scapegoat for all his failures.

I lifted the bat and swung, intending to strike his shoulders and knock him off her. But in that instant, he turned and the bat didn't connect with his back, but the side of his head.

He stood for several seconds, then staggered to his favorite chair at the head of the kitchen table. He pushed it back, dropped into the seat, then rocked forward and back. Finally, he rested his elbows on his knees and lowered his head, where he froze, like a mannequin.

CHAPTER 2

BISBEE, ARIZONA

IN 1877, JACK DUNN WAS leading an expedition in the Mule Mountains of the Arizona Territory. A desert patch of wilderness, Arizona would not become a state until Valentine's Day, thirty-five years later. The purpose of the expedition was to provide safe passage from Apache Indian raids for various prospectors and travelers moving between the silver mining town of Tombstone, Arizona, and Mexico.

During one of these expeditions, Jack discovered that his horse refused to drink surface water. He knew that meant the water contained excessive mineral content. Jack documented his observations and sought feedback from his friend George Warren, a local prospector working the Mule Mountains. Warren immediately understood the significance of the find, and the two men filed a claim together. However, Jack and George would not share in the potential wealth their discovery promised. Shortly after recording their claim, Warren, in a drunken state, wagered that he could outrun another saloon patron's horse on foot, using the claim as his bet. He lost. Warren would die drunk and penniless, despite his multi-million dollar find.

In 1881, however, investors led by Judge Dewitt Bisbee recognized the land's value. They created a financial syndicate to launch the Copper Queen Mine and establish a town that would bear the judge's name: Bisbee, Arizona—a name that would endure despite the fact that the judge never set foot there.

The Bisbee find was unprecedented. The copper ore showed productivity between 9 and 20 percent, where most ore yielded less than one-half of one percent. Bisbee quickly attracted thousands of opportunists seeking their fortune in copper, silver, and gold. In 1889, a rail spur connected Bisbee to both the northern and coastal United States. By 1890, the town had exploded in size, boasting over fifty saloons and thirty-six brothels, relieving miners of their hard-earned wages. Bisbee quickly gained a reputation as the most corrupt, dirtiest, and most violent town in the West.

Though film and literature often romanticized its northern neighbor Tombstone, Bisbee was the true center of commerce and lawlessness. It offered another unique benefit to criminals: just eleven miles from the Mexican border, it provided a convenient escape route for those willing to prey on the weak and flee consequences. By the end of the century, civic leaders could no longer tolerate the lawlessness and began efforts to bring order to the community.

At the same time, Phelps Dodge purchased the mine and provided the capital needed to civilize the city. Roads, sewers, schools, and even a hospital were constructed in the now-booming downtown. Suburbs like Lowell and Warren grew to meet the increasing demand for housing. A modest settlement transformed into a city of 25,000 within three decades. By 1910, Bisbee was the largest city between St. Louis and San Francisco. The Copper Queen Mine became the second most productive copper mine in the world, and its sister operation, the Lavender Mine, emerged as one of the largest open-pit mines of its day. Two thousand miles of tunnel lay beneath Bisbee, yielding thousands of tons of ore each year. When World War I created a surge in demand for copper, prices soared, and Bisbee thrived. This prosperity brought unprecedented wealth to the town, fueling the rise of lavish homes, hotels, restaurants, and theaters.

But mining was a business that flourished—or failed—based on labor costs. Profits and labor were inextricably tied. Management understood this and continuously imported lower-cost labor from Mexico and other parts of the country. The resulting population boom created a downward spiral in wages and an upward surge in housing costs. Miners were caught in the middle. Bisbee became a city of "haves and have-nots." The miners' answer was unionization; management's response was union suppression through violence.

On July 12, 1917, two thousand armed men rounded up 1,286 miners suspected of supporting union efforts and forced them into cattle cars. The miners endured a twelve-hour journey in 90-degree heat without food or water, eventually being dropped off at Tres Hermanas, New Mexico. Outraged by the arrival of penniless vagrants on his doorstep, the governor of New Mexico protested to President Woodrow Wilson.

This highly publicized conflict prompted calls for action and led to superficial federal legislation addressing union rights across the United States. The real response, however, came more subtly in the case of United States v. Wheeler, in which the Supreme Court ruled that the federal government had no authority to intervene in such private disputes, even those involving kidnapping or deportation. No one was ever prosecuted for the events of 1917, and none of the deported miners ever returned to Bisbee.

Though future tactics would be more discreet, both sides learned from the episode. Labor understood that any gains would require solidarity, and management learned that violence could be effective—if employed quietly.

***

In 1950, a young Irishman from Boston calling himself Finn Rome arrived in Bisbee to take advantage of the boom. At six feet two and 250 pounds, he was a large man for his time and considered himself an ideal candidate for the physical demands of mining. He had a great propensity for bragging, drinking, and fighting, all of which were enhanced by his fondness for Irish whiskey. Not much was known about Finn before he came to Bisbee. I don't think anyone was even certain that his real name was Finn Rome. When intoxicated, I had also heard him refer to himself as Sean or Kyle. But in Bisbee, he went by Finn, and he, like thousands of others, was a miner.

Finn spent his first five years down in the Copper Queen performing the world's most dangerous profession alongside his coworkers. One Tuesday in 1955, a fight broke out between one of the foremen and several of the miners. This was commonplace in the Copper Queen. Finn would always tell the story heroically, but my bet is that he was drunk, lost his temper, and stepped in. The foreman was spared, and Finn's life changed. He received a new job title, placing him in charge of "Special Projects," and his pay went from $4,000 a year to over $8,000—a small fortune for a man of his stature. Most importantly, Finn no longer toiled in the mines. In fact, the only time he went underground was to deal with a special problem.

Most of his work involved visiting people at night or waiting outside a tavern to "explain" a new policy decision regarding that employee's activities. Though Finn was never directly instructed to take another person's life, his "explanations" often involved a conversation punctuated by a broken limb, busted nose, or missing teeth. Finn became both respected and feared in Bisbee. He was the tool of intimidation used by the city's largest employer to make a point, and local law enforcement understood the immunity his job afforded him.

Like many miners, Finn headed eleven miles south to Naco, Mexico, when he needed to blow off steam. The community preferred that young men take their drunken, illicit behavior out of Bisbee. At the time, the border was nearly invisible, and travel between Naco and various border towns was commonplace. Finn drove a bright red 1953 Ford Sunliner convertible with a red and white interior and kept his ever-present polished chrome Colt revolver within easy reach in the glove compartment. The years of abuse had not yet taken their toll on his appearance. His eyes were still bright blue, and his hair, a sun-bleached strawberry blond. The desert bronzed his skin to a glistening sheen. When he saw himself in the mirror of his Ford, Finn was certain he was irresistible to the local Mexican women. And to many, he was.

Finn's weekly trip included a stop at the local market, several hours of drinking at his favorite saloon, Fuego, and a final stop at one of the local bordellos. Around the time Finn turned thirty, he noticed a young girl at the vegetable stand. Though he didn't know her age, he guessed she was sixteen or seventeen. She spoke enough English, and he enough Spanish, to flirt. The young girl was Carmen Martinez. Five foot four, barely 110 pounds, with jet-black hair and eyes nearly as dark, she had a glint like polished blue steel. Finn, ever conscious of his image, parked his Ford in front of the market where she could see it. He continually asked her if she would like to go for a ride in his convertible. Carmen thought the handsome man was too old for her but eventually concluded she couldn't resist the gringo.

This courting ritual of a drive and then a meal continued for several months. It was a level of attention and easy money Carmen had never experienced. She was actually fifteen, not seventeen as Finn believed.

Carmen could still recall the times when Finn was gentle, funny, and kind. In time, there was young lovers' passion. Naturally, at first, Carmen was afraid. Finn would be her first. But he was patient as she discovered him and herself. She grew to love and trust the American and looked forward to the weekly visits. However, despite the excitement of their relationship, she already saw flashes of the future where Finn would explode with jealousy over any conversation she had with another man.

Three months before her sixteenth birthday, Carmen discovered she was with child. She told Finn and asked him to marry her, to be a father for their baby.

Finn exploded. "It's not my child," he insisted. "It could belong to any one of the dozen beaners you've been fucking in the market."

Carmen collapsed at his feet. "Finn, why are you saying that? You're the only one, the first one! Please don't be angry. This is a child we'll love. We'll be a family—the three of us."

Finn stepped close to her, inches away. "You think I'm a fool? A meal ticket out of here for you and your bastard? Well, not this one. This boy won't be dragged down by some Mexican whore." Carmen sobbed on her knees in front of him.

Finn turned, spat on the floor, and disappeared into Fuego for the night. Without another word to Carmen, he returned to Bisbee the next morning with no intention of ever seeing her again.

Carmen was terrified and devastated. How could Finn possibly believe the things he'd said? She confided in her parents, seeking both guidance and assistance. Their answer was simple. They drove her to Finn Rome's home and left her on his doorstep—where Finn ignored her, leaving her to cry through the chilly night until the next morning, when he reluctantly agreed to let her in.

Two years later, Finn ultimately married Carmen. But he refused to give what he called her "bastard child" his name. She alone named her first son Jackson and changed his last name from Martinez to Martin. Having a Mexican name would have been an untenable burden for a boy growing up in 1950s Arizona. Despite Finn's disavowal, Jackson would grow to look identical to his father, who steadfastly maintained that Jackson was adopted. Finn was beyond stubborn. Once his mind was made up, it did not change, and the subject was never broached again.

One year after Jackson's birth, when Carmen was almost seventeen, she had her second child. Born in wedlock, this boy was given his father's name and called Jordan Rome. Jordan's birth required a cesarean section, and just before the surgery, Carmen instructed the doctor to make sure she could never have children again. She swore everyone involved to silence. Finn never found out and believed nature had simply chosen to make his wife barren.

I know all these things because my mother told me on her thirty-first birthday, celebrated over a Hamburger Helper feast for two. I am Jordan Rome.

CHAPTER 3

NOTHING LASTS FOREVER

GROWING UP IN BISBEE DURING the period from 1960 through the mid-70s was unlike a childhood in almost any other town. The central nature of the mines dominated commerce, education, and family life. Every aspect of every business relied on the mines and the income generated from their operation. The Phelps Dodge management placed strong emphasis on religion, athletics, and education. As a result, the public schools were among the best in the state, and churches dotted the landscape. Bisbee boasted the state's first regulation-size baseball diamond and the first golf course in Arizona.

Each Sunday, my mother took my brother Jackson and me to the Catholic Church. It was a day when my father would sleep in, waiting for her return to prepare her usual Sunday masterpiece of huevos rancheros, tortillas, and fresh fruit salad with greens.

Jackson and I were as close as brothers could be. Barely a year apart, we went to school together, competed in athletics together, and hunted and fished with our father. Both of us lettered in baseball and football in high school. Our father was a devoted taskmaster when it came to sports, ensuring that nothing was left on the field and that respect was paid to both our coaches and our teammates. He never failed to remind us of the opportunities we had that he did not.

Dad's most-used line was, "You should be thankful for what you have. The only thing my father ever gave me was the back of his hand." As he began the phrase, my brother and I would finish it in three-part harmony. Our father never spoke specifically about his childhood. All we knew was that he'd been poor, and that his father gave him the gift of violence he seemed determined to pass on to us.

A child cannot fully understand what is happening in the marriage of his parents. I have specific memories of my father caressing my mother as she cooked our meals, and of my mother responding with what seemed like reciprocal affection. That did not change the fact that my father was two men. He could be attentive, teaching us how to aim a rifle, make a campfire, or throw a baseball. This was the Good and Sober Finn. But when intoxicated, he became the Bad Finn—violent, aggressive, and verbally abusive to anyone in his crosshairs. We learned to stay clear of the Bad Finn. In earlier years, there was a road map. On weekend nights, when he came home late, we made sure we were in our beds. No one made a sound. Over time, those weekend nights turned into weeknights, then nearly every night.

Jackson spent his entire childhood trying to prove he was worthy of our father's love. He excelled in sports, was an exceptional student, and held a job consistently from the age of fourteen. Finn bragged about Jackson's accomplishments as if they were his own. Yet he made no attempt to hide his favoritism for the boy he called "his" son, as opposed to "her" son. Our mother did whatever she could to compensate for Jackson's pain. This manifested in small ways—notes in his lunch box clipped from magazines, or lipstick kisses on the folded lunch bag. When we stood together as a family, her arm always seemed to find its way around Jackson's shoulders. I don't think she was even aware of the extra attention she gave him. I could never reconcile my father's commitment to his sons with the cruelty he inflicted on my brother.

I can't ever recall Carmen complaining. She was the first to rise and the last to retire each night. She was younger and prettier than any other mother among our friends. Because boys don't know better, our friends frequently commented on her appearance. They only stopped when Jackson loosened the front tooth of our third baseman, who had repeated to Jackson what they all said behind his back.

We knew our mother had grown up poor. But we hadn't understood how poor until her father died and we went to her mother's home for the wake. I was twelve, Jackson thirteen. Our father refused to attend. Our grandmother lived with one of her three sisters in a two-room corrugated metal shack without water or electricity. They scraped by performing menial labor and raising a few goats and chickens. My mother saw the shock on my face—I hadn't known people could be that poor. We were by no means wealthy, but to her family, my mother had married a Rockefeller. When we left the wake, the $100 my mother gave her mother was received like a grand inheritance.

In addition to maintaining our home, Mom had worked since we entered school—first as a maid at the Copper Queen Hotel, and later in her dream job at the Copper Queen Library on Main Street. It was there she devoured books and began evolving from the impoverished Mexican girl she had refused to remain.

The Copper Queen Mine was legendary. It had birthed over eight billion pounds of copper and was believed to promise wealth and opportunity for generations. Like the other 20,000 souls in Bisbee, our lives were tied to that assumption, which proved to be false.

"Nothing lasts forever," Mom said. I first experienced this in 1970, when I was ten. One evening, my father came home with a bright blue 1965 Thunderbird convertible. He was over the moon. We all had to pile in because we were going out to dinner to celebrate—he had just been interviewed for the position of head of security for the entire mine. This would be a massive promotion. The interviewer was an executive from Phelps Dodge, all the way from New York City.

Of course, there were other candidates, he explained over dinner, but his local drinking buddy and mine foreman, Albert Coolidge, had put in a good word for him. Finn felt confident that this would tip the scales. He would no longer be a knuckle-dragging skull-buster but a corporate executive. We'd move from our two-bedroom home on Oak Street to a more fitting house in Warren, the suburb where Phelps Dodge executives lived.

He spent the next few weeks cruising Warren, scouting homes that suited our new lifestyle. He laid out brochures on the kitchen table, inviting everyone's opinion on which home looked prettiest. Two weeks and one day after the Thunderbird's arrival, Albert Coolidge stopped by and spoke to Dad on the front porch. My father didn't come home for two days.

In 1972, the mine announced downsizing as ore productivity declined. People speculated. Some believed the company would seek new mineral finds, as it had done before. Others finally admitted what they had long feared: the mine's useful life was nearing its end. Bisbee could not, and would not, exist without it.

Two days before Christmas, 1973, my father was told his position had been eliminated. The reality was that a man of his background no longer had a place in the modern, downsized Phelps Dodge operation. Once again, it was Albert Coolidge who helped him find a job—as a night watchman in one of the closed sections of the mine. For half the pay, he now sat alone eight hours a night in a four-by-four-foot wooden guardhouse. This was a job he went to drunk and returned from even drunker.

In the years that followed, our home became a tinderbox. Jackson and I did everything we could to avoid being there. The only saving grace was that Dad worked nights. In 1975, the mine shut down completely. Bisbee's population fell from over 20,000 to 9,000, then to 6,000. Businesses closed as the town's economic engine seized. Families left in droves, abandoning homes they couldn't sell. Phelps Dodge and civic leaders scrambled to repurpose the city for tourism or recreation. People relocated to Tucson, Phoenix, California—anywhere but Bisbee. New open-pit mines opened south of Tucson, so large they could be seen from space.

Guarding the abandoned mines was one of the few jobs that remained, and Finn was lucky to have it—until 1977, when the supervisor responsible for overseeing the vacant mines checked in on him. He found Finn unconscious in the guard shack. He had been drinking for days, and passing out there was nothing new. He was fired on the spot.

Now he was broke, drunk, and unemployable. Worse for the family—he was home all the time. Jackson, eighteen, was finishing high school and planning to join the Marines. I had one year left.

Our mother bought a used futon from one of the many fire-sale furniture shops in town and moved into our room. It was obvious, though unspoken, that she would leave Finn after I graduated.

One week after Finn was fired, the Thunderbird finally gave out. There was no money to repair it. Jackson had a blue Camaro he'd bought after years of saving. It was his pride and joy, and he kept it immaculate. Our father demanded to use the car to "look for work."

"Not happening. You don't need my car to get loaded at some bar," Jackson said.

A fight broke out. Finn lunged at Jackson and shoved him. Carmen stepped between them. Jackson tried to pull her back, and Finn struck her with a right hook to the side of her face. Blood poured from her mouth as she fell to the floor.

Jackson dropped to his knees beside her. She clutched him, repeating, "I'm fine, bebé, I'm fine."

I stood frozen, watching. Jackson, now a fully grown man, broader than our father, rose with the same linebacker energy he had shown on the field. He charged. Finn's back crashed into the curio cabinet, shattering the glass behind him. He breathed deeply, checked himself, then raised his hands like windshield wipers.

"No more. No more, young man," he said, grinning. "Goddamn. I trained you well. You ought to thank me for that."

"Go ahead. Touch her again. I dare you. It'll be the last thing you ever do." Jackson was seething. Then he picked up our mother and carried her to our room. I followed, walking backward, while Finn—bloated, balding, and beaten—sat on the floor, rubbing the back of his head and cursing under his breath.

CHAPTER 4

YOU MUST GO NOW

THE HOUSE WAS EERILY QUIET for several days. My mother, brother, and I walked on eggshells, avoiding any conversation with my father. Finn also honored the truce by sleeping until noon, leaving the house at six, and not returning until well after midnight.

The truce was broken when he demanded that Carmen hand over the savings he suspected she had hidden in the house. For the first time I can recall, Carmen stood her ground at the dinner table.

"I will feed our children. I will even feed you, though I know you wouldn't do the same for me. But I will not give you money to keep poisoning yourself. Can't you see what you're doing? Look in the mirror. You're not even fifty years old, and you look seventy. If you won't help yourself, why should I help you?"

Finn shoved the table, shaking its contents, and stood up. Carmen rose slowly and walked around to stand inches from him. She was nearly a foot shorter but glared at him face to face.

Finn grabbed her hair and lifted her head until she was on the balls of her feet.

Again, Jackson rose from the table. Before he could move toward our father, Finn froze, his lower lip quivering, then let Carmen go.

Like fighters returning to their corners, we all sat again in silence. I had never seen Carmen stand up for herself before. And now, for the first time, I saw my father apologize. It was the only time I ever heard him say he was sorry to anyone.

"Boys, I'm sorry. Carmen, I am sorry. You're right on every front. I will change. I will work hard to change starting now."

I sat in amazement. It was as if my parents were putting on some sort of theater, each adopting a new role.

Finn didn't go out that night. He was up early the next morning tending the yard. My father never worked in the yard; it was something he insisted was his boys' responsibility.

This new routine continued for nearly a week. We all went our separate ways during the day and returned home in the evening. The next Monday, my father announced that he wanted to bury the hatchet with Jackson. He said it should happen over a steak dinner.

With my mother's encouragement, Jackson accepted the peace offering. Finn and Jackson both changed into one of their few respectable outfits and drove off in Jackson's Camaro.

Just past 2:00 a.m., Finn returned home. Jackson wasn't with him. Finn was staggeringly drunk. Carmen confronted him immediately, demanding to know where Jackson was.

"He met up with some floozy and went home with her. He likes them loose, like his mom," he slurred.

Nobody believed him. Jackson would never leave his car with Finn, and he had never stayed out without discussing it with his mother. Finn was lying.

The next day, Mom took off work and checked every steakhouse, every restaurant. None had seen either my father or my brother.

That night, Carmen confronted Finn. She was shaking with rage.

"What have you done with him? I checked every restaurant in town. You weren't there. Where is my son? Do not lie to me!"

Finn stuck his head over the refrigerator door as he rummaged for something to eat.

"I told you, we went out and decided to take a little drive up toward Tombstone for dinner. He met some cheap slut... he'll be back when he tires of her. You just want him back so you can get on my ass. Well, your little bodyguard is gone for a while, and the man of the house is back in charge."

He grabbed a piece of chicken with a paper towel. As he walked out, he shoved Carmen, forcing her off her feet and out of the doorway.

"I'll be back at... Forget it. I'll be back when I'm back."

Finn started the Camaro and peeled out of the driveway, gravel spinning.

He came home around midnight. Carmen was hysterical, desperate for news about Jackson. She lost all sense of self-preservation and followed the drunken man around the house, staying inches behind him as he paced.

He turned and exploded, striking her with the back of his hand. Her head hit the oven handle and began to bleed.

Carmen stood up and, holding a cast iron pan, swung at her husband with all her strength. He caught her arm, absorbing most of the blow, then reached for her throat with his free hand. Carmen screamed.

I jumped from my bed and grabbed my baseball bat.

This would be the last time Finn hit Carmen.

I've replayed that moment a hundred times since. I've rationalized it as self-defense, or an accident. But if I'm honest, it wasn't an accident. I removed a man from this world who had killed my brother and would have killed my mother if given the chance. I did it because it needed to be done.

Carmen placed her hand on his neck, searching for a pulse. Then she checked his chest for breath. There was none.

We stood there, staring at each other, motionless for what felt like forever. Neither of us cried.

My mother walked to the sink and dampened a paper towel, washing her face and inspecting the blood now staining the towel crimson. She repeated the process until the bleeding was under control. Then, holding a fresh paper towel to her cut, she carried on.

She walked into the bedroom we shared and retrieved the passports she had gotten five years earlier when she took her sons to her father's funeral. Then she opened the freezer and removed a bag labeled Green Giant Frozen Spinach, Family Size. It was the one bag she knew her husband would never touch.

She unsealed it and pulled out four stacks of one-hundred-dollar bills, each bound with a hairband. Each stack had fifty bills. She handed me two.

Then she stood up straight, composed and calm, looking taller than her petite frame.

"You did not kill your father. That man died years ago. It just took time for his heart to stop beating. But you should know Finn still has some friends in the police department. Not good people. Although they know who he was, their truth may not be our truth. It could take a long time to sort out and ruin you in the process. I won't let him destroy both my boys.

Go pack your clothes. Pack your brother's clothes too. I'll tell the police Jackson left a few days ago, and you went to meet him

21

in Phoenix. Do not go to Phoenix. Go as far from Phoenix as possible."

She turned to face my father's body.

"I know my son is dead. He's buried or, worse, lying somewhere in the desert or the mountains. I can never forgive your father for this—his own son."

She walked up to him, inches away.

"How could one do such a thing?" she screamed in the face of the dead man.

My mother stopped, hands over her mouth, tears rushing down her face.

"Mi bebé, mi bebé," she said, trembling.

I walked behind her and wrapped my arms across her chest. She collapsed to her knees. I bent with her, trying to keep her upright. She stood again, wiped her tears with her sleeve, and looked up at me.

"You must go now."

I started the Camaro and drove through the night, north to the 10, then east. I drove for twenty-seven hours before pulling over to rest.

I tried to make sense of things no seventeen-year-old could understand.

Bisbee was dying. My brother was dead. My father had killed him. In turn, I had taken my father's life to protect my mother.

My mother was now alone for the first time in her life.

At that moment, it was impossible to know that Jackson Martin was not really done yet—nor was my mother and the town of Bisbee.

Finn Rome, however, was gone for good. And anyone who knew him would have to admit the world was better off.

PART II

IBRAHIM ASSAD

Beirut Lebanon
1983: 18 Years Before

CHAPTER 5

ONE OF TWO LIVES

IN 1862, AMERICAN MISSIONARIES IN Lebanon asked Daniel Bliss to form an educational institution for higher learning. The university was originally chartered under the name Syrian Protestant College, opening with sixteen students in 1866. In 1920, the name was changed to the American University. The school quickly became one of the most prestigious academic centers in the Middle East.

Throughout the 20th century, Beirut experienced extraordinary success and earned the nickname "Paris of the Middle East," only to be ravaged by bloody violence in 1975. Despite these challenges, the university remained one of the leading engineering and medical schools in the Arab world. Originally, it served Europeans and American expatriates, but it has since grown to welcome individuals of all backgrounds, regardless of race or religion.

It was once unheard of for someone of my background to stand on these hallowed grounds, graduating today. The majestic limestone and brick Moorish architecture was surrounded by mature cypress, juniper, and pine trees—trees native to Lebanon, and a far cry from the dry, arid desert I grew up in.

Until this university, everything in my life had been brown and relentlessly hot. This lush, green space kissed by the Mediterranean breeze was its opposite in every way. Yet here I stood, receiving my diploma on a sunny day in May. This education, handed to me in a hardback leather-bound case, would be the key to freedom from the shackles placed upon my family and my people by the Jews and colonizers of Europe.

They called the names in alphabetical order, using the English alphabet. Mine, Ibrahim Assad, was the eighth name in a class of 203. As is the tradition at all American universities, I walked up the steps to the podium, received my diploma, and shook the hand of the dean.

As I descended, I could see the deep blue sky blending with the glistening Mediterranean, separated only by the silhouettes of cypress trees. In the front row sat my mother and my little sister, Lulú, along with my oldest friend, Aaliyah. My mother was sobbing, watching her son realize her dream, now armed with a degree in civil engineering and headed to a job in Dubai that would pay him the astounding annual sum of $65,000 starting just three weeks from today.

These events made it clear that I could take a different path from my father, grandfather, and uncles. It would be the path of a multilingual, cosmopolitan professional—a man who straddled the East and the West. This version of Ibrahim would travel the world, buoyed by the petroleum wealth Allah had provided to his people. Others would have to soil their hands to do battle with the infidels.

My mother, along with her escorts, rose from her seat to greet me.

My oldest friend in the world—no, my only real friend—followed my sister and mother, her hands clasped over her chest, beaming. Aaliyah had been living in Cairo, serving her residency for the past year. She was one year older than I was, but she had carried the gravitas of a grown woman since we first met when she was eight. She was by far the smartest person I knew and had matriculated to Cairo University just as she turned seventeen. There, she enrolled in an accelerated medical program and now had her sights set on becoming a surgeon.

I had known many young people who bragged about the roles they would someday play and the success that would surely follow, only to wind up as laborers or street thugs. But when Aaliyah said she would do something, it happened. At first, I thought her bold proclamations were only that. But they weren't. She matter-of-factly told me she would finish first in our elementary school. She did. Then she said she would graduate at the top of her secondary school class a year early. She did. Then she said she would defy the odds and obtain a scholarship to attend medical school in Cairo. Of course, she did.

When I told her I wanted to study engineering at the American University, she cocked her head and held her chin. "You will." And I did—largely because she would not allow any other outcome. She insisted on studying with me for every exam. There was no rest until every answer could be recited by heart. Our evening study sessions were rewarded with shaved ice or some other sweet treat she had dreamed up.

Aaliyah was the rock the sea broke upon—immovable, confident, and unflappable. Men—serious men—pursued her. She had no interest. Her mother challenged every decision she made, warning that her hardheaded nature would be unappealing to a prospective mate. Her answer was simple: "Any man who would want me to be less than I am is not a man who cares for me. Nor should I have interest in him."

The three women approached me in the order of respect our culture demanded. My mother wore a traditional chador. The long black robes were modest, covering her entire body except for her now mature face. Though just over forty years old, the difficult years had aged her, and the lines on her face made her appear twenty years older. My little sister, Lulú, barely able to stay in line behind our mother, had rebelled slightly. She wore a hijab with a bright green dress that covered her arms down to her ankles. This attire would be considered quite progressive in our religious community.

Aaliyah stood out from the crowd. She looked like one of the women in the windows of Zamalek Boulevard's storefronts in Cairo, wearing suede Wellington heeled boots, form-fitting European jeans, and a bold, flowing black silk top. Her only nod to our faith was the bright blue hijab framing her fair-skinned face and large wraparound sunglasses. Every man she passed took note of her undeniable beauty.

CHAPTER 6

TWO OF TWO LIVES

THE ASSAD FAMILY HAD ENDURED a long and complicated path through history to arrive at this place and time. When al-Ikhwan besieged the Grand Mosque in Mecca to protest corruption within the House of Saud, over 300 militants stormed the grounds and took control of Islam's most sacred site. The Saudis claimed there were 600 armed militants to account for the vast number of innocents killed by Saudi forces, but in truth, there were only 300 brave souls. The government assembled over 10,000 troops to overtake the militants who were holed up inside the mosque.

On the Arab Street, the siege was quickly blamed on the Americans and the Israelis, sparking riots in Baghdad, Tehran, and Amman. But the siege was, in fact, the final act of desperation by true believers who felt the Kingdom had been corrupted by decades of Western decadence and Christian infidels. Saudi forces made several disastrous attempts to retake the mosque, each one adding to the slaughter of innocent bystanders. The Kingdom appeared impotent before the world. Only then did they enlist French special forces to lead the counterattack.

After two weeks, 117 militants were killed, 68 captured, and nearly 600 innocent people killed or injured. The leader of the siege, Juhayman al-Otaybi, was publicly beheaded. The 68 captured were publicly executed by hanging. Violent crackdowns in Egypt, Jordan, Iran, Iraq, and Saudi Arabia became the standard tool for controlling unrest. Middle Eastern leaders were not afraid of the West or even Allah; they were afraid of their own people. And they had good reason to be. New leaders, with access to education, wealth, and communication, were emerging to threaten their grip on power.

However, another outcome of the siege hit closer to home. My father, Amir Assad, along with his elder brother, was among the 68 martyred for our faith at the hands of the corrupt king.

This was not the first sacrifice made by my father's family. My grandfather was one of the earliest members of the Egyptian Muslim Brotherhood's 1928 movement. He studied directly under its founder, Hassan al-Banna. The movement arose to protect our ancestral home, land held by my family for over 2,000 years.

By 1928, Egypt, like so much of the Middle East—had been poisoned. It's often said that the British conquest of the Ottoman Empire introduced Western culture to the Arab world. But what truly changed Arab Muslim culture was the brief three-year visit by the French under Napoleon. Between July 1798 and September 1801, the French overtook the Ottoman-installed Pasha who ruled Egypt and Syria. For the French, it was a chance to establish another trade foothold along the Mediterranean. What the French really exported was not weapons—but corrupt Western liberal thought and bureaucracy.

Even after the Ottomans joined forces with the British to expel the French in 1801, their legacy remained. Local government offices, trade, and worse—political thought—became entangled with European influence. For the first time, Sunni Muslims were governed by laws outside of Sharia. Religious leaders and devout citizens found this irreconcilable.

When Hassan al-Banna traveled the world, he took note of this conflict. He concluded that the secular institutions introduced by the West could never be compatible with the caliphate that once ruled. Under Ottoman rule, the Sultan also served as Khalif, the religious leader and protector of Islam's holiest sites including Mecca and Baghdad—all governed under Sharia. Al-Banna wrote extensively about this perspective and concluded that resistance by force was the only way to expel the infidels.

But the corruption had taken root in every facet of life. The military, merchants, and even religious scholars prospered from their dealings with the West. Oil-fueled American dollars and British pounds flowed into national coffers. Corrupt kings, shahs, and strongmen lived in palaces, drove European automobiles, and violated Sharia in the most flagrant ways, while their people remained barefoot and hungry.

Change could only come through rebellion. The Muslim Brotherhood and related groups emerged in Sunni-dominated countries. Militant actions, including bombings and armed attacks were taken against the ruling class. In response, occupying Europeans deployed brutal mercenary forces and bribed tribal sheikhs to thwart any effort toward organization. Mass roundups and disappearances became common.

As dramatized in the film Lawrence of Arabia, the escalation grew increasingly violent until the British could bear it no longer.

The costs of occupation began to outweigh the benefits, creating political liabilities at home. The solution was to divide the land and install cooperative leaders. The British agreed to mandate territories back to their indigenous populations. But this was not to rebuild a caliphate; it was to disperse power. In Egypt, Iraq, Syria, Jordan, Iran, and Saudi Arabia, figureheads were placed in power who could be easily controlled.

The Jews, however, presented another problem. European powers sought to avoid having Jews return to their countries after World War II and to shed the guilt of their treatment. A solution emerged: move them to Palestine. The first sign of this betrayal came through the infamous Balfour Agreement, which proposed separating Palestine into Jewish and Arab territories. Zionist funding from Europe and America facilitated the influx of Jews into our homeland.

The ultimate betrayal came in 1948 with the establishment of the state of Israel, what we call the Nakba, or "catastrophe." Zionism stole our ancestral land and gave it to the Jews so Europe could ease its conscience. The Muslim world had no choice but to respond. Five Arab nations united against Israel, only to be humiliated once more by Western-backed power.

It was during this war that my grandfather died. My grandmother then committed her three sons to the destruction of Israel and the restoration of our land. But nothing truly changed. The corrupt kings, shahs, and elected leaders continued to live lavishly while their people starved. The Arab Street knew this all too well. In the shadows, the struggle for truth and Allah endured.

The defeat by the Jews in 1967 crystallized the failure of corrupt Arab leadership. Jews, who had long lived as subordinates in Christian Europe and under Ottoman rule since the 1200s, now ruled over a once-proud Arab people. It was the ultimate humiliation made possible by the West.

From this injustice, a new struggle was born. Lebanon, Iran, Gaza, the East Bank, Saudi Arabia, Yemen, Afghanistan, and other Muslim nations became recruitment grounds for the cause. The Jews would be first. The Americans next. And eventually, the dream of reviving the Muslim empire and expanding it into Europe would be realized. Our jihad knew no time limits—nor limits in method. God would bless the martyrs and damn the infidels. Paradise awaited the faithful; hell awaited the rest.

This was not a perspective I shared with my family. After my father's death, my mother deliberately moved us from Cairo to Ramallah, a difficult decision. She refused to offer her only son to the cause. Though she had no means to support us, her brother in Ramallah managed a meager living through his vegetable stand beneath the apartment he rented. Her goal was clear: to end the generational cost and place her children on a new path.

But truth is not easily buried. Though Ramallah was one of the more progressive cities in the East Bank, believers still offered prayer and guidance for the cause. When I entered university, I sought out like minds. It wasn't difficult. Prominent speakers gave sermons and lectures in Beirut. I was fortunate to hear the Egyptian author and surgeon Ayman al-Zawahiri and the young Hezbollah spiritual leader Hassan Nasrallah.

The struggle was alive, now burning in Afghanistan. The Americans had become a temporary ally, supplying weapons and aid against the Russians. There was poetry in Allah's wisdom, using one devil to defeat another. A charismatic Saudi leader offered money and spiritual leadership. In Pakistan, many Muslim soldiers of God trained to bring war to the Russians in Afghanistan.

I was convinced this was a call believers must answer.

CHAPTER 7

ONE OF TWO LIVES

MY MOTHER HUGGED ME. THIS act of affection would be tolerated between myself and no other woman. She went on, her face beaming.

"I have told everyone. My brother, your aunt, and your cousins are all so thrilled and impressed by what you've done. The first engineer in the family! And from such a prestigious school."

She then came close and whispered, "They are also jealous. I know they thought you would never finish. My sister-in-law kept telling me I was foolish to send you my savings. Now it will be you who supports the family. Who is foolish now?"

I smiled back at my mother. She was blessed in her ignorance of who her son really was. I would not spoil that delusion. My sister suspected that I harbored different ambitions than to be an engineer. But she, too, thought my next position in life would be at a desk in Dubai.

"What kind of car will you get?" she asked. "The BMWs are befitting of an engineer's position. I know they are expensive, but the smaller ones can be bought secondhand for a reasonable amount."

"I don't know, Lulú. I have so much to consider. The car selection doesn't seem like the first priority."

"Well, when you get one, send me a photo. I'm still working on Mom to see if I can come visit. This travel by myself will not be easy. I will try… I promise."

My sister then continued to review the many details regarding the transportation and lodging that would be required for her visit to Dubai. But my attention was diverted over her shoulder to Aaliyah, who waited patiently, standing so erect she looked military in her posture. My friend could communicate simply through her eyes, which were now staring at me from beneath her oversized sunglasses, perched atop her head.

"Pardon me, sister. Would you mind if I took a moment to talk to Aaliyah?"

My sister turned and looked at me, then at my friend. She smiled and touched my shoulder.

"Of course, brother, of course."

Aaliyah came very close to me and whispered, "Ibrahim, let's go for a walk, just you and I."

The panic in my face must have been visible. My mother's eyes grew to the size of saucers whenever any woman approached her son. Aaliyah turned to my mother and sister.

"Ibrahim and I are going for a walk. We won't be far. Will you please excuse us?"

My mother started to speak, but Aaliyah cut her off—politely.

"We will be fine. We will not be far and will return in just a few minutes."

Again, my mother tried to speak, but she faced the gaze of an immovable force.

"All right, just a few minutes," was the concession my mother made to maintain her now illusory authority.

We turned and walked up the campus path, shaded by a row of junipers. Several minutes of silence passed as two friends—bound by time, experience, and an unspoken love—basked in each other's company.

"I think your mother is prouder than if you became president of Egypt. She has not stopped talking about you to all her friends to make sure they knew of this day. I am happy for her. And I am happy for you."

After a short silence, the conversation resumed.

"When do you start work?"

She knew the answer to that question, but she also suspected that the answer she had been told might not be the correct one.

"In three weeks. I start work in three weeks," I said, refusing to make eye contact.

"Really? In three weeks, huh? Ibrahim, you're speaking to me. There is no aspect of you I do not know, and it is not possible for you to lie to me. And you are lying now."

Of course, Aaliyah was right. There was no lying to my best friend. We had grown up as youngsters playing hide-and-seek in her mother's home, dining at her parents' table as if I were her brother. We shared every secret, from childhood crushes to the changes we observed in our own bodies. As children grew into young adults, our feelings changed from siblings to something more. It was the discipline of our beliefs that maintained the boundaries of our behavior and our fidelity to Allah.

"I have other plans before Dubai." This would be no surprise to Aaliyah. She was aware of how I felt about the political landscape in the Middle East.

"There is a holy war in Afghanistan. They need men of my strength and education. They need brave men, men willing to sacrifice for Allah. I will train in Pakistan. We will cast the Russians from Muslim soil. If we accomplish this task, the West will see the might of a committed Muslim army. This will be the beginning of expelling them from our homelands. They are paper tigers who do not wish to battle longer than one news cycle. It will be only one year, I promise. I will then return to Dubai, and no one will be the wiser."

Sensing I was losing ground, I picked up the tenor of my explanation.

"The sponsor where I was to work in Dubai is a large construction company. There is a great man, a learned man, who is part of the family that owns the company. They will send money home to my mother as if I were doing so myself. She will not know, and please, do not tell her."

Aaliyah stopped in her tracks. She turned and looked up at me, tears at first trickling, then flooding down her cheeks.

"Do not do this. You talk like the peacocks who present themselves on the pulpits. They would have you die while they profit. I had hoped that this celebration of your studies would be a new chapter for us."

She paused to compose herself. Then, in the firmest voice she could muster:

"We are to have children. Four children. Two boys and two girls. The boys will be handsome, tall, and strong like you. The girls will be beautiful and brilliant."

Her lips trembled as she struggled to finish the sentence. She wiped her tears with the palm of her hand.

"I know it is wrong for a woman to talk like this, but I do not care. This is what should be. We will be happy, and the world will be better for the gifts we provide it. Beautiful children, roads and buildings, and healthy patients. This is the path Allah wants for us."

I could not return her gaze. And then she did something unspeakably inappropriate, for which I loved her all the more. She took my hand and placed it over her chest.

"This heart beats because you are in its world. It would cease if you were not. Please... don't go."

I started to pull my hand away, then left it there for a moment.

"I will return, I promise. Your dreams are my dreams. But there are higher callings than the needs of two people. When I come back, we will marry, and we will have eight children, not four. All girls as beautiful as their mother."

We both laughed, and silence fell between us.

"We should be getting back now. My mother has probably already called somebody to look for us," I said, smiling at my future mate.

Aaliyah gathered herself and pulled her sunglasses from her head to cover her now bloodshot eyes. We walked side by side back to my sister and mother, closer than ever and careful not to touch.

PART III

REBECCA ROME

New York, New York
2018: 17 Years After

CHAPTER 8

SEEMS LIKE A BAD IDEA

THE PHYSICIAN'S DESK REFERENCE DOES not specify what happens when you mix various drugs. It covers a wide range of narcotics, their appropriate uses, and their dangers. But if you combine a few bumps of cocaine with a microdose of ketamine, there's really no clear outcome. Unfortunately, I self-medicated with this concoction, hoping it would give me the strength to get through my wedding rehearsal. Instead, it brought on alternating waves of euphoria, paranoia, and significant physical discomfort. Looking back, what I thought was a brilliant idea now seems like a terrible one.

My fiancé, Eric, had his whole family there as expected. My side was represented solely by my stepfather, Richard. It may have been my wedding, but both Richard and my future in-laws were running the show. They are always in charge. It was only a small comfort to see them jockeying for control while doing their best to maintain civility and the appearance of decorum. Every directive came with a caveat: "I'm open to suggestions, but I think…" or "I know there are many ways to do this, but I've always done it like…" or "I'm normally flexible about these things, but on this particular issue…"

Decisions were easier given that neither my in-laws nor my stepfather were financially responsible for any part of the event. My mother had committed to paying for everything before she passed. Since she and Richard had been estranged for nearly five years, we never discussed what role, if any, he'd have in the event. But now that she's gone, Richard has assumed a paternal role he showed no interest in during the ten years he lived with my mother.

I don't care for Richard, and for good reason. It's not fair to say my mother didn't like him either. I know she must have felt something for him at one point after all, she did marry him.

Just as we were getting started, Eric's brother Russ joined us. Russ works in San Francisco for a private bank, so we had never met in person. Eric's father introduced us. "Becca, this is Russ, a derivatives trader." I turned and looked at Eric. He knew what I was thinking. Everyone in his family comes with a title. No one is ever just "my brother" or "my cousin." They are introduced as "my brother, the derivatives trader" or "my cousin, the brain surgeon." It's like royalty. They're nothing without their titles.

My title is Becca, Duchess of Sleeping Late. I've teased Eric about the pretentiousness of these introductions, so nothing needed to be said.

The rehearsal took place at the same church where we planned to marry in three weeks: Marble Collegiate Church in New York. I must admit, it is stunning, an 1854 Romanesque masterpiece in the heart of Manhattan on Fifth Avenue. This was one of the things Eric's family felt "quite strongly" about. The grandeur of the space did nothing to help my body metabolize the drugs in my system. I could've really used an edible, a Valium, a drink or all of the above to come down a few notches.

Eric could sense my anxiety. He left his mother's side and came over to hold my hand. Whispering in my ear, he asked, "Becca, are you okay? You're not, you know, taking anything?"

"I'm fine," I said. "I'm just nervous. And this is so hard without Mom. I never imagined this day without her." He squeezed my hand.

Eric is not a bad guy. He, like everyone else I went to Columbia with, is Type A ambitious. He comes from an ambitious family and expects me to be ambitious—but only to a point. Ambitious, yet femininely docile. Strong, yet demure. Beautiful, yet natural. Smart, but not so smart that I interrupt when he's talking about business. Of course, I'm also expected to remain stick-thin with a tight ass and perky breasts until I'm sixty. And, most importantly, I should want to fuck him every time I look at him.

It sounds cynical, but I'm certain that if he answered these questions honestly, he'd admit my reading of the room was spot-on.

We met after graduation. I think if Eric had known me before, he would've found my behavior unworthy of matrimony. He now only knows the PG version of my life—BE, Before Eric. Back then, I lived what could be politely described as a promiscuous life, which sounds much better than "slutty." Some might say I had "Daddy issues," but that's not possible. I hardly knew my father; he died when I was seven. I'm not even sure my memories of him are real or pieced together from photos and my mother's stories.

I know he was tall and dark, while my mother was fine-featured and fair. I look like her—some say almost identically. When he died, we were left with debts and little else. Like many who died that day, he left before his time. My mother returned to her craft as a musician, teaching lessons and playing weddings, bar mitzvahs, and anniversaries. It made for an impossible schedule for a single mother.

On the day my father died, 2,977 other people also perished. That number doesn't capture the real damage that was done. Thousands more died in the aftermath from diseases no one anticipated. And these losses don't include the tens of thousands of lives that were irreparably damaged ;widows, orphans, fathers, mothers, brothers, and sisters who had gaping holes torn through their lives and souls. How does one reassemble life after such a loss? They do not.

To this day, the image of my mother hysterical, trying to drive my father's abandoned car back from the train station two days later remains the most vivid memory of my youth.

That's when a coworker of my father stepped in as "the knight in shining armor." He courted Mom obsessively, but his real, unspoken offering was security for her and for her daughter. My mother retained her beauty and made the same trade that so many other single mothers made: she compromised her happiness for the love of her child.

An eight-year-old girl does not understand these concepts. Nor does she grasp the desire of her new stepfather to exclude his wife's child in order to indulge a man's needs over a family's. My mother was trapped in this conflict, as the two people who shared her household competed for her attention. Over the years, my resentment of Richard hardened into disdain. My mother knew it, and so did Richard. He simply did not care.

When I was twenty years old, the world somehow changed. I visited home from school during Christmas. Richard was not at home.

"Where is Dick?" I asked. I chose to call Richard "Dick" for two reasons. First, it seemed like such an appropriate name, so much more fitting to the individual. Second, I knew he hated it. My mother would sternly correct me when he was in the room but let it go when he wasn't. I saw the difference as an unspoken acknowledgment of her concurrence.

"Richard has moved out. Last month. We are taking some time to reassess what is best for everybody."

"Why now, Mom? You should have thrown him out ten years ago. He is such an asshole. Mom, I could tell you stories..." I stopped to take a breath, knowing the potential hurt of finishing that thought. "You deserve better."

"It is not so easy, Becca. We have a house, you have school. These things cost money—lots of money. Your grandmother didn't have it, and neither did I. Sometimes you do what you must. You'll see, my beautiful one, life isn't always so clear."

"And what has changed to fix these adult problems I'm apparently unable to understand?" I asked sarcastically.

Mom adjusted her posture on the couch and fussed with the edge of a silk pillow.

"Our family has inherited some money. Quite a bit of money. I'm hoping to take this and change direction for the two of us."

"Mom, who do we know that has money? This seems very strange. Are you sure it's okay to receive it? Maybe it's illegal I mean, it kind of sounds like a scam."

"I thought so too at first. A law firm, a big one, called and asked if I'd be okay to meet. It seemed strange, but this is a very prestigious firm. So, I met with a partner, a Mrs. Blackman," she said, staring at the ceiling as if Blackman's phone number was written on it. "She told me that an individual set up a trust in the Cayman Islands for you and me. With a substantial sum. So, I was still skeptical. I talked to my cousin Jessica, the attorney in Jersey, and asked her to investigate. She did, and…it's legit. She said if we pay taxes, it shouldn't be a problem."

"And we still don't know who this is? So sketchy, Mom. There have got to be some strings attached."

She shrugged.

I continued, "So, what are you going to do?"

"I agree it needs more digging. Jessica is going to see if she can get to the bottom of where this is coming from. But in the meantime, we're going to fix what's broken starting with us. Starting with you. You need to get help."

I looked at my mom incredulously. "What do you mean? I'm fine. My grades are good. I don't need help."

Mom slid over and held my hand.

"Becca, you're angry. You've been angry for so long I can't remember when you weren't. You self-medicate. You think I don't know? Of course I know. You look for love… in places that don't love you back. Your road has been hard. Our road has been hard. Believe me, I know."

Our life changed that day. My mother was reenergized in her career. She took only those jobs that interested her. Her demeanor, her attitude, her self-esteem changed overnight. Three days after our chat, I had the first meeting with Dr. Sharon Green, the therapist my mother found for me.

It sounds like an exaggeration, but Sharon saved my life. She turned me into a different Rebecca Rome; one who had freed herself from the shackles of her past. This was the woman Eric had met and decided to marry. Now my mother, too, was gone. In the most awful way. As a result, old habits, bad habits crept back into my life.

The paranoia and body aches had completely replaced the euphoria. My body was withdrawing, crying for more poison. I needed to hold it together long enough to follow the directions of our wedding planner: where I stand, how we walk up the aisle, what the pastor will say, how we will respond. The instructions weren't complex, and even in an altered state, I could follow them.

We ran through an expedited version of the ceremony. Richard was to walk me down the aisle. This was announced matter-of-factly by the wedding planner. I was too disoriented to protest.

During the practice, he took my hand. I froze.

"Dick, let go of my hand." He looked at me and smiled.

"You let go of my hand this moment, or I will throw a tantrum that will make your experience at my seventeenth birthday party look like a group hug."

Richard's hand immediately dropped from mine. The smile on his face fell as if he'd eaten something rancid. Richard understood exactly what I meant.

At my seventeenth birthday, Richard had hit on one of my friends. Of course, he was intoxicated. A seventeen-year-old girl can have the body of an adult with the mind of a child. Richard had been flirting with one of my most attractive friends, Beth, throughout the party. It clearly made her uncomfortable. As she sought distance, Richard kept moving closer. He whispered in her ear, then placed his hand on her bottom. She froze in horror, unable to respond.

I knew what was happening. There were countless times Richard had made comments about my appearance or the fact that "we really weren't related." Unwarranted touching, innuendo, or double entendre were commonplace if my mother wasn't in the room. My strategy was to simply avoid him. But this was beyond the pale.

Being stoned out of my mind at the time didn't help me moderate my response. I started beating him with the cake spatula until my mom stepped in.

The party abruptly broke up. Mom tried to mediate some sort of resolution, but there was no common ground. My girlfriend was too freaked out to say anything of real value, simply hoping to leave without further incident. Dick claimed that nothing really happened, that he was just ushering the guest to another part of the room. I was too high to put together a coherent story for my mother to explain my outburst. But she knew what I was saying had truth to it. After all, she knew Richard better than anyone. From that point on, Mom's radar was always up, and Richard was careful to steer clear of my wrath.

After the first walkthrough, everyone seemed to be talking at once. I reached into my back pocket and found my phone. Without looking, I pressed speed dial one. Cat would be my savior. I picked up my phone as if I had felt it vibrate.

I began talking to myself. Within the first few moments, Cat had picked up the other line.

"Becca, how are you?"

"Oh, hi, Cat. I think I can. We're almost done here. What time? Okay, let me see if I can make it. Really nice of you to set that up."

"I'm not sure what's going on, but I assume you want me to pretend I'm asking you to go out. So, I'm guessing you're trying to get away from a dramatic in-law experience during the rehearsal. No problem. Where do you want to meet?"

"A half hour from now at Pancho's. Okay, let me just check with Eric for a moment," I said, taking the phone from my ear.

"Eric, Cat has set up a bunch of friends to meet at Pancho's for drinks to celebrate the rehearsal. It's just going to be the girls. We're meeting in half an hour, OK?"

Eric looked back at me with disapproval. I didn't acknowledge the glare and took advantage of the fact that he wouldn't start a spat in front of his parents. That would ruin the image he'd so carefully cultivated of our perfect, progressive relationship. I put the phone back to my ear.

"We're all good. I'll see you in half an hour. Thanks again for setting this up... so sweet of you all," I said into the phone. Then I announced to the group that I had to run—my friends had planned a celebratory get-together for me. I thanked everyone and left before anyone had a chance to change my mind.

Eric was not okay. He followed close behind until we were out of earshot of his parents.

"I don't want you going out. I was thinking we could have dinner with my folks. If this was something you wanted to do, you should've cleared it in advance."

He sounded like a father talking to a child.

"I'm sorry. I should've cleared this with who? And how was I supposed to know about an event I hadn't even been told about?" My tone was hostile. In fairness, I was being a bitch. I wasn't really running from the rehearsal. I was running from this... the wedding.

My mom has not even been gone three weeks, and here we are pushing forward with this 'celebration' like her death never happened. I've been told this is what she would want—as if they know. Everyone seems to think it's right, except me. "After all, life must go on," I've heard again and again.

I'm suffocating, and I have no one to talk to.

Looking down, I whispered with a shudder, "I need my mother."

Eric looked at me in disbelief, clenched his teeth, then turned around and resumed his cavalier gait as he walked back to his parents. I could tell he was smiling because they were smiling back.

As I exited the church, I noticed a man in the back row. He was impeccably dressed in a tailored three-piece gray suit, only missing a tie. His hair and beard were tightly groomed. We made brief eye contact as I passed.

My mother was killed by a stranger. Did this man mean me harm? Worse, I recognized him.

Did he look like the man from the pirated online tape? The tape of my mother being pushed in front of a subway train. The grainy footage played again in my head. Her panicked expression, then the glare of the perpetrator staring directly into the camera. I'd seen it a hundred times. I shouldn't have watched it. Now I can never unsee it.

A wave of panic surged through me. Was this stranger following me?

Before leaving the church, I ducked into the bathroom for another bump from the vial in my pocket. My body flushed with instant euphoria. Then I remembered where I'd seen the man. He wasn't the man on the tape. He was the one I'd seen in the coffee shop probably just a local resident.

This realization, combined with the drug, brought a mild wave of optimism. I stepped back out to check the pew where he had been sitting, but he was gone.

I exhaled and made my way to Pancho's.

CHAPTER 9

ARE YOU SOME SORT OF SUPERHERO?

HERE IS WHAT I CAN remember after arriving at Pancho's...

Pancho's is a hole-in-the-wall biker bar that has become trendy on West 18th Street and 10th Avenue. Only in New York is grungy considered prestigious. It's around 6:30, September evenings are shorter, and dusk has fallen. The small place is buzzing with an eclectic crowd, and I don't see Cat. I force my way up to the bar with the intent of ordering a beer, but at the last moment I change my mind and order a cosmopolitan instead. I'm halfway through my drink before Catherine comes up behind me and grabs my breasts while thrusting her hips into my buttocks.

"If you can't find it here, it doesn't exist," Cat shouts with a smile. One has to talk at 90 decibels at Pancho's to be heard. "Sorry I was late—couldn't get an Uber." I turn around, face Cat, and give her a hug. The gentleman next to me at the bar is grinning.

"Do you two know each other?" His grin widens.

"We will before the night's over," Cat replies, taking her two fingers and sticking her tongue between them. Our bar neighbor laughs and shakes his head.

Catherine and I went to school together. She insists on Cat. To the extent that I am capable of having friends, she is my best friend. She knows me before everything and after. Our ability to consume at Columbia was legendary. The difference between Cat and me is that I couldn't stop, and she could.

I walk Cat through the rehearsal, doing my best to explain how I feel trapped and manipulated. "You are a lifesaver. I couldn't take one second more," I tell her while trying to attract the bartender's attention. The bartender at Pancho's at 6:30 on a Friday night is like a grizzly trying to catch salmon swimming upstream to spawn. There's no catching up; you can only do your best to harvest as much as possible.

"Well, look on the bright side. Once you're married, you only have to put up with it for the rest of your life. After that, you're free and clear," Cat says. She then puts her fingers in a circle and whistles so loudly that even the frazzled bartender responds, if only to avoid a repeat of the ear-piercing sound. "I'll have what she's having, and to make things easy, if our glasses are empty, they shouldn't be." She winks and blows an air kiss at the bartender, who cracks a smile despite the chaos.

Cat has her own rules. In fact, she makes them. She grew up in Nebraska and moved to New York to pursue a career in fashion. But she's a planner, not a dreamer. She harbors no fantasy of living a comfortable, artsy life in Manhattan on her meager earnings. She believes it's only a matter of time before the whole city collapses from its decadence. Her plan is simple. Actually, she has two.

Plan A: She will marry the man of her dreams—handsome, filthy rich. They'll have two kids, a Mercedes convertible, and a big house on the island.

Plan B is just as straightforward. At thirty-two, she will move back home, marry her high school sweetheart, and work in her father's lumberyard. Amazingly, she seems equally at ease with either outcome. Cat looks like a Barbie doll: tiny ass, big boobs, and an electric smile. Damn near indestructible. Men gravitate to her like moths to light.

"Becca, what are you thinking? Now me, I could put up with any amount of crap as long as it came with the right amount of money. But sweetheart, you are not cut out for that. Why don't you just tell him you want to wait a year before tying the knot? Stay together and play house. You could still agree to any kink he's into for that year—no holes barred. So it's not like he's really missing out on anything. Hell, just have him make the list and then you can initial it." Cat gets a look on her face that tells me she's really proud of herself. "You know, this is a really interesting twist on a prenup." Her flash of brilliant advice is interrupted by the arrival of her cosmopolitan.

She lifts her glass. "To the best friend, who should have the best man." Cat downs half her cosmo in one swig. "There, now we're caught up."

After a second round of cosmos, the B-52s are blaring "Love Shack" on the jukebox. Pancho's doesn't really have a dance floor—more like a space of about 100 square feet in front of the jukebox where people mash together. The two of us slide off our stools and embarrass ourselves on the floor with some kind of native ritual dance interpretation. We intentionally exclude the wolves trying to join in. I need a bathroom break for the vial. When I return, the third round of cosmos is waiting on the bar top. We each drink half and spend the next half hour gathering our wits. Cat makes a small howling sound and shakes her head.

"Ready?" she asks.

Together, we revisit the floor, now in motion with no particular relationship to the music—just thrusting our bodies in an activity that looks more like aerobics than dance. We morph into new versions of ourselves: Cat on air guitar, me handling the fist microphone, leading the bar in our rendition of "Jumpin' Jack Flash." The dance floor intoxicants join us in the debauchery as each lost soul offers their own interpretation. We make it back to our seats, sweating, and finish the third cosmopolitan. I turn to look at Cat. I'm pretty sure she's cross-eyed. I mimic her look. We both break into cackles, and the remnants of my cosmo start dripping from my nose. The sight makes Cat convulse, nearly falling off her stool before barely catching herself. The wheels are falling off the operation.

"Becca, Rebecca Rome," says a vaguely familiar but distant voice from somewhere over my left shoulder. Behind me stands an over-muscled surfer dude in a three-piece suit. He looks noticeably uncomfortable in the attire.

"We went to school together. You dated my roommate sophomore year. His name was John Burns. Surely you remember."

But I didn't. That doesn't mean I didn't date his roommate. Shit, I might even have slept with his roommate.

"Sure. I think I remember him," I say, not having a clue who he's talking about. But muscle man has appeal—a pretty face, athletic build, and a nice smile. And I am hammered.

"My name is Kent. Kent Darcy. Can I buy you a drink?"

Cat chimes in, "Sure, you can buy us a drink." She makes a "two" signal to the bartender, then points at Kent. "These are on him." The bartender begins mixing two more cosmos.

"Hi, I'm Catherine. Friends call me Cat. Thanks for the drinks. That's a really nice suit. Men's Wearhouse has a better selection than people give them credit for." I turn and shoot Cat the dirtiest look I can manage in my state—before I can stop myself from smiling. She responds by flipping me off. In fact, she gives me two fingers. Our drinks arrive and we each take a more-than-adequate first draw.

"Do you want to dance?" Kent asks.

"I think I'm danced out," I say.

"Come on. It's a slow one." The Foreigner song "I Want to Know What Love Is" glides through the stereo speakers. He takes off his Men's Wearhouse jacket and sets it on the back of the chair. Then he lifts my hand and tugs until I submit to the dance floor. It's a slow dance, and soon enough, his hand is on my back.

I can feel his muscled body beneath his shirt and the dampness on his skin. My body is aroused, despite the lack of familiarity— or maybe because of it. Ridiculous, drunken schoolgirl thoughts stream through my pickled head. Fabio comes on his white steed and carries me away. The alcohol and drugs have dulled my inhibitions. The song saves me by ending.

We walk back to our stools. Cat leans over and whispers, "I thought maybe you were going to fuck him on the dance floor. Show some class and take him to the bathroom." I flash her my best dirty look.

Our drinks are empty. Kent puts up two fingers to the bartender. The bar is noticeably quieter. It's just after midnight, and I've been here for five hours. I'm not sure how many drinks I've had on an empty stomach, bolstered only by a cocaine supplement.

"You know, I always liked you. I thought that John was an asshole to you. You probably don't remember me. I was a much smaller guy—think I've grown four inches and maybe fifty pounds. You know I have a job at Morgan Stanley now. Just getting started, of course, but it's a great company."

I can't believe it, but I'm feeling an attraction—and almost sympathy—for my newfound friend.

"Becca, we should get going. It's late, and I've got a full day tomorrow." Cat is chiming in, but I know the real goal is to rescue me from bad decisions.

"Catherine, I can get her home. She's in safe hands," Kent says as he gently places his safe-feeling hand on my shoulder.

I stop for a moment to assess. Four or five cosmopolitans have removed any critical thought from my mind, and I don't want to be alone. I turn and look at Kent. He's handsome, athletic, and he seems nice. My mind works to rationalize why this is not a problem.

"We'll get home okay, Cat. I know Kent from school. We'll be fine."

Cat leans close and whispers to me, "Are you sure you're okay? If you want out, just grab my hand and I'll know not to leave."

I look at Cat and struggle to focus and speak without a slur. "No, we're fine."

"Okay then, Becca. If you need anything—anything—call me, and I will come."

Cat reaches over and kisses me on the cheek. Kent and I remain at the bar, making small talk and finishing cosmopolitan number unknown.

"Ready to go?" Kent asks. But now I'm having second thoughts.

"Kent, I think I'm going to catch a cab. I'm quite drunk, and I'm afraid I wouldn't be good company."

"Well then, I'll walk you out and flag down a cab for you," says Kent.

I stagger off my bar stool toward the door—the same door I came in almost six hours ago. As we walk out, there's a large silver Bentley parked in front of the bar. Now, a Bentley is not that rare in New York, but a Bentley in front of this bar, at this time is quite strange.

There's a man in a gray suit with a white shirt and silver tie standing in front of the expensive automobile. He is dark, but not African American—maybe Asian—with a military-style haircut. When I exit the bar, he changes posture, standing erect. I am certain he is looking at me.

Like the flip of a switch, Kent becomes very handsy. His hands are on my back, my ass, my neck. I am uncomfortable and feeling a bit nauseous as the world begins to spin. Kent grabs the back of my head and forces his tongue down my throat. His hands make it to my breasts. I push back and he walks away briefly to hail a cab. He pulls on my arm and I resist, but I am very wobbly and lightheaded. He opens the cab door and grabs my waist to pull me into the car.

Whatever romantic feeling I had has now turned into drunken panic. I take my free arm and press it against Kent's muscled bicep and whisper, "No." I know it is barely audible.

"Rebecca, I know you. I know what you like. And you definitely don't mean no."

A new voice enters the periphery of my hearing. "Mate, I think she means no. Why don't you leave the young lady? She's obviously had too much to drink." It's the driver of the expensive car.

"Listen, Sanjay—or whoever the fuck you are—this is none of your goddamned business. If you know what's good for you, you'll stay clear and just stick to driving the boss's car."

The coffee-colored man steps between Kent and me. Kent easily has three inches and forty pounds on him. Kent grabs the man by his tie and lifts. "Now fuck off, I said," Kent sneers.

The driver takes his left hand and pushes me back behind him. In one motion, he lifts his right hand and strikes Kent's chin with the heel of his palm. That move is seamlessly followed by his left hand to the right side of Kent's torso. Kent is stunned. He releases the driver's tie and stumbles, trying to regain balance.

But the smaller man is not done. He steps forward, places his right leg behind Kent's left, and rotates his torso, landing a fist to the center of Kent's chest, immediately followed by a second left to the torso. Kent is reeling. A final blow is delivered by the smaller man's right hand to Kent's neck. Kent wobbles on his heels. The driver adjusts his tie back into place. As Kent staggers backward, ready to fall, the man catches his upper arm and sits him on the stoop of the clothing store next to Pancho's.

"Spread your legs and put your head between them. Try to take deep breaths. That's right, deep breaths. Okay, look up for a moment." The driver provides instructions to the larger man as Kent starts to regain his composure. "You'll be okay. Had the wind knocked out of you, that's all."

Kent lifts his head, and the darker man opens his eyelids, checking each pupil. "I think you've had enough for tonight, young man."

"Miss Rome, it's time you called it a day as well. It's my job to get you home, so please..." He walks over to the Bentley and opens the back door. "Need a hand, Miss?" he asks.

"Do you even know where I live?"

He whispers; "Rebecca Rome, you live at 89th and First, Unit 3206."

I assume one of Eric's family members has arranged this ride. I'll be in deep shit when they hear about this outing. At this point, I'm also certain I'm going to be sick. But still, I walk to the car the best I can. Whatever judgment I have left is all bad.

The man in the suit remains standing, holding the door open. I get to the door and turn to see Kent, still with his head between his legs, trying to catch his breath. He looks up and we briefly exchange glances before he lowers his head again.

I look at the man holding the door, then back at Kent. The man's military haircut doesn't have a strand out of place. His shirt looks impeccably pressed, as if he just put it on. There's not a drop of sweat on his face.

"Who are you, some sort of superhero?"

The driver responds, "Rebecca, if you feel like you're going to be sick, please let me know, and I'll pull the car over. My employer wouldn't be happy if your insides ended up all over the interior."

CHAPTER 10

I DIDN'T GET YOUR NAME

WAKING UP REQUIRED AN INVENTORY of my faculties. I recognized the room because it was mine. My hair was gummed and crunchy. There was a stench of vomit on my pillowcase. I sat up in bed only to immediately feel so sick that I lay down again. My head throbbed. I struggled to turn my head to see my clock mocking me: 9:30. At least it was Saturday, I think. I wouldn't have to feign some deathly illness to escape work.

I felt my body... I was only wearing a T-shirt. Yet, I didn't recall how I got into the T-shirt, nor did I remember getting into my room. I slowly sat up in bed. The shades had been drawn, allowing small slivers of light to illuminate the otherwise dark space. My phone sat on the charger pad by my nightstand. I picked it up. Six messages. Four missed calls. Eric accounted for all but one; the other was Cat, asking if I had made it back home. I struggled to type a one-word response: Alive. A smiley face immediately flashed on the screen.

On my third attempt, I rose and made it to the bathroom. My clothes were in the tub, still damp. A small residue of my insides, both on my clothing and around the drain, resembled some sort of roadkill. This was some world-class damage I had done. Then a second wave of nausea came over me, raising the bar for how shitty I felt.

There was a man who took me home. I remembered now. A vague discussion with my doorman in the lobby, and me puking my guts up as I made a break for the bathroom. I was sure this had already been relayed to my fiancé, Eric. Worse than the nausea would be the endless waves of bullshit coming in my direction.

I picked up the clothes from the tub and tossed them into the plastic bag that lined the trash can. Then I turned the water to the hottest level I could stand. There I sat, underneath the running shower for a full fifteen minutes. I threw on some yoga pants and a sweatshirt top and made my way toward the bedroom door.

I was too wounded to say anything when I entered the living room. Sitting on the couch, reading one of my John Grisham novels, was a man in a gray suit. The man from last night. His jacket was set over the back of the couch. I could see the burgundy sateen interior of the neatly folded garment. He looked up at me, said nothing, and simply raised the coffee cup from the saucer to his mouth, blew on it for a moment, then took a sip.

My first thought was that I didn't know I had saucers that matched those coffee cups. My second thought was how striking the man looked—chiseled features, coffee-colored skin, and a tailored shirt over his hardbody build. When he looked up at me, his green eyes looked fake against his dark skin. I shook my head to clear the cobwebs.

"I didn't get your name," I said.

"Harkirat, but my friends call me Hart. Sikh names aren't all that common, and it makes things simple. Would you like a cup of coffee? I took the liberty of making some. I hope you don't mind." He glanced at the book cover. "Also picked this up. Kind of a fan." Hart spoke with a distinct English accent.

I got right to the point. "If you can keep this misadventure to yourself, I'll compensate you for your discretion."

"I'm afraid that ship has sailed. My employer insists on being informed of my activities."

"Shit. I think I'll have some of that coffee." I slinked into the closet-sized space my landlord labeled as a kitchen, poured myself a cup, then walked back and plopped down opposite Hart.

We sat in silence as I drank most of my first cup of wakefulness. That's not to say there weren't moments when I started a sentence. I did, but I simply lacked the brainpower to finish it.

"You're Sikh? Huh. You sound English."

"My father was Sikh, my mother British, but both are gone now. I was raised outside of London."

"Well, that makes sense... I mean, the accent and the darker complexion." Hart raised an eyebrow, and I wanted to crawl between the couch cushions after my clearly—but unintentionally—racist comment. I drained my cup of coffee in silence, noticing that my companion's cup was also empty.

"Pointing out the obvious, I woke up in different clothing than I was wearing last night. I'm assuming you coordinated that."

"Rebecca, I couldn't very well have left you as you were. You were feeling quite ill. I think they call it the Irish flu. So I cleaned up the place a little bit—and you as well."

62

"We didn't, we didn't... do anything else, did we?" I asked, unable to make eye contact.

"Rest assured your virginity is intact. Nothing I haven't seen before." A moment of uncomfortable silence hung in the room before Hart filled it. "Well, it looks like you're on the mend. I'll be going now. Just wanted to make sure you were okay. I told Mr. Martin that I would."

"Mr. Martin? Who is Martin?" I asked.

"Jackson Martin. My employer asked me to look out for you last night. Must be honest, more of an errand than I anticipated."

"You mean you don't work for Eric or his family?"

"I'm sorry, ma'am. I don't know who that is, but I'm certain I don't work for them. Just Mr. Martin."

"Finally, some news that does not make me want to kill myself. Thank God. Well, I guess I owe you a thank you for getting me home safely—and not raping me while I was passed out."

"You are entirely welcome on both accounts."

Hart picked up his jacket, adjusted the cuffs of each sleeve, and aligned his tie. Continuing with precision, he buttoned his jacket, placed the coffee cup and saucer in the sink, and walked out the door without another word.

I sat in silence for ten minutes, then picked up my phone and hit speed dial number two. It went to voicemail. "You have reached the voicemail of Dr. Sharon Green..."

PART IV

JORDAN ROME

Miami, Florida
1979: 22 Years Before

CHAPTER 11

9 AT NIGHT TILL 4 IN THE MORNING?

THE CONSTRUCTION WORK IN ATLANTA had come to a near standstill. In the year I spent building apartments in Buckhead, I managed to put together a small nest egg that I used to move further south—to Miami. I was eighteen, with an extra twenty pounds on my six-foot-one frame, courtesy of my work as a concrete laborer. My face and features had changed too. Staring back at me each morning in the mirror was a darker image of the man I loathed most in my short life: my father.

I had also lost track of Mom. We exchanged one letter, in which she informed me she was moving to Phoenix. I was unable to find her new address or stay in one place long enough for her to find me. I was alone, but Miami felt like my opportunity. The town seemed immune to the economic malaise gripping the rest of the country. This would be where I made my new start.

I drove up and down Coconut Grove and Biscayne Bay. Money looked like it was falling from the palm trees. Fancy cars, beautiful women, nightclubs, and hotels all pulsed with activity, twenty-four hours a day. I tried my luck at several construction sites, restaurants, and hotels, but to no avail. I needed work, and I needed it soon.

One day, I spotted a sign outside a small industrial building that looked out of place in such a flashy part of town. The sign advertised automobile detailing, with a bumper-sticker-sized banner taped across it at an angle. "HELP WANTED." I went inside.

The building was a sixty-foot-wide garage supported by clear-span bow trusses. Oversized fans roared, circulating the stale, humid air. Beneath the open space was a flurry of activity—various Black and brown men working feverishly on Ferraris, Lamborghinis, Porsches, and every other imaginable high-priced car. I'd never seen so much wealth concentrated in such a small space.

In the corner of the building, a metal stairway led to a small mezzanine office surrounded by glass on two sides. I climbed the stairs and knocked on the door, dodging the constant drip from the small AC unit above the entrance. An overweight man looked up from his desk and signaled for me to come in. Without removing the phone from his ear, he raised one finger in the air. I opened the door, and a small Latin woman with comically large breast implants and skintight spandex told me to sit on the vinyl couch—one that had been granted multiple extra lives thanks to the miracle of duct tape.

The office was a disaster. Papers, food boxes, and beer bottles covered the coffee table in front of the couch. A greasy film coated the cushions, impossible to avoid.

"What the fuck do you want?" the man behind the desk barked, swigging the last of a Tab before setting the empty can on the desk.

He stood up, exposing his ample gut, hairy chest, and a ridiculous thick gold chain around his neck.

"I saw you were looking for help. I'm new in town and could use a job." I avoided eye contact with his assistant.

"Job pays six an hour. I pay on Fridays. The tips for any given car are split among the crew that works on it. I take ten percent of the tips off the top. If you're ten minutes late, you're fired. If you miss a day, you're fired. If you steal anything out of the cars, I'll break your face. And then you're fired. I'd ask if you had any questions, but I just don't give a fuck if you do." He smirked. "Do you want the job?"

I took a moment to think—a moment too long for Mr. I-Don't-Give-a-Fuck.

"Look, Einstein. It's a simple yes or no. If you want to work, go see Hector downstairs. If not, get the fuck out of my office." He picked up the Tab can, easily crumpled the pink aluminum, and tossed the mangled metal into the trash.

"Yes," I said.

"Yes you want the job?" He let out a snort.

"Yes, I want the job."

The girl in spandex finally spoke. "OK, young man, I will introduce you to Hector."

As we walked down the stairs, I stayed several steps behind her. Her perfume was overwhelming. When she got to the ground floor, she turned to me, standing two stairs back.

"Just so you know, we are not together. He thinks he owns me, but he does not. Jesus, I mean. He is the manager, but he does not own it. She owns it." She paused for a moment. "If you want, maybe we can have a drink sometime, me and you."

"I'm not sure that having a drink with my new boss's girlfriend— or friend, or whatever your relationship is—would be a good start, especially if I value my life. But thank you for the offer. Maybe things will change, and we could have that drink sometime later." I said this as politely as possible, but she was angry—I could see it.

"OK, Whitey, suit yourself. But believe me, you don't know what you're missing."

The ground floor buzzed with the sound of buffing machines, vacuums, air hoses, and a blaring boombox playing Spanish-language music. The spandex girl introduced me in Spanish to Hector. They exchanged a joke in Spanish at my expense, outlining how estúpido a white man must be to take this loco trabajo.

There was no way for them to know that, having grown up in southern Arizona, the language was as native to me as it was to them. I responded, "Los hombres blancos también comen"— roughly translated as "white men eat also." Spandex girl turned on her heel, adjusted her breasts, and returned to her office.

Hector and Jesus ran a tight ship. The six bucks an hour was starvation wages, but I needed the income. What I didn't know was how the clientele viewed money. Young men, not much older than I was, brought in cars that cost upwards of $50,000. They would casually tip $100 for their car to look showroom-ready.

Two men could do four cars a day if they worked ten hours. Jesus and Hector didn't take 10% off the top. They skimmed 15%—each. Still, I could clear $150 a day in cash. I had never seen that much money. So I worked and kept my head down. I befriended my coworkers, who were largely Spanish-speaking, from the Caribbean, Central America, or Mexico.

It was hard work and hot. Our clothes clung to our bodies as if we'd showered in them.

At night, we went out and spent the cash we'd replenish the next day. I discovered I could drink it as fast as I could make it.

But I learned something else in those bars as well: women liked money. Looking good was helpful, but money was a necessity. It didn't make a difference what you looked like if you had it, and it didn't make a difference what you looked like if you didn't.

After six months, I had settled into a rhythm at the shop. I worked six days a week and became the requested laborer for the most expensive cars. The drivers knew me by name and would refuse to bring their prized chariot in without a commitment that I would handle it. I demanded—and got—a renegotiation of how we split our tips. I went from 70% to 80%.

Owners would frequently and discreetly slip me a $20 in addition to the tip they left with Hector. In my young mind, I felt I was successful.

Friday morning, March 7, changed everything. A stretch white Rolls rolled into the garage. I had seen this beast before but had never worked on it. Hector handled it himself. Two giant men loomed in the front seat, with a woman in the rear. She exited the automobile and called Hector over. She pointed to me, then exited the building with the two men, one in front and one behind her.

"Jordan, I want you to do this one today. This is the boss's car. It better be perfect or you're a dead man," Hector said, his voice thick with anger.

"I thought you did this car. Why aren't you doing it today?" I asked.

"What, do I look like I make the decisions here? She wants you to do it. I don't give a fuck why. You do it. And quit asking so many fucking questions." Hector tossed me the keys.

I worked with one other guy on the car for six hours. The Rolls was enormous before it was stretched, and about the size of a small studio apartment afterward. The doors and glass were

71

bulletproof, making each item four times its weight. Just moving the parts around was an effort.

When we were done, the engine bay was as clean as a surgery center. The finish on the car was polished to where it wouldn't hold a handkerchief without it sliding off. The brightwork and wheels looked like mirrors. The automobile hadn't looked this good coming off the assembly line.

When the woman returned, she arrived in a black Suburban, attended by the same two men she'd left with. For fifteen minutes, she inspected the car's every detail as if she were buying it. I stood back thirty feet to show due respect for my position versus hers.

The larger of the two men, the driver, opened the rear door. The owner of the car made eye contact with me, smiled, then entered the rear of the spotless automobile. The second man returned to the Suburban, and the larger man walked up to me.

"Mrs. Cassandra has instructed me to offer you a job at the front door of the Mutiny Hotel Club. It's in the lower level of the hotel. The job starts Monday."

I responded with my best effort to look polite but firm. "I appreciate the offer. But I believe I can make more money here than as a doorman at a hotel. So if you would, please tell your employer I'd prefer to keep the job that I have."

The man let out such a loud belly laugh that it almost scared me. He raised his right hand and put it on my left shoulder.

"I may not have been clear. This is not an offer from 'my employer.' This place—the place you're working in now—is hers. The hotel where you'll work is hers. Half the buildings on this street are hers. She's already your employer, and you start on Monday. And don't worry about the money."

The driver reached into his pocket and pulled out a fat wallet, from which he counted ten $100 bills. "Think of it as a signing bonus." He almost smiled for a second, then his face went dark and serious again.

"Monday."

The man turned and walked back to the Rolls.

"What time do I start? I mean, what time should I be there, and what do I wear?" I shouted.

The man returned from the car once more and reached into his vest pocket. This time, he handed me a card.

"Call this person. She'll meet you tomorrow and get you the necessary clothing. You should plan on coming in between 9 and 10. The place closes around 4."

The man again walked back to his car.

"I assume you mean 9 at night and 4 in the morning," I said, thinking it could just as easily be the other way around.

"That's right, Jordan. You got it right."

The man smiled and shook his head as he sat behind the wheel of the enormous white Rolls-Royce.

CHAPTER 12

LEAVE THE SUIT ON

I REMEMBER WATCHING RERUNS OF The Jackie Gleason Show, which my father seemed to enjoy. It was filmed "Live from Miami Beach." They would show clips of Collins Avenue and the magnificent hotels along the waterfront. This was how I imagined the city.

Miami during the late 70s and early 80s was a different place than The Jackie Gleason Show portrayed. There was one reason for that difference: cocaine. Though other drugs ran through South Florida, nothing changed Miami like the importation of cocaine. I was clueless to this fact before my arrival.

The statistics were staggering. The DEA believed that approximately 75 tons of cocaine came through Dade County each year. The actual amount was closer to 175 tons. This accounted for one-third of Miami's economic activity. Seventy percent of the cocaine that entered the United States and Canada passed through Miami, bringing $12 billion a year into the economy.

The amount of cash was unprecedented. The Federal Reserve Bank in Miami held twice as much cash as the other eleven Federal Reserve banks combined. One-third of the homes purchased in Miami were paid for in cash. Exotic cars and jewelry outsold every city in the country, including New York and Los Angeles. The mayor of Miami famously said that "the skyline of Miami was built on cocaine."

Young people, often Latin Americans in their twenties and thirties, lived like sultans, flaunting cars, yachts, and oceanside mansions indiscreetly.

One of those people was Cassandra Diego. She was a thirty-four-year-old Guatemalan widow of a Colombian man who died at the hands of two assassins on the streets of Medellín. Her now-deceased husband was twenty-five years older than Cassandra. As one might imagine, there was no estate planning, so Cassandra took it upon herself to "inherit" the distribution business he had so carefully set up in Miami.

She was twenty-nine at the time, with a thirteen-year-old son. This distribution business generated $80 million a month in revenue. By comparison, Apple Computers generated $28 million per month.

The unspoken rumor surrounding her husband's death was that Cassandra herself had him executed to avoid being discarded for his then-current teenage mistress. That mistress, too, would become collateral damage in the corporate shake-up that followed Cassandra's hostile takeover of the Miami business.

The dramatic infusion of wealth into the economy ultimately had other impacts beyond financial. Though cocaine was widely used in social circles across the country, it remained illegal. Territorial control was fought over tenaciously, with violent outcomes.

Miami became the murder capital of the United States. In 1980, a record 573 people were slain. This was only surpassed in 1981 with 621 murders. Shootouts with automatic weapons occurred in broad daylight on major thoroughfares. Ten percent of the police force would eventually be indicted. Five municipal judges went to jail. But this came later in the story.

In 1979, the day I started working at the Mutiny Hotel, the only thing anyone could see was money.

The Friday night I was offered the job at the Mutiny, I called the phone number on the card given to me earlier that afternoon.

"Hello, this is Gabriel," said the sultry voice that answered.

"Hello, Gabriel, my name is Jordan Rome. I was given your number by an associate of Mrs. Diego. This man told me that you would..."

Gabriel cut me off mid-sentence.

"I assume you're another hillbilly pretty boy they're trying to make presentable. I can meet you tomorrow at 12 o'clock. You can buy me breakfast. We'll meet at the coffee shop in the Fontainebleau Hotel. Try not to embarrass me."

Click. No goodbye. No confirmation that I got the message. Just click.

I had one button-down shirt that had belonged to my brother. I also had the cleanest pair of khakis he'd owned. I didn't have any good shoes, so I washed my tennis shoes with bleach to make them as white as possible.

I arrived at the Fontainebleau Hotel fifteen minutes early. At 12:30, Gabriel walked in, stood at the hostess stand, and looked around. She didn't need to be told whom she was meeting. It was obvious who looked most out of place.

She walked past the hostess without acknowledgment. She paid no attention to the heads that turned as she moved through the room, her silk sundress clinging to her figure, accentuating her rotating hips.

Before sitting down, she stopped a random waiter. "I'll take a Bloody Mary—make it a double," she said.

When she sat down, she pulled her sunglasses down just enough for me to see her eyes. She looked me up and down.

"Well, I can see why you got the job. They're always looking for a certain, you know, look." She reset her sunglasses. "So, which backwater armpit did you come from? Mississippi? Arkansas? No, don't tell me—Alabama?"

"Bisbee, Arizona, actually. That's in southern Arizona, just north of Mexico," I said, fumbling with the napkin in my lap.

"How the hell did you end up out here? How old are you anyway?"

"I'm twenty-one," I lied. "Just making my own way and thought Miami would be a good place." I paused, unaware that I was staring. "I'm sure you're told this all the time, but you're really a beautiful woman," I said without thinking—and immediately regretted it.

I'd never seen a woman like her. I mean, with a figure and face like that.

She acted as if she hadn't heard me and waved at our waiter, asking where her Bloody Mary was.

"Easy, Tiger. Believe me, you can't afford the payments. So, let's focus on getting you out of this clown costume and into something that will fool the idiots you'll meet Monday night."

The waiter scurried over. I ordered an omelet; she ordered toast and a second Bloody Mary. She took one bite of the toast but quickly finished both drinks. As her straw made a slurping sound at the bottom of the second Bloody, she stood up.

"Take care of this, won't you, sweetheart? I need to powder my nose. I'll meet you at the front door."

I spent the afternoon shopping with Gabriel. She had a credit card she used for every purchase. There was no discussion of repayment—or of who was footing the bill. She never asked the price of anything. She simply told me to try something on, and if she approved, she instructed the employee, whom she usually knew by name, to wrap it and send it to the address I gave.

I couldn't help but smile, imagining the delivery drivers' expressions when they showed up at my ramshackle apartment with absurdly priced garments.

At each stop, Gabriel was offered a glass of champagne, which she gladly accepted.

It was at our third stop that Gabriel first addressed me by name. I didn't know how to interpret that change. Maybe it was the two Bloodies and four glasses of champagne.

Our last stop was a boutique that specialized in men's suits. It was around 6:30. Gabriel picked out a gray suit, a white shirt, and brown shoes. The suit needed tailoring, but the tailor had already gone home. The salesperson informed her it would be ready by the middle of next week.

She looked at her. "Well, that won't work. We need the suit now. Call him up and have him come back. We'll wait while he makes the necessary adjustments." Gabriel said this as if she were asking someone to pass the salt.

The salesperson was speechless and thought it best to confer with the manager before dismissing the request outright. She walked over and spoke to the manager in a whisper. He looked up at Gabriel and picked up the phone. Then he walked over. "The tailor will be here shortly. Would you like us to order anything for you while you wait?"

"Some caviar and toast with cream cheese would be nice. I don't want to spoil my appetite."

The salesperson walked out the door to fulfill Gabriel's request. Not ten minutes later, the tailor was altering my suit, a bottle of champagne had been opened, and we were nibbling on a snack I had never tasted. I was a long way from Bisbee, and I liked it.

The suit was completed at 8:30. I tried it on again. The man in the mirror was a new person — a person I had never seen. Gabriel came up and adjusted my hair, the lapels, and the collar of my suit and shirt. "Fuck, maybe you're dumb as a box of rocks, but you're definitely a looker." She took her hand and rubbed the side of my face despite the two-day stubble. "Leave the suit on. I think we'll wear it out to dinner."

CHAPTER 13

EVEN LOOKS GOOD WITHOUT THE SHIRT

LOCATED AT **2951 S BAYSHORE** Dr in Coconut Grove, The Mutiny Hotel boasted 105 luxury suites, each decorated differently. The lower level housed a bar and disco that rivaled Manhattan's Studio 54. The clientele was unique, high-end, and celebrity-focused. Fleetwood Mac, The Rolling Stones, Tom Jones—any celebrity vacationing in Miami would make a stop to see and be seen. The club opened at 10:00 pm and closed whenever it closed. Although the posted closing time was 4:00 am, most nights it buzzed until daylight.

The hotel was titled to a corporate holding company out of Panama, but the real owner was Cassandra Diego, as was the club. Aside from luxury accommodations, the Mutiny was known for unique services unavailable elsewhere in Miami. The rooms upstairs offered oversized tubs and beds featuring mirrored ceilings, leather restraints, and a variety of other paraphernalia to meet the special needs of their guests.

The most important feature of the hotel was security. Beautiful women called Mutiny Girls worked as "hostesses" and "escorts" while providing the other "personal services" requested by patrons, and at the same time, ensured none of the guests were carrying weapons. Gabriel was a Mutiny Girl. The unspoken truth about the Mutiny was that gangsters and drug runners, as well as politicians, policemen, and judges, could mingle there without fear for their safety. Competitors out to kill each other would sit side by side talking business. When a guest arrived at the entry, I would politely ask if they had any weapons they would like to check. I also provided a superficial pat down to anyone suspicious. If I suspected they were carrying, I would let the Mutiny Girls know, and they would confirm with a pat down of a different type. If anyone refused to relinquish their weapon, they were asked to leave and barred from the club. After meeting my coworkers and the rest of the Mutiny Girls, I understood the game: the personal presentation of an athletic, well-groomed individual lent both the illusion of security and the perception of an upscale operation. Everything about The Mutiny Club was image-driven, and that made me an ideal candidate for the job.

Every night the place was packed. The Mutiny served more Dom Perignon than any club in the country. Music blared as beautiful bodies, capitalizing on their chemically altered state, danced all through the night. Entry without knowing someone— or being breathtakingly attractive—was impossible. This created the opportunity to receive handsome gratuities as the gatekeeper. On a good night, I could easily clear $500. I kept my nose clean, avoided confrontation whenever possible, and started to print money. After a short time, I knew most patrons by first name: who had power, who had money, who was potentially violent. Cassandra's son Eduardo fit each of these categories. In current parlance, he would be diagnosed with bipolar disorder aggravated by drug addiction. At least once a week, I had to step between him and another patron to avert a brawl. I would separate the two, buy the patron a drink, and do my best to smooth over Eduardo's temper. Five months and three days into my job, that task became impossible. I was called to assist in a skirmish in the women's bathroom, where inside a stall Eduardo had taken a toilet seat to the side of a woman's head. She was naked and badly injured. Her husband, unaware of who Eduardo was, had responded in kind, taking a blade to Eduardo's throat before rescuing his wife. When I entered the bathroom, he had Eduardo pinned to the floor and was cursing at him, knife raised in the air. There was no time to think or respond; just as my brother had hit my father like a linebacker, I body-slammed Eduardo's assailant. We tumbled across the room, both momentarily stunned. He then stood up, looked around for his knife, and grabbed it to come back at me. But he was clearly injured from the tackle's impact, slowing him as he limped in my direction.

I squared off, ready for his charge.

"Stop, just stop for a goddamned second and listen to me. You and your wife have one chance to live through this night—if you take her to a hospital and get the fuck out of here. You have no idea the trouble you're in. Take her. Take her to a hospital now and don't ever come back. Any other decision, and you'll be a dead man. I promise."

For whatever reason, I was able to speak this in a composed monotone.

Eduardo struggled to his feet to face the man holding the knife. I turned to him.

"Eduardo, you don't want this. You don't want to bring the heat down on this place by killing this guy here. Your mom will kick your ass if you do."

There was rustling behind me. A small group of patrons stood in the doorway to the women's bathroom, guaranteeing witnesses to whatever happened next. Eduardo took a vial from his pocket, walked over to the mirror, and snorted once in each nostril. Then he bulled his way out the door.

I went into the stall to assist the woman who had confused a hat for a toilet seat. A nasty cut on the side of her head was bleeding heavily. I took off my jacket and shirt and tied the shirt tightly around her head. Then I called out to the other security doorman, Erin, who was working with me that night. He was standing stunned in the doorway with the others.

"Erin, call a cab for this girl. She's going to the hospital."

I picked her up and carried her to the covered drive, where a cab was already waiting. Her husband was right behind me. I looked at him.

"Get in the cab. Your car will be parked on the street two blocks up on the north side. The keys will be under the floor mat. Don't come back here. Ever. Understand?"

He nodded.

When I turned around, a crowd was staring at me, shirtless and covered in blood. Gabriel walked forward and handed me my suit jacket. I put it on and thanked her.

She gave me a broad smile. "The suit even looks good without the shirt."

Gabriel took me upstairs and opened the door to one of the suites.

"Take a shower. I'll send some clothes up for you. Cassandra wants to talk to you later."

When I got out of the shower, there were carhop slacks and a golf shirt with the hotel's name on the breast. I helped myself to a beer from the mini-bar and sat down in front of the television. Then, at three in the morning, the large man who was the driver for Mrs. Diego knocked on the door.

"She'll see you now," he said, opening the door.

The two of us entered the elevator. He took out a key and unlocked an unlabeled button. The elevator ascended and didn't stop until we reached the top floor. During the ride, we made no eye contact and said nothing.

On the landing, two men stood in a small vestibule flanked by heavy wooden double doors. When we reached one set of doors, the large man looked up at a small glass plate near the ceiling. With a click, the doors opened.

We entered a small lobby with yet another man at a desk. Another click, and we stepped into a sprawling office. The back wall was glass, with the city lights twinkling beyond. To the right sat a large, vacant antique desk, flanked by four white leather club chairs. To the left was a larger seating group in a sunken living room configuration. Two couches faced each other across a large glass and chrome coffee table. On the table were white lines of powder and heavy cocktail glasses.

Behind the seating area, four large aquariums spanned twelve feet, floor to ceiling. Mrs. Diego sat on one couch. Eduardo and another man sat on the second.

To the boy from Bisbee, this was hard to absorb.

"Jordan, please join us. You've met Ricardo." She looked over at the large man who had brought me up the elevator and now stood behind the couch with the other two men. "This is my husband, Alexander, and I believe you know Eduardo quite well." The three of us nodded at one another. "Can we get you a drink?"

"A beer would be nice, thank you."

"Ricardo, please get Jordan a beer. A Budweiser, I assume for the Gringo."

"Budweiser is fine."

Cassandra shifted on the couch, turning and recrossing her legs in the opposite direction. "In a very short time, you've made quite an impression, young man. I wanted to thank you for helping Eduardo through an unfortunate and delicate matter tonight. You displayed a cool head and intelligent behavior. The Mutiny prides itself on avoiding unnecessary public attention."

"I was just doing what I thought was my job, Mrs. Diego. There's no reason to thank me."

"Nonsense. Good work deserves recognition, and loyalty should be commended and rewarded." She continued as Ricardo handed me my beer. "I like to think of myself as a good judge of talent. It's hard to know for sure if your instincts are correct, but surrounding yourself with the right people can make all the difference between success and failure."

"Well, Mrs. Diego—" She interrupted me.

"Please, my friends call me Cassandra."

"Cassandra, I want to do a good job, and I appreciate the money I've made working here."

"Very good. What do you think about taking a job that comes with more responsibility—and, of course, more money?" It almost sounds like a question, but given who I'm working for, I know it's not. She reached over and placed her finger in the white powder, then brought it to her lips, pressing it between her lip and front teeth. She lifted a glass of brown liquor off the table, took a draw, and pulled her mouth back over her teeth before returning her face to its resting position.

"Our work involves some risk. I assume you've figured that out by now. But it also comes with extraordinary rewards for a skilled young man like yourself. You'd work with Ricardo, running special tasks for the organization. Is that something you'd be interested in?" Again, I know she's not really asking.

Before I could respond, the door opened, and Gabriel entered, struggling with a banker's box that looked far too heavy to hold just files. Ricardo took it from her and walked into a room behind the oversized desk.

Gabriel made eye contact with me, then looked back at Cassandra.

"It was a very good night. Unfortunately, that also makes for a very heavy box," she said, smiling at Cassandra.

Eduardo stood and moved inches from Gabriel. "Hi, Gabby. Want to blow this pop stand and head over to my house for a nightcap?"

"No, Eddy. I think I'm done for tonight, but thank you anyway." She turned back to the couch and stepped sideways away from Eduardo. "Will you be needing anything else, Cassandra?"

Alexander chimed in uninvited. "Eduardo, sit down. You're embarrassing yourself. Just leave her alone already."

"Fuck you...not my dad," Eduardo growled.

"Eduardo, please sit down. We're trying to have a civil conversation," Cassandra interjected.

Eduardo sat without another word.

"Okay then, I'll be going." As always, I stared at her like everyone else in the room. She turned and looked at me, holding momentary eye contact. "Good night, Jordan," she said, omitting any other names from her farewell.

"Good night, Gabriel." Her smile, directed at me, didn't go unnoticed by anyone in the room.

Gabriel walked out the door, and Cassandra returned to her ritual of powder and brown liquor. Several moments of silence followed.

"Eduardo, why don't you run along with your friends? I'd like to finish this conversation with Jordan."

Eduardo shook his head, teeth clenched, muttering something no one could hear—or cared to. He stood and stomped out of the room in what could only be called a tantrum.

Once he left, Cassandra spoke in a near whisper. "My son has always been a hot-headed boy. He lost his father very young, you know. I think it's taken a toll."

I remained quiet.

Cassandra leaned back, looking up at the ceiling. "Do you like that one? Gabriel, I mean. She's very popular with the men. She's also quite valuable for special projects of mine. Maybe I can put in a good word for you."

Again, I didn't answer.

"Well, there is much to think about. And as you can see, there is another day coming to welcome us." Cassandra turned toward the massive glass windows at the end of her office. I could see the sun just breaking over the horizon. "Each day we're on this earth is a blessing, don't you think?" She stood and walked to the window, staring at the bold yellow light now creeping into the day. "We'll talk tomorrow. Tell me what you think then."

She said nothing more. Ricardo gave me a nod and tilted his head toward the door. I stood and followed him.

"Thank you for the beer. Alexander, it was nice to meet you."

"Good night, Jordan," Cassandra said without turning around. Alexander just nodded.

Ricardo took me down to the room where my formerly soiled suit, now freshly dry-cleaned, awaited me in a plastic hotel bag. I picked it up and went back down in the elevator with Ricardo to the lobby. The new day was now clearly presenting itself. I could hear lawn mower engines humming as the landscapers worked to beat the full heat of the day. I looked up at the cloudless sky and took a large breath of the warm, moist Florida air.

This was more than a new day. Perhaps it was the start of a new life.

As I looked down, a small white BMW convertible pulled up. Behind the wheel was Gabriel, now changed out of her hotel uniform, wearing athletic shorts and a loose AC/DC T-shirt.

"Come on, Jordan. I'll give you a ride. Maybe this time I'll buy breakfast."

I threw my suit bag in the back and slid into the passenger seat of the convertible. Gabriel started to drive, then stopped just short of turning onto Bayshore. She reached over, gently took the back of my neck, pulled my head toward hers, and kissed me on the mouth. Then she smiled and made a hard right up Bayshore Drive.

CHAPTER 14

YOU CAN FIX THE GARBAGE DISPOSAL

"I DID PROMISE YOU BREAKFAST. I'll make us some eggs."

Gabriel climbed out of bed and walked naked to the bathroom, where she brushed her teeth and combed her hair with the door open. I rolled over to her side of the bed to watch the sunlight catch her figure as she stood unclothed before the sink. She looked at me and smiled, toothbrush in her mouth, toothpaste trailing down her chin. She made no effort to deny me the pleasure of visually appreciating the body I had embraced just moments ago.

"Do not go all puppy dog on me here, Jordan. We're both adults. There's no reason we can't spend time together. It doesn't mean anything more than that."

I hadn't expected more—and yet, her words stung. But I wasn't going to show it.

"Of course not. It's just that you... you look like you do. I'm sure you know that."

I looked up at her, my head on my hand, elbow on her pillow.

"All people have a pretty good idea of how they look to others. They see photographs. They're told out loud. Sometimes they're told by people they really don't want to hear it from."

Gabriel rinsed her mouth, spat, and wiped her face with a towel. She walked over and sat on the side of the bed, still without a stitch of clothing.

"You seem like a nice guy. But acting as a greeter at a nightclub is different from working for her directly. You do know that, right? These people don't mess around. They'd feed you to the wolves for a dollar."

Gabriel stood and walked to her dresser, opened a drawer, and pulled an oversized Rolling Stones T-shirt over her head.

"I'll start on breakfast."

I started in on the scramble—with cheese, onion, and tomato—which was surprisingly good and the first food I'd eaten since lunch yesterday. We made eye contact, both too busy chewing to talk.

Breaking the silence, I said, "Am I here because she asked you?"

Her face remained composed, but I could sense a tectonic shift of mood behind her eyes.

"What do you mean?"

"You work for Cassandra. I know that. Did she ask you to look after me? Did you pick me up from the hotel this morning because she told you to?"

Now her eyes flashed with anger, though her tone stayed calm.

"Jordan, you're asking me if fucking you this morning was work—if I fucked you because she told me to. You're suggesting I'd screw somebody because I got paid for it. The word for that is puta. Whore. Yes, she did ask me to talk to you, but fucking you was my choice. I sleep with who I want, when I want. And you're an asshole for asking... a fucking idiot. Now, finish your breakfast and leave."

She stood, put her plate in the sink, walked into her bedroom, and shut the door behind her.

Half my eggs remained, but my appetite was gone. I scraped my plate into the sink and put it and the other dishes into the dishwasher. I tried the disposal to flush down the eggs, but it didn't start.

"Your disposal doesn't work," I yelled, getting no response. I was utterly out of my element. I had been with girls before, but I'd never really had a relationship—especially not with someone like this.

I walked to the bedroom door and knocked. No response. I opened it. On her bed was a small mirror with several white powder lines. She was dressed and applying makeup in her bathroom. I cleared my throat, but she ignored me.

"I'm sorry. I didn't mean to suggest..."

She turned and gave me a dirty look.

"I mean, I'm really sorry. I know I got it wrong. It's just... I see what goes on with other people at the club. I've never been in an environment like this."

She continued applying her eyeliner.

I had hurt her badly, but I wasn't going to give up this easily. Summoning my courage, I walked up behind her and laced my hands around her waist, resting my forehead on her shoulder. She didn't move and continued with her face.

I looked in the mirror and saw her eyes water. She stopped and placed both hands on the vanity, then lowered her head.

"You are a fool. I know the world I live in. I know the assholes and scumbags I spend my days with. I know where I came from. I know what your own family can do to you. I know I shouldn't poison myself. But for a moment, I thought you were different. I confused your naiveté with innocence. I thought this was a real connection. I thought this person didn't see me as a possession or a conquest—because he didn't see anyone that way. But I was wrong, and it stings. I'm a big girl. I'll be okay."

She straightened up and dabbed her eyes with a tissue, continuing her makeup as I remained standing behind her.

I had no words. I was very young. Gabriel was 26, and I was 19. I hadn't yet corrected the lie that I was 21. The notion that such a confident, beautiful woman could be fragile or wanting for anything seemed impossible to reconcile.

I looked at Gabriel with a focused gaze.

"There's something you should know about me. When I do things for the first time, I frequently do them wrong. But I learn from doing them wrong. I pay attention and process whatever information I can to do better and not repeat mistakes. I see now how hurtful my question was... and I am sorry. Genuinely sorry."

Gabriel walked over to her bed and ingested two lines of the white powder on the mirror.

"I have some errands to run. Let yourself out and lock the door behind you."

"Wait. You mean... there's nothing I can do here?"

Gabriel threw her purse over her shoulder and walked out the door. A moment later, it opened again.

"You can fix the disposal. It hasn't worked in a month. I hate the smell, and the landlord is useless. And cheap."

"OK. I'll look at it," I said as she slammed the door on her way out.

PART V

REBECCA ROME

New York, New York
2018: 17 Years After

CHAPTER 15

SO BECCA, WHAT IS IT THAT YOU DO?

DR. GREEN CALLED ME BACK. She agreed to meet at 11:30. I thanked her for the rapid response and for accommodating me on a Saturday morning. 11:30 didn't leave much time. I made it downstairs and stopped at my coffee shop for a to-go cup.

Osborne's was a one-location, independent coffee shop whose stated ambition was great coffee and never becoming a chain. The owner and operator was a gentleman by the name of Kerry Osborne, who ran it with his husband, Jeremy. I don't believe I was ever there when one of them wasn't. It was unusual to find an indie establishment in the prime location of an NYC high-rise, but Kerry had a relationship with the developer—possibly his uncle. With an obvious aesthetic flair, Jeremy had designed the shabby-chic interior to feel like a comfortable living room, complete with secondhand vintage furnishings. They knew each of their customers by name if they had visited more than once.

My head was throbbing. I was definitely still on the mend. As I've gotten older, I've recognized that benders come with a recovery time measured in days, not hours. I walked in, still partially blinded, and Kerry handed me my usual coffee mix without a word.

When I turned around, the man was there. The same man from the church.

I turned back and whispered to Kerry, "Do you know who that is?" I tilted my head toward where the man was sitting and covered my pointing thumb with my body so he couldn't see it.

"He's been here a lot over the last couple of weeks or so. I don't know where he lives, but I assume it's nearby. He's here most mornings. His name is Jack. Kinda hot for an old guy, don't you think?" Kerry leaned forward while whispering.

I walked past the man, taking note of the full library of newspapers on the small coffee table beside him. He was drinking tea. He looked up and smiled at me as if he knew me.

"I'm sorry, do I know you?" I asked. Immediately, I became aware of my hungover state and wondered if everyone else was too.

"I don't believe so," said the man.

He stood up, removed his reading glasses, and reached out his hand. "My name is Jack. How do you do?" He said it like he was introducing himself to a prospective banking client.

I couldn't help myself. I found myself inspecting Jack's every detail. A man in his fifties, or possibly sixties, impeccably groomed. Tightly cropped salt-and-pepper hair and an extremely close-cut beard. My immediate impression was that he might be a model for a men's skincare ad. His double-breasted blue jacket lay open over a crisply pressed white shirt. His camel linen pants were wrinkled in a way that looked intentionally fashionable. His shoes were suede driving loafers. I was uncertain about the watch he wore, but I was sure it was expensive. He caught me staring.

"I'm sorry. I don't believe I got your name."

"My name's Rebecca. My friends call me Becca."

"Would you like to join me? How about some pastry or a breakfast nosh?" he said, flashing a perfect smile.

"Thank you, but I don't think that's a good idea. And I really don't have much time." I pretended to look at my watch, though I knew I had about half an hour, accounting for travel time to Dr. Green's office.

"I think you could spare a few minutes. And I'm definitely sure you could use a little something in your tummy."

He turned to Kerry. "Could I trouble you for a couple of scones and some more hot water, please?" Kerry looked back at Jack and nodded.

Without thinking, I took a seat next to the stranger at whom I couldn't stop staring. He caught me, but just smiled. Before I could say another word, Kerry arrived with hot water and two scones on two plates.

Of course, I couldn't say what I was thinking. This man was twice my age, but those years didn't seem to have affected him at all. Ruggedly handsome. One of the many injustices of nature is that men can age so much better than women. Another justifiable reason for women to hate the opposite sex.

I knew anything I said would sound stupid, so I took a bite of my scone and washed it down with my third cup of coffee.

"So, Becca, what is it you do—I mean for a living, in New York?"

I covered my mouth because there was food in it. "I'm an actuary. One of those people who looks at probabilities for insurance companies. It's a pretty good job." I can never just say I'm an actuary. I always have to explain what it is and justify why someone would choose to do it for a living. I can't just say I like numbers, but not so much people. And I've heard all the jokes. An actuary is an accountant without a sense of humor. All actuaries are required to have their personalities surgically removed upon graduation. I could go on—but I do, in fact, enjoy the work.

"That's quite impressive. Takes a lot of discipline and schooling. What level tests have you passed?"

I was amazed that he even knew to ask that question. "I've passed my eighth exam. I'm hoping to pass the next two within the next year. I'll have all ten done—I'm certain of it." We discussed the importance of each level and the opportunities they presented within the profession. Jack seemed both knowledgeable and genuinely interested. I had now talked more to this stranger about my profession in fifteen minutes than I had with my future husband in eighteen months. That is really fucked up.

This thought ran laps around my mind until I forced it back and focused on the conversation.

"And Jack, what is it that you do? Because whatever it is, it looks like you're pretty good at it."

"Well, I'm more or less on sabbatical at this point. But over the last several years, I've been an investor. I have a particular interest in distressed debt instruments, and that has worked out pretty well."

My head was finally coming out of the fog. The scone actually helped. I took note of the time. If I left now, I could make it to my appointment with Dr. Green. I feigned surprise.

"It was really nice to chat. I have an appointment I need to make. Thank you so much for the scone." I paused for a moment. "I enjoyed meeting you." It came across as genuine, because it was.

As I walked out the door, I turned back to look at the man, once again seated in his chair, buried in his newspaper.

What the hell was this?

I answered myself: You are just very hungover... I will never drink again, I lie.

CHAPTER 16

IN THE LAST 20 HOURS...

DR. SHARON GREEN WAS A psychiatrist with a degree from the University of Pennsylvania. She was in her mid-forties, married with two children, and lived in a co-op on the Upper East Side. Originally from Chicago, she had never lost her Midwest common sense, despite treating New York City's one percent for their first-world problems. She was an excellent therapist. Like peeling an onion, she slowly removed layers of pretense and bullshit to uncover both malady and cause. I don't know if she had a guiding philosophy, but her recommendations always seemed driven by a genuine desire to find solutions.

"If you have a problem, and you don't actively pursue a solution, the chances of finding one are not that good." I think she said something like that, anyway.

My solution had been to recognize that I masked pain with chemicals. Not that I would "move on" from the things that nearly destroyed me, but I could learn to live with them. I could still find joy, satisfaction, and comfort alongside the scars that brought pain. This process had helped me a great deal.

I arrived at the garden apartment that had been converted into her office five minutes early. She was fumbling with the keys to open the door as I approached the four-story building. As always, she had Larry with her, the small mixed-breed dog who greeted me as if I'd just returned from war.

Dr. Green used to say she thought the presence of the dog helped bring calm to the conversation. I never asked if she meant for her patients, or for herself.

We hadn't seen each other in almost four months. I had never discussed the passing of my mother. Actually, my mother didn't pass. I had never discussed the murder of my mother with Dr. Green.

She had sent me a lovely note and left a voicemail offering her condolences and support, but I ignored the gesture and took refuge in a different, familiar remedy.

Dr. Green turned on the lights, reached into a cookie jar, and handed Larry a treat, which he carried to his bed and began chewing. She picked up her pad and sat cross-legged in her chair. I slumped on the overstuffed couch opposite her, as I had done so many times before.

"Thank you for coming in," I said.

"Not a problem. Again, I'm so sorry about your mom. I know it's a platitude, but she was a beautiful and wonderful woman. She'll be missed by many, and I'm sure she's missed by you."

Dr. Green adjusted herself in her chair and glanced over to see Larry contentedly chewing. "It sounded kind of urgent that we get together. We haven't spoken in some time, and I was concerned about how you're doing. Is there something specific you wanted to discuss?"

I drew a deep breath, uncertain whether I wanted to pull off this scab. I knew it would be painful. Dr. Green wasn't one to let me gloss over the facts. I started anyway.

"In the last twenty hours, I went to my wedding rehearsal, left after an explosive blowup with my fiancé, went out drinking, did drugs to the point of oblivion, and left the bar with a stranger."

Dr. Green's eyes widened.

"As that stranger was about to forcibly abduct me in a cab, another man I'd never seen before emerged from a silver Bentley, punched out my oversized kidnapper, and drove me home. I woke up hungover, blinded by pain, and found the rescuer sitting in my living room, calmly drinking coffee. After telling me he'd cleaned up my vomit-covered clothes, he left without another word.

"Then I walked into a coffee shop, talked to a strange man twice my age, and felt both connection and attraction. Do you think any of this is odd?"

Dr. Green had been taking notes feverishly—until halfway through my story.

"Are you doing drugs now?" was her first question.

"Are you asking that because you don't believe the story, or am I showing some mannerisms that make you think that? Because I'm not doing drugs."

I stopped and stared at the ceiling, then began talking again without looking down. Barely able to speak, I continued.

"I feel adrift. I feel alone. I fear my state of mind. And I'm painfully unhappy. Most of all, I'm concerned that I'm proceeding down a path I thought would fix these problems, but I think it's only making them worse."

Dr. Green stopped taking notes and looked up.

"First, the story—the elaborate story you just told—is that true? Or is it some fantasy your mind created from the chemistry you've been ingesting?"

"I know it sounds crazy. And as I think through the last hours, I'm not sure how much of it is real and how much is imagined. But I think most of it happened just as I described."

Dr. Green resumed.

"What are you about to do that you worry will make things worse? Get married? Or continue to self-medicate?"

"When I met Eric, my mind and body were in a different place—thanks to you, at least in part. My mom supported the relationship, and her encouragement validated a decision I might've otherwise postponed. I thought my second-guessing was just normal jitters.

"But now it feels different. Worse. I have no one to talk to about these doubts, and they keep growing. Meanwhile, Eric seems less patient and more insistent that we push forward.

"He thinks the wedding will help me. I know he means well, but in urging me to move past my grief, I think he just doesn't want to be caught in the drama of his mother-in-law's murder. Or face the perception that his perfect life might not be perfect. Every flaw is a reflection on me—one he neither wants nor tolerates. It makes me want to run."

"Becca, you need to tell him. Just as you've told me. Ask for the time and space you need. And your pause doesn't have to exclude him—unless you want it to."

"This wedding is important to him. It's important to his family. The planning, the celebration, the—"

Dr. Green cut me off.

"The purpose of getting married is to be married. And the purpose of being married is to be with someone you want to face life with. All of it. The good and the bad.

"Your life isn't wrapped up neatly with a bow. It's messy. And you need Eric to face that mess with you. If he can't do that, then you need to ask yourself what that means—not just tomorrow, but for the next fifteen thousand tomorrows.

"I can't answer that for you. But I can tell you this: if this wedding isn't something you want to do, it's not something you have to do."

She stopped.

I couldn't speak. What felt like eternity was probably only five minutes.

"Are you okay, Becca?" she asked gently.

I didn't answer. My throat was so dry I couldn't even swallow. I just shook my head.

Dr. Green stood, walked over, and sat beside me on the couch. She put her arm around my shoulder. I shuddered, then broke down sobbing.

She handed me a tissue. Then she wrapped both arms around me and pulled me close, the way a mother would hold her child.

"I miss my mom," I whimpered.

"I know," she said softly. "That will never change."

CHAPTER 17

MY MOTHER WAS A MUSICIAN

DURING THE NEXT WEEK I kept my nose to the grindstone at work and told Eric I was busy going through mom's things at her house. I had put her condominium up for sale, and after weeks of procrastination I started going through her belongings. This is an extraordinarily difficult task for anyone. I enlisted Cat to help, and she was supportive beyond what any friend could ask. We started in the kitchen, postponing the most personal items for a later time. I spoke to Eric numerous times but did not share the intimate thoughts I outlined to Dr. Green. I felt cowardly not being able to communicate with the man I was to face the rest of my life with.

On Thursday night I stayed at my apartment. Eric surprised me, bringing in my favorite Thai food. We watched a movie and fell into our easy and comfortable companionship. At night, he initiated love making and I added an enthusiastic attitude to convince myself as much as him of my feelings. When we were done, I could hear his quiet snoring as I lay in bed, dreading the conversation I would have to have in the morning. Despite my wishes, morning in fact did come.

We both got up and started our dressing for work routines. With only a few minutes before the starting gun required us to leave the apartment, I built up the nerve for the conversation.

"Eric, I need to talk to you."

"Hon, can it wait? We're running short here and I gotta catch a ride to work," he said, looking at his watch.

"No, it really can't. I need to talk to you—and it's serious. I think I've put it off too long already."

" Oh shit… sounds bad. If it's about the fight at the church last week, let's just forget about it."

"It's about the fight, but I can't forget about it. We need to talk this through." I stopped and sat on the couch, tapping the seat next to mine. A moment later, he sat next to me, and I took his hand.

"I'm going through a rough time." He nodded. "I know this wedding is very important to you. And I have done what I could to keep it on track. But it's…it's crushing me. I feel trapped, scared, and manipulated." I could see his face changing, so I squeezed his hand a little tighter. "Wait. I didn't mean it that way. I mean, the wedding to you is important and the only thing important to me is being with you. So I want to put it off—the wedding—for a few months, or better yet for a year. I'm not putting *us* off—we can still live together. In fact, I really don't care if we have a wedding at all. I would be just as happy to elope over the holidays."

Eric let go of my hand and started rubbing his temples. "Becca, I don't know what the fuck is wrong with you. Our family has worked so hard to plan this, we've sent out invitations, we've reserved rooms. Lots of people have bought airplane tickets, booked hotels. What the fuck do we tell everybody, not to mention the money? You're acting crazy."

Now everyone in the world knows there are two things you don't say to a woman if you are seeking a resolution. The first is "calm down." The second is "you are acting crazy." The result is anything but calm and definitely more of what you thought was crazy.

I turned and faced my future husband. "I don't give a shit what anyone thinks. I only care what we think." And then I said something I regretted before I finished the sentence." And as for the money, it's not yours, it's not your parents, it's my mom's. And she wants what I want.'

I wanted to apologize. But he beat me to the punch." Fuck you, Becca. You want it off, it's OFF. We don't need to put it off for a year and then 'revisit.' Maybe it's just wrong and we both can't admit it." He then stood up and walked out the front door of my apartment. I wasn't sure what had just happened. My fiancé and I might have just broken up. That was not the plan. Most definitely not the plan.

I sat on my couch, stunned, trying to assess how I felt. Was I okay because I believed it was just a flare of his temper and not anything he meant? Or was I okay because I agreed with him that we both knew it wasn't right? I wasn't sure, but I felt better, lighter, less damaged.

I went downstairs to Osborn's for coffee. The man, Jack, was at his usual table. Always smartly dressed, reading the paper with his tortoise shell frame glasses. I had seen him earlier in the week, but only exchanged smiles. Today I stopped to ask how he was doing.

"Good morning, Becca. It's nice of you to ask. I am well. How are you today?"

"You're not going to offer me a scone?" I said with a smile.

"Of course." He smiled back and signaled to Kerry with two fingers while mouthing the word, Scone.

Kerry immediately brought the scones over, and I sat next to Jack. "So, Becca, what's new in your young life?" he asked in an upbeat tone.

Sometimes you meet a stranger, and you feel relief that sharing your story has little exposure because this person is so many degrees of separation from you. You might as well be talking to yourself. I started blabbing.

"That's quite a question, Jack. My life is, being honest with myself things are, well, pretty fucked up. I sometimes do things that in hindsight appear self-destructive. I don't know why. I was about to be married. Don't know if I am anymore. Did I just blow that up because I wanted to make sure I couldn't be happy? Hell, I'm not sure I should be getting married anyways, at least not till my head's on straight." "Jack didn't flinch. I think I surely must have freaked him out with that little tidbit.

"Oh, and another little factoid; I am an orphan. Have no brothers or sisters either. I have some friends, but friends are not family you know. So now I'll go to work and start this wonderful life all over, really by myself." I said this as if I was describing my major in college. It came across with no regrets, only an observation of the facts. I look at Jack and he must not hear my words. He is listening to what I am saying. His eyes are drilling a hole through my face. He does not move a muscle.

"But first I'm going to finish this scone which I did not pay for. Thank you for that."

"You are welcome." We both chew in silence". Becca, what is it that you enjoy? Are there any things that you do for you? Certainly, there must be aspects of your life besides your work?"

"I don't know, lots of things. I like sports, I like to read, I love music. Symphony really. My mother was a musician. An excellent musician. She used to take me to the Symphony when I was younger. I liked that."

"Well, this is a remarkable coincidence. I have tickets to the symphony for tomorrow night. My guest has canceled on me. Would you be my guest tomorrow night?" Jack asked.

I stopped to digest the offer. I should have been fearful, but I wasn't. "That would be wonderful. How exciting. Thank you so much for the invitation."

I stand up with the new sense of optimism that there is now something to look forward to, albeit a small thing. Still, it lifts my spirits. Jack speaks to me again." Plan on meeting in front of the building tomorrow around 4:00 o'clock. Is that okay? We can grab something to eat on the way there."

"That's fine," I said. I started walking towards the front door of Osborne's when a discomforting thought entered my mind. I returned to Jack's table.

"Jack, something just occurred to me. You should know I don't sleep with men…well men of your…"

I was unable to finish my sentence before Jack interrupted." Well, that should work out. Cause I don't sleep with women half my age either. But I'm glad we got that out of the way. I look forward to tomorrow."

I returned Jack's smile expressing solidarity in our joint affirmation. I felt confident that he meant what he said and I was also pretty sure about my commitment as well.

CHAPTER 18

THESE WERE MY MOM'S

AT 4:00 O'CLOCK SHARP, I was down in the lobby waiting for Jack, wearing a form-fitting green satin dress with a scoop neck and a deeply plunging back. This was the dress I had purchased for my rehearsal dinner, and I saw little downside to wearing it tonight. With my hair pulled back, I topped off the look with a pearl necklace and earrings my mother had owned for as long as I could remember. I felt very Audrey Hepburn. It didn't occur to me that the Hepburn and Cary Grant analogy would be obvious.

"Something else to talk to Dr. Green about," I said aloud.

At 4:10, I walked outside looking for him. I didn't see Jack, but a large silver Bentley was parked at the curb. I thought it was the same car from my near-death experience a little over a week ago. I was certain of it when the gentleman who exited the vehicle turned out to be the coffee-colored man—this time in a blue suit.

"Rebecca, it is nice to see you. You look absolutely lovely tonight." He opened the door for me.

"Hart, do I have that right?"

"Yes, Rebecca, that is correct. You may have been a bit injured the last time we met, but you've got the name right."

"And you're the one taking me to the symphony?"

"Correct again. Jackson Martin, my employer, is going as well. I've been asked to pick you up this evening."

"And Jack was the one who asked you to rescue me at the bar?" I asked as we stood in front of the open car door.

"Well, that's not exactly correct. Mr. Martin saw you at a church earlier that evening. I went to pick him up, and he asked me to check on you. He said you appeared quite distraught and wanted to make sure you got home safely. The 'rescue' wasn't really planned."

"Is this something Mr. Martin asks you to do often? I mean, look after a total stranger?" I hesitated to get in the car.

"Well, from time to time, things like this can happen. But to be honest, I think his exact request was just to follow you home, to make sure you arrived safely. The rest of the evening's adventure was unplanned—but it was no trouble."

Feeling a bit more at ease, I got into the rear seat. Before Hart began driving, he handed me an 8 ½ by 11 sheet of paper listing food options.

"Rebecca, if you can look through the options and pick something, it'll help us stay on schedule. I'll order from the car on the way."

I looked through the menu and chose a spinach salad with tuna and walnuts. I passed on dessert. I handed the menu back and identified my selection. Hart made the call and read off the order on speakerphone while a feminine voice on the other end acknowledged it.

"Where will we be eating? Is there a restaurant on the way?"

Hart replied, "The plan is to eat on the way there. Timing is up to you. It should take no more than a couple of hours, door to door."

"A couple of hours? To where?" I asked. "I thought we were going to the symphony."

"We are. But there's no symphony playing in New York or Philadelphia tonight. Cleveland has an excellent symphony. They're performing at 7:30, so we'll go to Cleveland. We should reach Teterboro just before 5:00 and arrive at the concert hall in time for the opening."

"Hart, we're going to the airport now... and flying to Cleveland tonight?"

"Yes, to both. You, Mr. Martin, and I will attend the symphony. It's a pleasure Mr. Martin has passed on to me. I was pleasantly surprised to learn we were going tonight. They'll be performing Beethoven. We should consider ourselves fortunate."

I sat stupefied in the back of the car for the rest of the ride.

When we arrived at the airport, Hart exited the car and Jack approached him. They exchanged a bro hug. This was more than just an employee-employer relationship. I wondered for a moment—are they gay? No, these weren't gay men. And they weren't related.

I stayed in the car until Jack came around and opened the door.

"Come on, Becca, we're cutting it close." I sat frozen, unable to move. Jack misread the source of my fear. "Don't be afraid. It's a Challenger 300—quite a reliable aircraft. And the crew is very experienced. You'll be fine."

Jack took my hand, and I stepped out. For a moment, I thought he was staring at my chest, but he wasn't. He was staring at my pearls. I raised my hand instinctively and touched them.

"They were my mom's," I said.

Jack looked up and smiled. "They're beautiful—but pale compared to the woman who wears them. You look stunning tonight."

We boarded the plane and began to taxi. It was my first time flying in a private aircraft. The convenience and luxury could easily spoil anyone. The seating was two across, so three people couldn't sit side by side. I sat first, and Hart took the seat opposite me. Jack sat behind us both. Within five minutes, we were airborne.

I had moved past the idea that this might be a kidnapping or murder. Hart had had plenty of opportunities earlier. My only conclusion now was that this was some kind of grand seduction. I was curious to see if it would work.

After a few minutes in the air, Jack stood and made small talk with me. The lone flight attendant offered us drinks and asked when we'd like to eat. I was the only one who ordered alcohol—a glass of wine. Jack told me he'd be working during the flight and asked if I'd be okay entertaining myself.

Hart struck up a conversation, getting quite personal about my engagement before I turned the tables and asked about the relationship between the two men.

"He's really more of a father to me than anything else. We've been together for eight years now, but I've known him my whole life. My father was with the SAS, sort of a British equivalent of special forces. He and Jackson served together—very close friends. There's a lot of history there."

"Unfortunately, Dad did not come home. Anyway, to make a long story short, Mother fell on hard times with the lung cancer you know. Dastardly stuff, a bad way to go.

I got out of the SAS myself after my vehicle got all shot to hell. I sort of fell off when Mom was ill. I was very messed up from the opioids they gave me for the injury in the field. Couldn't quite get off them, and couldn't quite get any more. H became the least expensive replacement. Jack got wind, and well, he stepped in. Took me off the street and into his home. It was very ugly at first, but he would not give up until we got it done—until I got it out of my system. I'm not sure I could put up with the same crap I put him through. We've been together ever since."

I just stared in disbelief. You couldn't make this stuff up, but could any of it be true? I vacillated, taking the story into account while looking for telltale signs of fabrication. Hart interrupted my thoughts.

"You're a beautiful woman, you know. I'm sure you're told that all the time." As Hart said that, he leaned over to ensure no one else could hear. I couldn't help but notice that Jack looked up from his work for a moment, then looked back down.

I smiled back at him. "Hart, are you hitting on me?"

"I might be. If I was, what about it?" he asked as he leaned back in his seat.

"Just asking, that's all. Like to know the lay of the land, if that's possible around here."

The pilot called out over the speaker that we would be landing in fifteen minutes. When we touched down, a waiting Escalade shuttled us to the theater.

Severance Hall is reported to be the most beautiful music center in the country. The 1930s neoclassical building blends Art Deco sculpture with soaring limestone columns. The massive rotunda lobby creates a scene out of a Paris painting, with overdressed elites milling from one spot to the next, creating a show of their own before the symphony. The Cleveland Symphony is one of the four best symphonies in the country, competing with

Philadelphia, Chicago, and New York. The Beethoven repertoire was extraordinary. Our box seats provided acoustics and sight lines that I had never experienced with my mother, who always bought the more affordable seats. As I sat between my two hosts, my eyes stung. It hurt that this experience was not one I could share with my mother.

The two-hour production flew by. By midnight, we were jetting back to New York. I thought of thanking Jack but was uncertain exactly how I would do that. Before I could speak, he kissed me on the forehead and put me in the car. "Becca, this was an extraordinary night for me. Thank you so much for coming."

Hart started the car, and we headed back to the city. I pinched myself to see if I was dreaming before I started in.

"Hart, I know I'm missing something here. I don't know if this is some creep who gets his kicks out of seducing young women or maybe he thinks I have some money and he can trick me out of it, because I have none. Not really."

"Rebecca, I don't think you need to worry about either of those circumstances." Hart made another sound as if he was going to continue, but he did not. The only noise was the muted wheel whine of the Bentley.

"Hart, my friends call me Becca. You should call me Becca."

I saw him look in the rearview mirror, and our eyes made contact. He smiled. "Okay, Becca, would you like to stop for a nightcap before we call it?"

"Yes, I would," I said.

PART VI

JORDAN ROME

Miami, Florida
1979: 22 Years Before

CHAPTER 19

IT'S HARD TO GET A GOOD REPAIRMAN

THE EXPRESSION THAT ONE NEVER forgets their first love rings true because it is. Gabriel ignored me. I tried to reapproach her every day for the next week. There was no reciprocation.

In the meantime, I started my new job under Ricardo. This usually meant running errands for Cassandra. In my second week, Ricardo informed me I would need to carry some kind of weapon—specifically, a nine-millimeter handgun. The rationale was that we often carried significant amounts of cash and needed to protect the company's assets. It became expected that I would always carry a weapon. No one seemed worried about registration or licensing requirements because we thought we were above it all.

I began my instruction at a firing range. What was scheduled for two hours was cut to fifteen minutes when Ricardo observed my expertise. I was a marksman. Hunting was part of the culture growing up in southern Arizona. Guns were in every home, and everyone was expected to know how to use them. Ricardo was not impressed. "Shooting a target is different from shooting a person. The difference between your death or his is the ability to identify your target and fire. No hesitation. You can't think—only act. By the time you finish thinking, you're dead, and he's alive. Remember: target, fire; target, fire; target, fire," he said as he pulled off three rapid shots to the head of our paper target.

The "life" sneaks up on you. Everyone around you is consuming—food, liquor, drugs, and people. There was camaraderie and swagger among the crew I worked with. We were not the same as the club employees. We were gangsters. We made money, dressed expensively, and people were afraid of us. My head became stuffed with poisonous substances and poisonous ideas. It would be a lie to say I didn't love it.

The errands began to change. We were assigned to collect money. If you didn't have the money, we leaned on you. If we had to come back, you could have a bone broken. If we came back again, you could disappear. We moved every type of contraband—guns, drugs, cash—whatever was necessary. The drugs arrived in Miami in every imaginable way. Fast boats met runners off the shore in international waters. By morning, they were unloaded in our warehouses. By afternoon, they were on the streets or headed up I-95 to the East Coast. Huge containers, concealed in ways you'd never think of, brought hundreds of pounds of cocaine at a time—disguised as canned goods, hollowed-out fruit, or inside gutted fish. We kept one step ahead of the DEA through bribery and ingenuity. Once, we brought a load of tropical fish—100,000 of them in various bags. The bags were inserted inside a double bag filled with liquefied cocaine. We smuggled over a ton of cocaine before the scheme was discovered. I was making more money than I'd ever seen and thought it would never end.

I continued to unsuccessfully pursue Gabriel, now more confident—or maybe arrogant—in my approach. After months of trying, she finally approached me.

"You're a big shot now, huh?" she said as I waited in the hotel lobby to ride along with Ricardo while looking after Cassandra.

"I think I'm doing okay for myself. Are you talking to me now?"

"Well, I never thanked you for fixing the garbage disposal. So, thank you."

"The switch over the counter was broken. Really wasn't much to fix. And you're welcome."

"It's hard to get a good repairman nowadays," she said, lifting her sunglasses atop her head to hold her hair back. "I think now I have something wrong with my plumbing. Would you mind looking at it?"

I started to speak but couldn't—I could only laugh. "You got something wrong with your plumbing? Have you thought of calling a plumber?"

"I have. But I'm really looking for someone who's more of a specialist. If this is beyond your expertise, I would understand. I'll find another plumber elsewhere." She looked straight at me. There are certain women you can't make eye contact with. Gabriel was that woman for me. She could have asked me for anything at that moment, and I would have agreed.

"Do you mind if I come over and look at it after work? That might be around 3:00 or 4:00."

"I look forward to it," she said. "I'll make sure the door is open."

I arrived at Gabriel's three-story walk-up apartment just after 3:30. I had butterflies reminiscent of my first high school date. Gabriel lived in a one-bedroom on the third floor of a six-unit 1950s vintage building three blocks off South Beach. The door was unlocked and slightly ajar. I walked in and called her name.

"I'm in here," she responded. "In the bathroom."

I walked into the bathroom, and she was in her robe brushing her teeth. She dropped the robe on the floor and turned on the shower.

"So, the water pressure isn't what it used to be. Could you look at it for me?" she asked as she stepped into the shower and closed the curtain behind her. "I think you need to experience the problem firsthand before any repair can be initiated."

When I woke in the morning, Gabriel was gone. She left a note saying she ran out to get coffee and would be back. When she returned, we sat outside on her small balcony on two café chairs at a small round table. We could hear the ocean in the distance.

I looked up and began. "Not that I'm complaining, but I'm curious why all of a sudden you would talk to me again."

"Because you're persistent. And sweet. And I liked—like—you." She took a sip of her coffee, mouthing the words too hot. "Jordan, what you said that morning a few months back was really shitty. It hurt me. I'm not a prude, but I don't just jump in the sack with anybody. So, if this is something you want to try, I'm on board. But if it's something you see as a passing fancy, I'd prefer we address that now. We can part as friends; we'll both be okay."

I took a moment and drew a breath. "Gabriel, I'm not experienced here. But when I'm around you, when I look at you, my shoulders hurt. I find it hard to breathe. No matter how close I am, I want to be closer. I've never met or seen anyone like you."

Gabriel stood, bent over, and kissed me. Then she sat in my lap. "Why don't you come back tonight? I'll see if I can get you the night off. I know people there. I'll make you dinner. I'm really quite a good cook."

"You have a deal," I said.

She wrapped her arms around me and whispered into my ear. "Before you go, do you think you can check that plumbing one more time?""

CHAPTER 20

IT IS A DANGEROUS
BUSINESS

As PROMISED, GABRIEL MADE ME dinner that night. I went back home one more time before staying at her apartment for good. Days turned into weeks, then into months. The sole purpose of my ramshackle place was now simply to store various goods.

Gabriel was a complex person with numerous demons from her past—demons that would wake her in the middle of the night and that she self-medicated to keep at bay. It was impossible to anticipate the immense mood swings, from euphoria to depression. Despite her best efforts, these could not be leveled out with chemicals.

That does not mean our life was bad. Just the opposite: a jet-fueled, nonstop party of substances and lovemaking. Together, we were always on the edge of disaster. Fancy restaurants with four-figure bar tabs. Incomprehensible parties at extraordinary mansions with a Gatsbyesque feel. Yacht parties that would last through the night.

We had no real friends. The people we associated with were in the same business, guided by the same morals. I couldn't take Gabriel to a party without her getting hit on, often right in front of me. It was a surreal time in a surreal place. Sometimes we partied for days, giving little thought to the implications of these bad decisions.

There came a stretch when Gabriel was up for a couple of nights straight. I couldn't keep up. I came out to the living room and found her sitting on the couch, lines of powder in front of her and an empty bottle of vodka on the table.

She looked awful. Her eyes were dark and drawn; her skin, almost gray.

"Baby, I can't go in today. I think I need help. There are red pills in the medicine cabinet. Can you get me two? Please," she said without looking at me or blinking. I brought the pills out, and she took four. I fought to take one back.

After she swallowed them with the last shot of vodka, I walked her to bed. I called Ricardo and told him she had caught something awful. I would look after her for a few days. He didn't seem to mind.

When Gabriel woke twenty hours later, she went to her dresser drawer looking for her vial. I stood in front of her, between her and the dresser.

"Let's stop for a moment. You're going to kill yourself. I can't watch that. Gabriel, I reserved a spot in the Keys. I let them know at work that we're going to take a few days off. Let's go there. Let's leave all this here, if only for a little while."

"I don't think I can. Jordan, I'm not afraid of dying. I think it would be worse to get old. What is a person like me when she's an old lady? Who would want to be with me as an old woman? There would be nothing left to want."

"I would. I would want to be with you. There can be another way. We can live like real people. Work for a living. People do it, you know." I said the lie with a straight face.

She touched the side of my face and smiled the way she smiled when I first tried on that suit almost a year ago. "You think you'll go back to washing cars, and I'll go back to cocktail waitressing? That's not how this goes. I'm not sure how it ends, but it doesn't end that way." She embraced me. I could smell days of body odor, but still, I could not let her go.

We took that trip to the Keys. She stayed dry for three days. We talked without the influence of alcohol or drugs for hours. I learned her entire story.

Gabriel was born in Los Angeles. Her mother was from a small, one-stoplight town outside of Memphis. She had gone to Los Angeles to be a star at the age of seventeen. She landed several bit roles, but never made her mark in Hollywood. Gabriel didn't know her father, but multiple men came in and out of her mother's life. They took what they wanted and believed they deserved the same opportunity with Gabriel.

When she was sixteen, her mother took her own life. Gabriel made a brief stop at her grandparents' home in Tennessee before making her way to Miami. While working as a cocktail waitress, a customer who worked at the Mutiny suggested she apply for work at the club. That was five years ago.

I worked up the nerve to also share my story. She listened intently while giving herself a pedicure, then looked up at me and laughed.

"I don't believe it. You made that all up."

I shook my head, but I didn't argue with her. We slept outside on the screened porch that night. We never discussed our pasts again.

When we returned from the Keys, old habits returned—slowly at first, then at the same furious pace of consumption. We talked about it. She agreed to modify her life, and then didn't. I reconciled that I loved a woman who did not love herself.

An event occurred on the periphery of my life. It was the start of a change that, like many changes, happened slowly and then all of a sudden.

Four men were shot at a shopping center just outside of Miami. They were gunned down in broad daylight by automatic weapon fire. Two weeks later, I learned the gunmen were Cubans hired by Cassandra to eliminate competition in our territory. The deaths were not extraordinary. What was extraordinary was the brazenness of the attack. The rules had changed. Our competition and the federal government took note.

Three weeks later, there was a shootout in the hallway of the Mutiny Hotel. One guest was killed. A month later, there were two more shootings in the hotel—one in a room, and one in the Club on the lower level. The Mutiny became a dangerous place to be. Business reflected it, falling off by half.

Between Thanksgiving and Christmas, Ricardo and I took the Escalade on a drive deep into the Everglades. When he opened the rear hatch, there was an oversized suitcase. Inside the suitcase was a man, his limbs broken to fit him in. I knew the man; he was in our crew. Despite my efforts, my stomach couldn't hold, and I retched.

Ricardo stared at me. "You want to give me a hand here? He ain't gonna jump in the swamp by himself." We tossed him from the case into the Everglades.

"The gators will take it from here," Ricardo said.

As we drove back to the city, there was silence in the car.

"He stole from her. About $100,000 over three months. Each time he carried a delivery, he put a few in his pocket. You can't steal from her. Don't forget it. She weighs it coming and going. She says you're stealing from her whole family. He's lucky he was alone. Otherwise, his wife and kids would be in the swamp with him."

We did not speak for the rest of the ride back to the Mutiny.

One week before New Year's, Gabriel called me from the police station. She needed me to pick her up. She had been pulled over for driving erratically and, of course, had alcohol and drugs in her system. I went and picked her up at two in the morning. I had not heard from her since ten at night.

"Are you okay?" I asked.

She stared out the side window and wouldn't look at me.

"I'm fine. It's just been a long day."

"Were you holding?" I asked. But I knew the answer. She was always holding.

"If it's okay, I'd really rather talk about this later," she said.

The remainder of this conversation never needed to occur. They found drugs on her. She did something or someone—to make it go away. Gabriel could not be confined in a cell, drying out. The mere thought would terrify her. She did what she had to do, and I would not ask about it or second-guess her decision.

On New Year's Eve, the Club was back in full swing. The Dom Perignon was flowing, the crowd was dancing, and life at the Mutiny had returned—at least for the moment. I got off at four in the morning. Gabriel had been given the night off. That struck me as strange, but she could have used the time, and I didn't press the reasoning.

When I got home, the door had been kicked in and the jamb was destroyed. Panic immediately overcame me. I called out and ran to each room in the small apartment. Gabriel was naked on the bed, her hands zip-tied over her head around the bedpost. Blood leaked from her nose, ears, and between her legs. She had been beaten to death after the worst of it.

I cut the ties from her wrists. Then I went to the bathroom and dampened several cloths. Methodically, I wiped every part of her body clean, my eyes tearing the entire time. I brushed her hair and placed her in her bed, with her head on her pillow and the sheets pulled up to her neck. Then I took the same small suitcase I'd moved in with and packed my belongings.

When I arrived at the Mutiny, the party was still going on in the penthouse. I stormed in. Ricardo rushed between me and the group in the living room, firmly grabbing my upper arm. Cassandra stood and walked over to the stereo, still blaring past daybreak. She turned it off. When she did, everyone looked at her. She announced the party was over and asked everybody to leave. Without a word, they immediately exited the room. The only remaining people were Cassandra, her husband Alex, Eduardo, Ricardo, and me.

"You look upset, Jordan. What is upsetting you?" she asked calmly as she walked back to the bar to freshen her drink. As she did, she pointed to the couch. "Please sit so we can discuss whatever is on your mind in a civilized way."

I reluctantly sat, my hands balled into fists.

"I've been home, Cassandra. Why would you do that? Why would anyone do that?"

"Gabriel was a nice girl. I know you were fond of her. But she was not strong, and she got in trouble. She made a deal. As you know, we have resources to inform us of these sorts of things. One needs to have resources everywhere, or else you can find yourself in quite a compromised position. She traded her freedom for mine. I could not have that. Certainly, you can understand. This is a dangerous business, something you should keep in mind as you think through what you do next."

"You could have sent her away. I would have taken her. You didn't have to kill her. And you didn't have to do those things to her. No one deserved that."

Cassandra looked at Eduardo. He put his eyes down, avoiding her gaze.

"Hmm. There was no reason for anything but her silence. I'll look into why more than that occurred. But I'm sure you can understand that I couldn't simply let her go. If the answer to anyone who decides to save themselves at my expense is to let them go, it's only a matter of days before I'm in jail or worse. We must have rules, and they can't be broken."

Cassandra sat next to me. It was all I could do not to grab her throat with both hands.

"Jordan, I like you. I really have since the first time we met. Maybe if I were a little younger or you a little older things could have worked out for us. But we don't always get what we want." She then looked at her husband and smirked. "We're going to put this behind us. It's a valuable lesson for both of us. Relationships inside the business can be challenging. Go home. Take a few days off. It's a new year, and we'll start fresh."

Ricardo walked over and hovered until I got off the couch. As we passed Eduardo, he said something under his breath. I couldn't understand the words, but I didn't need to. I already knew it was his doing that had brought such pain to Gabriel.

I went home to my abysmal apartment and sat in the dark, contemplating how justice could be meted out.

Chapter 21

Our Paths Will Cross Again

I RETURNED TO WORK, VACILLATING between trying to avenge Gabriel and running for my freedom. I had some money saved and thought I could go north or west. Every option came with risk. It wouldn't be possible for me to take Eduardo's life or Cassandra's without dying in the process. And if I ran, I wasn't sure I'd ever be safe. The "life" had become my prison.

I continued my job, doing no more than was required. I was certain I was being watched closely, with no attempt to conceal it. One of my new tasks was to bring the banker's box of money up after the Club closed. It was a job Gabriel had performed only weeks earlier. The boxes were lighter now and seemed to get lighter each week.

In March, I was making the usual trip to the penthouse, bringing the box to the vault behind the office. Ricardo wasn't there; he was off on some trip for Cassandra. Another crew member stood at the penthouse door, in addition to the two men in the elevator lobby. Alex was in his usual spot on the couch, watching soccer on the television. Cassandra was reading a fashion magazine. Eduardo was playing some kind of game on Cassandra's computer at her oversized desk.

I'm not certain what I first thought when I heard the explosion. I didn't know if it was thunder, an earthquake, or a bomb. When I heard small arms fire, I knew we were under attack. What I didn't know was how many were involved or where they were coming from. Moments later, a second explosion shook the next room. More gunfire, then silence. The entire assault lasted less than thirty seconds.

I left the safe and rounded the corner. Eduardo was hiding under the desk. Alex was bleeding on the couch but still moving. Cassandra was crawling, seeking refuge behind it. One man walked past me, his weapon raised and pointed at Cassandra. A second stood by the door, distracted, looking toward the elevator lobby. Eduardo and I made eye contact, but he didn't move.

I pulled my nine-millimeter Glock from my shoulder holster and fired—first at the man with his back to me, then immediately at the one aiming at Cassandra. Both men dropped. Eduardo emerged from behind the desk and checked their bodies, then put a round into each for good measure.

Alex was bleeding badly from an open chest wound. Cassandra stood, blood running down her leg. She pulled off her Armani jacket and tore off a sleeve to make a tourniquet.

"In the desk, top right-hand drawer. There's a key labeled 'elevator.' Get it." I walked over, opened the drawer, and rifled through a handful of keys until I found it. I held it up. Cassandra nodded.

"They're in the building. They'll either be coming up or waiting for us in the lobby. Either way, we're screwed. We need to get to the car, it's in the basement."

Cassandra hobbled to her husband and studied his wound. She held his hand.

"You're dying, my love. I'm sorry, but we have to leave you."

I walked over to Alex. It was a bad wound. He needed a hospital if he had any chance of surviving. I pulled Cassandra aside, out of his earshot.

"We need to call an ambulance. Get him to a hospital. We need to do that now."

She whispered back, "Alex isn't going to a hospital. They'll use him. To save his life, he'll tell them whatever they want. I know my husband. He's not a brave man. I'm afraid Alex dies here. You must take care of that."

I stepped back and looked at her. "Cassandra, if you're asking me to kill your husband, I can't. He's defenseless. He needs medical help, for Christ's sake."

Cassandra turned to Eduardo. "Eduardo, say goodbye to your stepfather. We have to go, and we can't take him with us."

Eduardo walked over to Alex, who was shaking his head. "Goodbye, Papa," he said, then shot him point-blank between the eyes.

"What the fuck, Eduardo? That was your father!" I screamed.

"No, not really and I never really liked him anyway," Eduardo replied, sliding his gun into the back of his pants.

Cassandra fixed me with her eyes. "Jordan, listen. If you want to leave this building alive, we need to get to the car in the basement. They can shoot whatever they want at us. Unless they have a tank, we'll drive right through them." She handed me the elevator key.

"The key will shut off all the elevators except the one we'll use. It only works from the control panel inside that elevator. The Rolls Royce is on the first lower level. If we can reach that car, we'll make it out."

I nodded. I thought about killing them both right then, but I didn't know where the car keys were. Maybe I'd get a second chance later but for now, I had to stick to the plan.

We ran through the death and debris in the elevator corridor. I turned the key in the unlabeled slot on the control panel and pressed the LL1 button. We waited through an eternity as the elevator descended.

When the doors opened, the three of us exited, guns drawn. The basement was empty. We moved toward the car. Eduardo pulled a small magnetic box from beneath the rear wheel well, took out the keys, and used them to unlock the vehicle. Then he tossed them to me.

"Jordan, you drive. Eduardo, front seat," Cassandra ordered as we climbed into the armored beast.

"Do not open the garage door. It will only draw their fire. Just drive through it as fast as you can. Eduardo will show you where to go from there. Eduardo, take us to the Ranch. Call Ricardo and tell him I'll need medical assistance. Now, get me the pills from the glove compartment and hand them to me."

She took a handful of the pills and sat back in her seat before saying her last words of the night. "If Jordan does anything except drive us to the Ranch, shoot him."

I started the Rolls and hit the roll-up door at fifty, jumping a curb as I drove across the landscaped island and through the bushes onto Bayshore Drive. I could hear bullets ricocheting off the car.

By the time I slid onto Bayshore, I was doing eighty. Cassandra lay sideways, passed out on the rear seat.

Ocala is five hours north along I-95 and then the Florida Turnpike. We stopped for gas in Orlando and drove straight through. I thought Cassandra might have died, but every couple of hours she'd shift with a groan and a sigh. We arrived in the early afternoon. Ricardo was there, along with a surgeon. I parked the Rolls in the designated shed, and the surgeon helped Cassandra out of the car.

The Ranch was a 1,500-acre spread with a mile-long drive, located in northeast Ocala. The massive equestrian estate was defined by white fencing outlining each pasture. The four large white barns were nicer than any home in Bisbee. The main house was a sprawling ranch-style home in an H-shaped configuration. When I entered, one of the many staff members showed me to my room, where I collapsed from exhaustion.

I woke up the next day at 11:00. Clothing and toiletries were laid out on a bench at the foot of the bed. The view from my room opened onto a large terrace adjacent to a pool and gardens. Sitting under an umbrella at a round table set with silver service was Cassandra. I showered, walked out the door, and joined her on the patio.

"Well, good morning. That was a memorable evening, don't you think?" she said. I stood at the table, taking in the massive grounds. "Won't you please join me for breakfast—or lunch, at this point?" I sat down and helped myself to coffee and fruit. Cassandra looked up from her plate.

"I think my leg will be okay. Nasty little shrapnel wound. I'm afraid it might affect how I look in a swimsuit."

I leaned back in the chair and looked out across the estate. The large gray horse grazing closest to us lifted her head, looked at us, then returned to the grass. Cassandra took another sip of coffee.

"It's nice here. The Ranch, I mean. Horses were a passion of my late husband. He had many passions—too many, I'm afraid."

I took my first sip of coffee and popped a strawberry into my mouth.

"Jordan, I think there are a number of things I'll need to start from scratch. You too, maybe. But first, I want to thank you for helping me and my son out of a very tight jam. I think this is the second time I've thanked you for something like that. Second, I'd like your help going forward. I believe we could make a good team. I could make your life a good one."

I sat in silence, mostly from disbelief. This was the same woman who, not twenty hours ago, had her husband executed and then instructed her son to shoot me if I didn't drive in the right direction. I didn't know how to respond.

"Cassandra, I'm done. I'm not a tough guy. What you've seen has been reaction, not forethought. I'm just not cut out for this gangster stuff."

She leaned back in her chair.

"So maybe you'll go back to washing cars. I don't think so. I think you like this. You're good at it, and you can't help flying close to the flame. It's in your blood. You just don't like to admit it because you think it makes you less of a person. A hunting lion isn't an evil lion—he's just doing what he does best. Believe me when I tell you, you can't and won't live the life of the average man. Not after what you've seen with me. You may tell yourself otherwise, but I know you. Maybe better than you know yourself."

"Well, assuming you don't kill me before tomorrow, I'm leaving anyway. My brother wanted to join the Marines. He thought he was doing a service to this country. I think I'll do that for him. In the meantime, I'm going to rest up, eat your food, and drink your liquor."

After my brief resignation speech, I walked back to my room. Three steps from the door, I heard her shout my name. I half thought she was going to shoot me right there.

"Jordan, you might be the first person to retire from this business alive. Go join the Marines. You have my blessing. I'm sure our paths will cross again."

PART VII

IBRAHIM ASSAD

Nuristan Province, Afghanistan
1984: 17 Years Before

CHAPTER 22

LETTERS BETWEEN IBRAHIM AND AALIYAH

Dear Aaliyah,

I'm sorry I have not written earlier. I have traveled for 4 days with little rest. From Cairo we took a plane to Istanbul and then another to Islamabad. After, there was a long bus ride to Peshawar, and then a two day walk to our camp. Peshawar is a cauldron of people from around the world. Weapons, foods and poppy are sold equally open. One can purchase Kalashnikovs, rocket-propelled grenades, and any type of explosives in street market stalls next to vegetables. I've heard five languages spoken inside an hour. It is like an exciting visit to another planet.

The final aspect of the journey was the two-day walk with pack mules carrying our supplies. It has been long and the most exhausting, but I am blessed by Allah to be here. The weather is quite cold, more than I anticipated and the camp is mostly primitive. I am sharing a tent with 8 others. There is no one from Ramallah. Many do not speak Arabic, but there is some English. I have already met people from Syria, Egypt, Yemen, Sudan, and throughout Afghanistan. Morale is high from each of the new arrivals. Every brother is committed to removing the Soviet Kuffar from Afghanistan. They speak of martyrdom, and we will carry the word of Allah to our enemies without fear.

I have met few soldiers. Most of the brothers are young and poor but seek adventure that they heard from sermons and books they have had at home. Here, they have received warm meals, and purpose. I share that purpose with them as our bond.

I miss you, but my heart soars with my blessing to carry out Allah's will. With his blessing I will carry his sword to defeat the Russian invaders and spread the word of Allah's power throughout Afghanistan.

Your friend Ibrahim.

Dear Aaliyah,

I have settled into a daily routine. Morning prayer is the first event of the day. Then we have a light breakfast of vegetables, fruits and broth. The weather remains very cold, and fires are frowned upon. The Russian bombers and helicopters patrol frequently. It could be deadly if we are spotted. There is a cleric that speaks to us in the mornings. It is as if Allah Is speaking from his mouth. This man is the Palestinian, Sheik Abdulla Azzam. I will send you his books. They have moved my soul. Azzam believes that able men are obligated as Muslims to help the Afghanis under siege by the Russians. If one does not, he betrays all Muslims. So profound. I now have learned, we are not here to fight a battle for land. It is for Allah. It is the opportunity to recreate a true Islamic State and prove its viability for the world to see. The West cannot understand this. The corrupt powers believe if they kill people, they kill ideas. This is about a higher power, guns cannot kill Allah, nothing can.

Still, we are battling the devil here. It is impossible to watch the Russians inflict such harm. They exhibit unspeakable cruelty. They bomb homes and towns. They murder people in their beds. They capture and rape Afghan women. They change the way the Afghans dress., how they study, how they pray. They pollute the morals of the young, the women. But they will still lose this war as the British did before them. Because we are not afraid. We will be rewarded in heaven for our battle.

There are times I get very lonely and miss you. Please write and tell me how my mother and sister are doing,

Your friend Ibrahim

Dear Aaliyah,

I know it has been months since my last letter. Please accept my apology. We have had calamitous events over the last several weeks. In the training camp Russian bombs and helicopters swarmed like hawks on a dove destroying everything in sight. Many martyrs were lost. We have moved into the mountains near Tora Bora. Still, sometimes our camp takes shelling that vibrates the ground, making it impossible to sleep. Last week we had. many new arrivals from Egypt. They are mostly from Egyptian prisons, but there are also some men with military experience. The men from prison openly flaunt their violent nature and brag that the Egyptians send them to be martyred in the war. They are adventurers not believers.

I cannot tell others that I have concerns about the strength of our leaders. They are pious good, Muslims, but we woefully lack the knowledge that is required for waging war and use of the necessary weapons to defeat he Russians. The Afghan Mujahideen belittle us behind our backs. They do not entrust us to travel into battle with them. Of the few weapons we have, they are old Chinese, or Czechoslovakian rifles with limited reliability. They are no match for the weapons the Russian use against us. When we go into battle young men throw themselves into the fire believing that their martyrdom alone is what they seek. This does not discourage the enemy. I pray all that is needed will be delivered to us.

I miss my home.

Please write to me to tell me you are well.

Your friend Ibrahim

Dearest Aaliyah,

A miracle has occurred. The Saudi Construction Bin Laden family has sent one of their sons, to save us. He is a brave, brilliant man. When he arrived, weapons, food and monies came with him. He speaks of the future on how we can defeat the Russian efforts. He is a quiet, pious, learned man. He has unlimited funds from Saudi Princes and Emirates that will fund our battle. He traveled with another man from The Pakistani intelligence. The Pakistanis will fight with us for the cause. With bin Laden's expertise, we have started an immense construction project, THE LION'S DEN, excavating large holes in the mountain. There we will be able to safely store weapons, ammunition, and food. Even a hospital. I've caught Bin Laden's attention because I both speak English and share his love of engineering. It is an honor to be in the inner circle of such a great man.

I must confess, I was fearful our effort might be in vain. My heart is now lifted with hope and strength. More people arrive daily and there is a renewed optimism that comes with the warmer temperatures of spring. With the newfound money, I believe that we will be armed in a way that we can mount the fight to destroy the Russian Kafir.

We will free Afghanistan. It will be a beacon for Islam throughout the world. It will be the first of many Islamic states. Allah shines on us.

I hope you are getting these letters. Please write back.

Your friend Ibrahim

My dearest Ibrahim,

I am sorry that I have not written earlier. I just received all your letters the same day. I did not know where to write until I received them. There is much to tell you. Your mother had taken ill and spent several days in the hospital. Her heart struggles, but she is getting good care, and I am hopeful that this is a condition which can be maintained over time.

Your sister is doing very well. She enjoys school and makes many friends quickly. She asks about you frequently. I believe she knows you are not in Dubai. I've asked her not to tell her mother for fear it will trouble her further. My work is going well. I am happy in the hospital environment and enjoy the work immensely. When you return, I will show you the hospital and introduce you to my coworkers. I talk of you all the time and they are excited to meet you.

I don't know what to think of your travel. It sounds so dangerous and that terrifies me. I am aware that many do not return. I pray every day that the same fate does not befall you.

When I sit outside at night with my tea, I look at the stars. I think these are the same stars you are looking up at, and this connection places us together for that moment in time. I know it is not right to speak from one's heart if you do not share marriage with that person. But my heart yearns for you. And I count the days to when you will return safely to me.

Your love always, Aaliyah

My dearest Ibrahim,

It has been over a month since your last letter. I worry incessantly.

Your sister is well. She asks about you Each day. She wants to know if there is a location where she can send a letter or make a phone call. I told her I would forward her letters on to you. Behind my letter is hers.

Your mother seems to be doing better. I am hopeful that she will be well for your return. My work is both challenging and exciting. I was recently contacted by a Muslim hospital in London. They would provide a work visa if I wanted to work there for a year. This may be something we could do together.

I read of the deaths of the fighters in Afghanistan. I cannot sleep because I worry. You have been gone 14 months, and you promised to return within a year. My heart fears that Allah has taken you. Please write at your earliest opportunity. I miss you and love you.

Your love always, Aaliyah

My dearest Ibrahim,

It has been months since your last letter. I tried every possible way to find out if you are alive or dead. I am heartbroken and unable to eat or sleep. If I do not hear from you by the end of this month, I'm going to Afghanistan to find you, whatever the circumstances. If you are able, please contact me.

Your love always, Aaliyah

Dearest Aaliyah,

I hope this letter finds you quickly. I have been wounded and hospitalized in Islamabad for several months. The battalion I was fighting with is gone except for myself and one other man, an American. In fact, that American is the reason that I am alive to write you today. There is no way to describe the horror of battle, let alone the loss of so many of my friends. These are images that my eyes cannot unsee. I am tired from it. I pray Allah will provide victory through others, but I can no longer assist in this war.

I leave for Cairo tomorrow. I will be home for Ramadan. Though my faith remains strong, my body will take time to heal. We have a new life to start together. Praise Allah for that opportunity.

Your Love, Ibrahim

My dearest Ibrahim

I received your letter. I am in such pain for your injury, but in such joy for your return. My heart soars like a dove finding freedom. I count the moments until I hold you. Yes, we will start our life anew as soon as you return. There is much to catch up on. I have such hopeful plans for us to share our life together. I am crying tears of joy as I write this letter.

Please send me the name of the man who saved you, returning you to me. I want to write him a letter to thank him. This man has made our life, the one I dreamt of, possible.

Your love always, Aaliyah

PART VIII

JORDAN ROME

Camp Pendleton, CA
1983: 18 Years Before

CHAPTER 23

ARE THERE ANY OTHER QUESTIONS?

AFTER SIX MONTHS AND TWO days of special training at Camp Pendleton, California, I was asked to take a series of written and oral exams. These tests were described as a method for the Marine Corps to identify potential officer candidates. Out of the 200 people in my training battalion, only four other men and I were selected. After the second day, I was the only one asked to continue.

The exams were abstract and unlike any other military requirements I had encountered. Hypothetical questions about ethics and judgment were posed; complex math problems had to be solved under intense time pressure; deductive logic puzzles were offered in the form of riddles and word problems. One week later came a battery of physical tests, measuring strength and endurance. These were conducted under conditions of limited sleep and without warning.

Four days into this grind, I refused to continue. There seemed to be no end. It appeared the testing would last indefinitely. Had I not refused, I'm certain they would have continued until I broke. I demanded to know the rationale behind the process and who was issuing these tests. It was clearly not the Marine Corps. By the end of the day, I was dismissed.

Three weeks passed before I was contacted again for an interview. It was held in a small, windowless room with sparse furnishings: a conference table and four chairs. Two of the chairs were occupied by men in slacks and shirt sleeves. Each had a three-ring binder in front of him. They carried a military demeanor but wore no uniforms. I sat in the third chair. The fourth remained empty.

The older man, seated on the right, appeared to be in his mid-forties. His hair was graying in a tight military buzz cut. He had a lean, muscular frame that stood out beneath his fitted shirt. A scar traced a sharp line from his cheek to the corner of his mouth. The second man was much larger and younger—no more than thirty. The older man spoke first.

"First off, we want to express our appreciation for your patience during the rather lengthy exam process. My name is Dan Murphy, and this is Reed Winters. We represent a different team from the Marine Corps within the DOD. Our agency coordinates with the military but operates independently. We focus on intelligence and operations the military cannot officially undertake. These are frequently covert missions. The agency that oversees this process works with several subcontractors, but we also conduct our own field operations. The larger umbrella organization behind this is the Central Intelligence Agency. We work on the recruitment side."

He turned a page in his binder and continued.

"We recruit from a variety of sources to match the best candidate with the task. These sources range from Ivy League schools to ROTC programs to enlisted men like yourself. One of our primary needs is for field agents, which, as you might imagine, involves a certain level of risk. It often requires relocation into zones of potential conflict. We've reviewed your records and test results—both intellectual and physical. Based on that review, we believe you may be a candidate for field work."

I had already suspected this was something other than officer candidate selection. The military often assumes an enlisted man is too dumb to recognize what's right in front of him, while simultaneously insisting what he sees isn't actually there. Don't believe your lying eyes.

Several moments passed before I spoke.

"Gentlemen, that's some fancy talking. A good speech if I've ever heard one. But I don't know how you came to the conclusion that I'm a good fit. Maybe the man you think I am isn't the one sitting in front of you. Ivy League? Hell, I didn't even finish high school. Did you know that? I'm guessing you also don't know I've lived on that fuzzy line between the good guys and the bad guys—and that may be putting it politely."

I tilted my head and looked at the tent I'd made with my fingers. Images flashed through my mind: my lover zip-tied on her deathbed, a dismembered body tossed into the Everglades for the gators, and the two would-be assassins I had shot.

"No, I think you're looking for the Captain America type. I'm not that guy."

The two men exchanged a look. The younger man spoke next.

"I can't tell you we know everything because by definition, you can't know everything. But we know enough. This isn't Boy Scout work. We think you're a good fit. And on the education front, we can help you. We'll support you through the GED and additional coursework. That's available and encouraged in our system."

The silence returned, this time stretching long enough to become uncomfortable. Finally, the older man spoke again.

"There are things we can teach and things we can't. You tested extraordinarily well, placing in the 98th percentile among your peers. Your physical capabilities are a significant asset in the field. Your familiarity with weapons is also critical. You're a few years older than the typical Marine recruit, and that maturity is a strength. You're single, and your family status is something we consider as well. As for your past... this isn't the angel business."

I knew exactly what they meant by family status. I didn't have a goddamned family. I could disappear and no one would know or care. And the men in front of me didn't need to explain that they weren't angels. It was literally written all over their faces.

I paused before responding.

"I don't know, guys. I've got a few more years to serve, then I'll figure out what's next. I think you need someone else to save the world. I'll say it again—I'm not one of the good guys."

The older man spoke as if I hadn't said a word.

"There will be a chopper here today at seventeen hundred hours. Bring all your belongings. You're due in Williamsburg, Virginia, the day after tomorrow. Your work begins the same day. You'll be briefed on your training upon arrival. Any questions?"

I opened my mouth to speak, but he raised a finger and began writing in his notebook. I doubt anything I said would have made a difference. My opinion clearly didn't matter. I sat in silence, watching him lower his head. The scar on his face seemed deeper now, more permanent. Without looking up, he said, "Then good day, Private Rome."

He stood, and I followed suit. We shook hands across the table.

When I returned to my barracks, they were empty—except for one man. My belongings were already packed in my duffel. A Marine stood at the foot of my bed.

"Private Rome, my name is Corporal Rogers. I think I packed everything, but you might want to double-check. Once you're ready, I'm instructed to take you directly to your ride. You'll be leaving in a couple of hours."

Lacking anything better to say, I thanked the man who was escorting me to the last place I should ever be going.

CHAPTER 24

WHAT COULD POSSIBLY GO WRONG?

THE FARM IS A 9,000-ACRE, sprawling campus in Williamsburg, Virginia. Its official name is Camp Peary, but to everyone stationed there, it's simply the Farm. If you were to ask where the CIA trains, the official response would be no response. So, the Farm doesn't really exist.

The CIA begins training personnel across multiple silos of expertise, ranging from technology to intelligence to fieldwork. In the first several months, all recruits undergo similar instruction covering self-defense, weapons, and operational protocols. Shortly after, individuals are separated based on their anticipated roles. The Middle East and Afghan theater, in particular, was an active sector for new recruits. That's where I was sent.

Because I spoke two languages, I was identified as having language skills. As such, I was given specific lessons in Dari, one of the most frequently used languages in Afghanistan. My GED classes never existed—I simply received the certificate. Instead, I spent six hours a day studying language, history, geography, and mapping. I became something of an expert in Islamic and Middle Eastern history, a passion that would continue for the rest of my life.

In addition to the coursework, there were four hours a day of exercise and weapons training. We became proficient in every type of motor vehicle operated by the Americans, Europeans, and Soviets. We received lessons in vehicle pursuit and flight. I could fire light arms in any configuration found on the Afghan battlefield. I could disassemble and reassemble American field rifles and pistols with my eyes closed. My hand-to-hand combat skills could rival any special forces in the American military. I soon felt invincible.

Nine months into training, we were sent into desert and mountain survival simulations in Colorado. With minimal clothing and almost no gear, we were required to survive for five days. Sourcing your own food and water was the only way to complete the task successfully. Participants had access to a radio for rescue, but it was understood that using it meant you were washing out.

All training in the CIA was delivered "just in time," meaning once you were taught a task, you were expected to perform it under pressure within a limited timeframe. Failure didn't mean you could try again later—it meant your role in the agency was over. Completing this field trial revealed a part of myself I otherwise wouldn't have known existed. Frigid nights and bone-aching hunger brought hallucinations and a kind of internal pain one would never experience in a life of comfort.

Of the eleven men who started training for field operations in Afghanistan, five remained after it was complete. The others were placed in various agency roles or left entirely. The five in my class became my closest friends. We knew our survival depended on complete trust and a team that could act as one. By the end of training, I realized a new person had emerged. The person who came out was not the same as the one who went in. I'm certain that was the intended outcome.

One might assume the most seasoned agents would be deployed to the Afghan theater. That wasn't the case. Everyone was a freshman in the fight. Genghis Khan, the British, and now the Soviets had all tried and failed to occupy the country. I didn't know it at the time, but America would take its turn in what came to be known as the "Graveyard of Empires." The five members of my team who deployed to Islamabad in 1983 had a combined combat experience of zero. That would change quickly.

The Russians invaded Afghanistan in 1979 and supported a puppet regime promoting communism. In the 1980s, the CIA began coordinating weapons and funds through various warlords and Mujahideen groups forming the resistance. The CIA already had a station in Islamabad before the invasion and had maintained relations with the Afghan government in Kabul since 1948, when they opened their first embassy there.

War is never what it seems. But Afghanistan took "fucked up" to another level. The Russians were fighting for mineral deposits and the spread of global communism. The warlords were fighting for control of the poppy fields. The Mujahideen were fighting for independence. The Taliban were fighting for an Islamic state. Radical Muslims from across the Middle East were fighting to defeat the West and secure a caliphate. The Gulf States were funding the war to keep their most extreme elements out of their own borders. Pakistan was fighting for regional dominance. And the Americans were fighting to defeat the Russians. What could possibly go wrong?

The earliest meetings were held in Peshawar, a remote mountain town that could have been Afghanistan's version of a Star Wars village, the kind with the bar scene. A collection of misfits, opportunists, and radicals gathered to carve out their share of the river of money coming from the Gulf States and the United States.

Those meetings were a who's who of rogues behind the Afghan resistance. From Saudi Arabia came Turki Al-Faisal, head of Saudi intelligence. From Afghanistan came the warlord Ahmad Shah Massoud and the Taliban leader Mullah Omar. From Pakistan came the ISI's General Hamid Gul, acting as host. Also in attendance were Saudi construction magnate Osama bin Laden and a noted Egyptian physician, Ayman al-Zawahiri. Bin Laden and Zawahiri represented the various radical Islamic interests seeking to establish a new caliphate based in Afghanistan. Representing the Americans was the CIA's Islamabad station chief, Milton Bearden. Three members of our team attended as his security detail. We didn't sit in on the conversation, but I did receive the summary of what was agreed upon.

Weapons and funds would be supplied by the Americans and Saudis to support the resistance against the Soviets. Sophisticated handheld weapons, including anti-tank and surface-to-air missiles, would be provided by the Americans. The CIA would embed personnel with the Arab fighters and the Mujahideen, offering technical expertise and instruction on operating the advanced equipment.

For some reason, no one agreed on who would be in charge of this operation. Each group would retain relative autonomy. It might have sounded like a recipe for disaster, but it was the only way to navigate the deep-rooted conflicts among the alliance members. Even then, it was clear that each party was eyeing the postwar power vacuum, hoping to seize control at the expense of the others. The Americans went along because arming the enemies of our enemies was reason enough. It would be years before the United States realized the consequences of a radical-controlled Afghanistan; one aimed at damaging its next adversary: the West.

The Saudis also failed to see the long-term risks. They sent radicals to fight, hoping they wouldn't return, eliminating internal threats. But they were wrong. Within a decade, those hardened veterans would return to sow chaos across the Middle East and threaten the very stability of the Kingdom.

So, through ignorance or willful blindness, the money and weapons flowed. And apparently, that's all you really need to start a good war.

CHAPTER 25

EAST/WEST;
A FOREVER WAR

THE AFGHAN RESISTANCE WAS OUTNUMBERED, outgunned, and undertrained. Its only saving grace was the topography, especially in the mountainous regions that bordered Afghanistan and Pakistan. For decades, no country had successfully policed this treacherous area, a fact that remains true to this day. The Afghans used their knowledge of the terrain to stage ambushes on Soviet troop movements, then quickly disappear into caves and mountains. The Soviets flailed, firing mortars and artillery shells blindly after their assailants. In this lawless terrain, various warlords ruled over small, fragmented kingdoms. Their power was fueled by the cultivation and sale of poppies. The same drug that flooded the streets of Europe and North America was, ironically, secured through protection offered by American military resources.

But the Soviets held unchallenged air superiority. They launched from Bagram Air Force Base with SU-25s, SU-17s, and MiG-21s, obliterating any sign of civilization. Entire villages vanished in moments, reduced to rubble and craters. For close-range support, Mi-8 and Mi-24 helicopter gunships delivered rockets, missiles, and high-caliber machine gun fire with devastating effect on both resistance fighters and civilians. The local population understandably grew to despise the Russians. Captured Russian soldiers were tortured or flayed, then left on the battlefield for their comrades to find. The Russians responded by bombing even more indiscriminately. It seemed only a matter of time before they would crush the resistance by leveling the entire country.

Then the Americans and Gulf states, particularly Saudi Arabia, changed the equation. Coordinated by the Pakistanis, manpower and money flowed into the country. More importantly, shoulder-mounted surface-to-air missiles (SAMs) inflicted massive losses on Soviet air power. The Soviets lost 333 helicopters and 118 jets during the occupation; unprecedented damage in modern warfare. These weapons shifted the balance and ultimately determined the war's outcome.

My task involved training and mission management embedded within the resistance corps. Though numbers fluctuated, our company typically consisted of forty-two fighters. The original group had little discipline, and casualties exceeded ten per month. It was a messy affair. I was stationed with two other men from the CIA. One was Derek Huntington, a Yale graduate from Boston who had gone through training with me. Derek was a buttoned-up patriot from a family with a long history of service. It was only a matter of time before he became a congressman, senator, or something higher. The second was Victor Rodman, a Navy

SEAL absorbed into the CIA through a path similar to mine. Victor, a Black man who graduated ROTC from the University of Alabama, stood six feet three and was the most intimidating man I had ever met. I was convinced he would be made into an action figure upon retirement. I had tremendous respect for both. Our communication with CIA command came through radio or biweekly meetings at predetermined locations. Otherwise, we were on our own.

Because our goal was to seek out the enemy, combat arose two or three times a week. We were instructed not to initiate direct contact with Soviet forces, but avoiding combat was impossible. One either died or became a hardened veteran quickly. The adrenaline became addictive overnight.

The Americans dressed like the local fighters. We all grew facial hair to blend in. None of us carried identification. But we were not invisible. Our complexions and distinctive weaponry marked us as foreigners. The greatest challenge was language. The three of us spoke broken forms of local dialects, but we could not communicate complex directions, especially under fire. This challenge was addressed by an interpreter who worked closely with us. His name was Ibrahim Assad, a man from the Palestinian territories, exactly one month older than I was.

Ibrahim was a study in contrasts. Educated at the American University of Beirut, he was deeply familiar with Western culture and Americans in particular. He could talk about baseball, politics, or fashion. His English was flawless. But that did not mean he embraced what he had learned. He saw the Soviets, Americans, and Europeans as indistinguishable, outsiders who came to take resources, not to understand the life or culture of those they claimed to help. In his eyes, they all lived in sin and decadence.

Still, Ibrahim understood the value the Americans brought to the war effort. He openly criticized the undisciplined behavior of the resistance, especially the Arab zealots eager to become martyrs. He leveraged the strengths of the three Americans to their fullest. He listened to our tactical suggestions and quickly became proficient with our weapons. He often stood up to his superiors when they questioned our strategies. They might know more about religion, but they didn't know how to fight wars. The Americans did.

Derek and Victor maintained a professional relationship with Ibrahim. Mine went deeper—but only because he chose for it to. I learned about his past, his love for a woman named Aaliyah, and his dream of starting a family after the war. He would read her letters aloud and ask for my perspective. I explained I had little experience to offer when it came to romance. He shrugged, assuming all Westerners were as experienced as those in the movies.

We often debated Middle Eastern history, but nothing could sway his beliefs. In his view, the world was divided into the oppressed and the oppressors. Historical boundaries only mattered when they supported his views; otherwise, they were dismissed as propaganda. I came to understand something from these talks, there are millions, maybe hundreds of millions, who believe this war between East and West will last forever. That fact would not change in my lifetime. So, I narrowed my focus. All I could control was staying alive and even that was uncertain.

After countless inconclusive discussions, I stopped engaging in philosophical debates. I would simply wave him off when he tried to reopen them. For the time being, we, like our countries, lived under a truce. A temporary truce, allowing us to fight the common enemy, the Russians.

CHAPTER 26

ALLAH'S WILL

IN APRIL OF 1985, WE were instructed to proceed toward the
Maravar Pass in Kunar Province. This was a hostile and combative
sector in Afghanistan. The Soviets had deployed the 334th Separate
Special Purpose Group from Asadabad to investigate Mujahideen
activity in Sangam. The 1st Company of Russians advanced into
Maravar Gorge in pursuit of their enemy. When they entered
the gorge, the trap snapped shut. Mujahideen fighters caught the
Russians in a crossfire of heavy machine guns. At the bottleneck
of the gorge, the Mujahideen effectively blocked the 2nd and 3rd
Companies of the 334th. It was a massacre, 31 Russian men were
killed. Those captured were beheaded or flayed, then tossed back
onto the battlefield to be seen by the remaining Russian combatants.

Although it took hours for the Russians to assemble
reinforcements, they arrived by the next day. A Russian armored
column moved in quickly, supported by the Air Assault Battalion
of the 66th Brigade in helicopters from Jalalabad. The Russians

showed no mercy as they sought to destroy the neighboring villages of Sangram and Daridam. Our goal was to get as many people out as possible before the Russian slaughter began. Our company used NSTVs (Nonstandard Tactical Vehicles), also referred to as Technicals, to ferry civilians to safety. We had eight vehicles in total. Though each was different, most were Toyota pickups mounted with .50 caliber machine guns and SAWs, along with armored Toyota Land Cruisers. I was in a partially armored Land Cruiser along with Ibrahim and two other fighters.

The sky was patrolled by three Russian Mi-8 and Mi-24 helicopter gunships. We had made the first three trips to Sangram successfully, dodging strafing runs and rocket attacks. We timed each leg of the trip to coincide with the helos' refueling. We had rescued approximately fifty civilians on those first three trips.

On the fourth trip, the last Technical in line was hit by a rocket. The explosion threw the vehicle ten feet off the ground and caused it to land on its side. The six civilians in the back were killed instantly, along with the driver. The passenger-side door, now atop the truck, opened, and an occupant consumed by flames threw himself out. He rose to his knees, then dropped into a smoldering heap, no longer recognizable as a man. The entire event happened in ten seconds.

The gunship flew past the convoy, then banked hard left for another pass at our remaining seven vehicles. Victor powered his Land Cruiser over the shoulder of the road, jumped out of the driver's seat, and popped the rear tailgate. He pulled out the infrared-guided Stinger surface-to-air missile, loaded it on his shoulder, and dropped to one knee. In an instant, the white trail of the projectile could be seen targeting the Mi-24. But before the SAM made contact, the gunship ejected another rocket, this time at

Victor's parked Land Cruiser. In the one-two beat of a bass drum, the helo exploded, followed immediately by the detonation of the Land Cruiser. The three remaining occupants, along with Victor, were decimated. The helo spun like a wounded boxer trying to right himself, but it couldn't. Black smoke and flames shot from the fuselage as it slipped into a spin and ultimately crashed into the desert floor. In the blink of an eye, the entire machine was in flames.

A second gunship approached from the horizon in front of us. Like Victor had done, I ran back to my vehicle and quickly loaded the surface-to-air missile, our last. I took the weapon and scrambled to the side of the road, knowing our vehicles were the least safe place to be. Ibrahim was screaming for each driver to exit and take shelter along the roadbank. The only vehicle that responded was Derek's. He stood on the road, dragging each civilian out of the rear of the vehicle and pushing them toward the embankment. The remaining five vehicles accelerated, hoping to outrun the helo. Ibrahim remained standing, screaming at his fleeing comrades in vain as they tried to escape. The vehicles, now several hundred yards ahead of us, were strafed by the autocannon on the Mi-24. The gunship made three passes before each vehicle lay in flames.

The gunship then turned and moved in our direction, unaware of our location except for the two vacant vehicles left on the road. We lay as close to the ground as possible, trying to blend into the sparse grass. As the helo slowed, I rose and targeted it with the missile. It was only 300 yards away. I fired. The helo pulled hard right, trying to outrun or dodge the weapon, but it was impossible. The infrared lock found the belly of the craft and struck its ammunition. The resulting explosion split the machine in half and brought it spiraling down.

I quickly took inventory of people and equipment. We had eight people remaining and two vehicles: Derek, myself, Ibrahim, one other fighter, and four civilians. Though we couldn't be sure of much, we were certain the Russians knew we were there. Additional air or armored ground assets would arrive soon. We would get off the road and drive our vehicles as far as possible toward the mountains. If we could reach them by dark, we might find refuge. Only there were the Soviets reluctant to pursue combatants in terrain they didn't understand.

We also took quick stock of our weaponry. Derek's vehicle had a .50 caliber machine gun mounted in a tripod in the bed. I had my CQBR rifle with 120 rounds, a Milkor MGL semi-automatic grenade launcher (more or less a six-shooter that fired grenades), and one RPG with an armor-penetrating round. We set a path due west across the desert floor. At 4:30 in the afternoon, the sun was starting to dip behind the mountains. Derek radioed that he thought we might survive to see another day. Before I could respond, I saw dust on the horizon, rising from the foothills. At first, I hoped it was from wind, or livestock, or anything but what it was—two pieces of armor: BTR-60 eight-wheeled armored personnel carriers. Each one could carry sixteen soldiers and two heavy machine guns. If they caught us, it would be game over.

Derek radioed again. "I gotta plan. We pull both vehicles off the road, 100 yards apart. We split up and try to get them caught in the middle. You use the RPG to blow the fuck out of one of the BTRs. Hopefully the second one runs, thinking we've got more. The men in the first will evacuate because they can't stay in the vehicle. I get on the .50 and take them out. You stand by with the MGL, and we do whatever we have to do."

"That's a shitty plan. They're going to blow your ass up while you're on that gun," I said. There was a pause; all I could hear was the rumble of his vehicle over the radio. I added, "We could just do a U-turn and try to outrun them until dark. Nah, that's a shitty idea too. We'll be driving straight into an ambush. OK, let's do yours… it's the least bad. We'll give it our best. But if that gun on the armor turns on you, get off your rig. Don't fuck around."

"Roger that," he said.

We stopped and sent the four civilians walking into the desert with all the water we had. Derek and the last remaining combatant in our company curled below the technical. Ibrahim and I lay in wait with the RPG, the MGL, and our rifles. It was 5:30 and the shadows dominated the vehicles, aiding our camouflage below. The two armored personnel carriers stopped at an idle 50 yards from us. The rear door of each vehicle opened, and eight men exited. They began walking towards our vehicles, weapons drawn. *Maybe the vehicles are not full. Maybe only eight men and the drivers.*

I checked the RPG, rolled over onto my side, rose to a knee, and fired the only round we had into the side of the first personnel carrier. It exploded in flames as it tried to maneuver backward. But with only one side of the propulsion system operable, the vehicle just turned in circles like some kind of wounded dinosaur.

I rolled back below the vehicle and grabbed the MLG grenade launcher. Before I could get back into action, I heard Derek on the heavy gun, burping rounds. The eight Russians were shredded by the .50 caliber gunfire. But the personnel carrier returned fire, tearing up the technical and silencing Derek's weapon.

The damaged armored vehicle stopped its helpless rotation and lowered the rear access ramp. As the ramp came down, I pumped a grenade into the cabin. The equipment exploded.

173

The second personnel carrier accelerated forward, then pivoted on a 180-degree axis, heading straight toward me. Within a second, the heavy gun on the armored vehicle destroyed our Land Cruiser. It turned again and rammed the Toyota, flipping it onto its side. I dove out of the way, but the Land Cruiser rolled past and over Ibrahim. He screamed in pain.

The vehicle then backed up several yards. When it stopped, three more men exited. It sat there, idling. I hoped these were the only three left. I took the rifle and sat with my back against the overturned vehicle, signaling to Ibrahim to stay quiet, but he couldn't. He bunched his sleeve and stuffed it into his mouth to muffle the pain.

One of the men came around, and I shot at him. He ran back to take cover behind the vehicle. The pattern repeated side to side. Then the Russians tried to reach around the vehicle and fire blindly. I shot back, striking the weapon and knocking it from the assailant's hands.

They paused. I could hear them speaking. I didn't need to know Russian to understand the plan. Two men would approach from either side of the vehicle, and when I fired at one, the second would round the corner and eliminate me. It's what I would've done.

But I developed a different plan.

I had three rounds left in the grenade chambers. I fired two almost straight up, hoping they would land on the other side of the vehicle. Then I covered myself and Ibrahim and waited to live or die.

I heard a short burst of Russian before the explosions. The remains of the Land Cruiser shuddered and shattered at the same time. Then everything went quiet. I lay in wait, anticipating the survivors to round the corner and finish their plan. After ten minutes, I took the chance and moved first.

Ibrahim and I were alone.

He lay on his back with tears streaming down the sides of his face. His skin was pale, and his eyes were squinted shut.

"Where are you hurt? How bad?" I asked.

"My back. I can't move my legs. There must be something lodged in my back. Can you look?"

I reached around and felt a hard distortion just beneath the skin—like a bone dislodged and trying to push outward.

"Can you move your feet?"

He lifted the ball of each foot a few inches before succumbing to the pain again.

"Leave me. Allah will come and look after me," he said, eyes still closed, fists clenched along his sides.

I rocked back onto my knees, placed my hands on my thighs, and lowered my head. I needed to think.

The religious fighters often exchanged stories about wounded men waking to full recoveries and walking off the battlefield. About people believed dead who never went cold. Most were probably concussions or comas mistaken for death. But Ibrahim's back wasn't going to heal on its own. He would die of starvation or worse in the desert.

I lifted my head and looked at him.

"I just received a message from Allah. He will heal you. But he set up his surgery center in the mountains. He's very busy with the war and all. He needs us to go there, where he has his equipment."

For the first time, Ibrahim turned his head and forced a smile.

"If that is Allah's wish, then maybe we should go," he said, then straightened his head and closed his eyes.

I dragged Ibrahim and Derek's lifeless body into the rear of the Russian personnel carrier. I searched the Russians for anything of value. Ammunition, weapons, rations, and water were loaded into the still-idling BTR. Hands shaking, I grabbed the controls of the armored vehicle, and we continued toward the mountains in the dark.

CHAPTER 27

I AM NOT SURE WHICH GOD

WE DROVE AN ADDITIONAL FORTY minutes before we hit the foothills. It was just past 7:00, and the silver cast of the moon provided the only light. Ibrahim was passed out on the carrier bed. I picked up all I could carry and followed a path up the mountain until I found what I thought would be an acceptable shelter. It was about five feet high and dug approximately fifteen feet into the mountainside. Best of all, it was not visible from the personnel carrier or the foothills. I made two more trips with supplies, then woke Ibrahim.

"I have found a place. Help me get you on this skid so I can drag you up."

Ibrahim looked at me and shook his head. "I can't move. Leave me, please leave me," he whispered.

I did not ask again. I grabbed the shoulders of his blouse and pulled him onto the skid. He screamed, but I ignored him. I then grabbed him under the thighs, straddling over his knees, and got his lower half situated. He screamed louder. I put the skid's straps over my shoulders and proceeded up the mountain goat path that led to our new home. Near halfway there, Ibrahim slipped into unconsciousness again.

I then returned to the personnel carrier and placed Derek on the skid. He had been shot under his left arm, creating a nasty mortal wound. It dawned on me that Derek had not died instantly. I held his hand and touched my head to his. To a man who could not hear, I apologized to him and his family for letting this happen. I then promised I would not leave him here. I covered the skid with a tarp, stuffing the edges underneath his body. I was exhausted. Derek was a big man, and getting him out of the carrier and up the side of the mountain would require every bit of my strength, strength I did not have left in me. In the morning, there would be aerial reconnaissance. I had to get Derek out and up the mountain and move the vehicle. Now. I grabbed hold of the straps and dragged them over the edge of the armored carrier.

Returning to the driver's seat, I started the vehicle one last time. I put it in gear and advanced the throttle, fixing it to the floor with an ammunition box. As the vehicle accelerated, I ran out of the back and dove through the opened ramp. I rolled over with my ass in the sand and my hands behind me, watching the vehicle drive itself back into the desert. With any luck, it would be miles away by daybreak.

I returned to Derek and dragged him to where the path started up the side of the mountain. I could go no further without rest. Leaning back for just a moment, I promised myself I would not sleep. But adrenaline had left my body, and I was unable to resist sleep as it overtook me.

At 5:30, I awoke to the whine of the rotors in the distance. A helicopter was doing concentric rings around where I anticipated the armored carrier had come to rest. I could not wait until it circled to our position. I grabbed hold of the skid and, with a new burst of energy, humped Derek up to our hideaway.

When I entered the cave, Ibrahim had awakened.

"I thought you had left me. I was not angry. In fact, I appreciated that you would have left me with this food. But you chose not to go. Why?"

"Fuck if I know. To be honest, Ibrahim, I'm not sure why I've done anything I've done since I got to this goddamned country."

"Jordan, why must you curse with every sentence? It does not make that sentence more important, nor does it make you sound more intelligent. It just makes you look less of a man than you are." Ibrahim's tone was preachy. He'd learned it from listening to other folks lecture him in the same way.

I stood and stared at him in disbelief. "Everyone we came out here with thirty-six hours ago is dead. You should be dead... I wish I was dead. We're forty klicks from anywhere, surrounded by the world's most dangerous people hunting for our skins. But the problem that is on your mind is whether I should use foul language or not?" I took a breath and lowered my tone. "OK, I will try and watch my language," I added under my breath, "like that's going to fucking help." Ibrahim just shook his head.

I opened the packs and took out the Russian MREs, which were just like ours: prepacked, awful food. Without being able to read the instructions, I kept adding water until it looked right. I made one for myself and one for Ibrahim. I tried to feed him, but he insisted on feeding himself. It was a messy but comical affair, with about a 50 percent entry rate into his mouth versus the side of his face. I continued my meal until I felt satiated, then dozed off a second time.

When I woke, it was five in the afternoon. I felt a burst of energy and the need to take some kind of action to remedy our situation. The only question I could not answer was what action. We had enough food for three days. It was possible we could stretch it to four, but I wasn't sure what that would get us.

The only search party that might be looking for us was the one we didn't want to be found by. I had a pretty good idea where we were. My guess was that Asmar lay forty klicks, twenty-five miles, northeast. It would be rough terrain and require a river crossing. I believed there was some sort of makeshift bridge at the village that would provide that. I also did not know what kind of reception I would get once I arrived. I told Ibrahim that maybe my team would send somebody out to look for us. Neither of us believed that. We made another meal that evening and slept through the night. Ibrahim was frustrated that he could not position himself to pray, but did so anyway in his immobile position on his back. I stared at him in silence, both amazed at his commitment and careful not to interrupt his holy sacrament.

"You think this is strange? What is important to me is that, though it appears Allah has abandoned us, he has not. You are alive, and so am I, because it is his will. It is his will that we will win this war, and it is his will that there will be another caliphate for believers in all lands."

"Ibrahim, I have no qualms with your prayer. A god is only as good as the people who worship him. So pray if you want, but your notion that there is a world that is one way or another is naïve.

Borders and peoples have moved, they have done so throughout history. Look at the Middle East and Eastern Europe. How many people have claimed some piece of land as theirs? There is no right place or wrong place for those borders. Only the place that exists now."

"Jordan, you are cursed by a mind that limits your vision."

"I agree I'm cursed, all right. But I think I'm cursed with a man who just won't shut the fuck up. I think you're all nuts. Keep killing each other if you want, but I wish you would leave me out of it."

I stood and walked over for one last inventory of our provisions. "I'm guessing we have one, possibly two days of food left. I'm going to leave it for you. I'll place everything within your reach. But when it gets dark, I'm heading to Asmar. If I travel through the night, I think I can make it in fourteen hours. If I see anything moving in the air, I'll have to hide out and try again the next evening. I'm taking water, but the food should last you at least two days. I'll find a vehicle and come back for you."

"You'll come back for me? Is that right?" A moment of uncomfortable silence settled in the damp cave. "You know, I think you will. Even if you believe I'm gone, you'll come back. You'll come back for him," he said, glancing over at Derek, now fully wrapped in the tarp.

"Damn straight I would," I said, also looking at the tarp. "But you'll be here. We'll get you to a hospital so you can go home and knock up that pretty little bride of yours."

"You are a bastard to speak of Aaliyah in such a manner. If I could stand, you would not say such things."

"Did you just call me a bastard? Ibrahim, wow... there just may be hope for you yet."

Two hours later, I picked up the small pack with water, a compass, binoculars, and a handgun with ammunition. In a straight line, I could have made the trip in five or six hours. But nothing was straight in this part of the world. I hoped that if I walked through the night, I could be there by morning.

As the sun rose in the east, I saw the tiny town perched on the bank of the Kunar River. I looked up and said thank you. I wasn't sure which God I was thanking, but only an act of God could have gotten me there.

CHAPTER 28

I NEED A DIFFERENT WAY
TO MAKE A LIVING

WHEN I WALKED INTO ASMAR, I could see the break of day casting shadows from the east. A row of one-story clay homes and commercial buildings defined the only real street in the village. Beyond the main street, the buildings thinned out until only terraced ground and poppy fields remained. My mind swirled with both optimism and the urgency to return to my companion.

As I walked up the street, merchants and residents noticed the stranger in their midst and quickly corralled the women and children back into the buildings. The largest of these was a kind of general store, marked with worn Western-labeled signs for consumer products. Outside, a stand of fruits and vegetables was operated by a middle-aged woman with graying hair and few teeth. I did my best to speak in Dari. The woman raised a hand, held up one finger, and walked into the rear apartment of the building. I stood and waited, knowing one finger meant one minute.

But I didn't have to wait that long. From each direction and from the rear of the building, armed men appeared with weapons trained on me. I tried again to speak in Dari, but they gave no response. One of the men approached and forcefully removed my Russian backpack. He dumped the contents on the ground, revealing various Russian supplies, including a handgun—all taken from the armored vehicle. The immediate reaction was heightened alarm from my hosts. The tone shifted quickly; the conversation became volatile. One man broke ranks and began beating my back, shouting words of revenge for the death of his family. Covering my head, I repeatedly cried out in Dari that I was American. The response was the same each time: I was a lying Russian pig.

At that time in Afghanistan, Americans were still something of a novelty. American culture had seeped into even the most remote areas, but Americans in the flesh were rare. Russians were not. Deserters, too, were commonplace. To an Afghan in Asmar, there was little visible difference between an American Caucasian and a Russian one. And the Russians were reviled beyond description.

My Dari was good enough to understand that a debate had begun over how—and when—I should be executed. The final decision was to wait until the Council could be convened the following day. I tried to explain the urgency of my companion's condition, but there was no response, not even a flicker of concern that it might be real.

Just an hour earlier, I had believed I was saved. Now, I expected to be beheaded in the morning. I was also nearing exhaustion. There was no jail in Asmar. In fact, there were no public buildings of any kind. The only option available was a wire vegetable bin in the cellar of the commercial building. I was given water and a bucket. When the door to the cellar closed, I sat in pitch black, awaiting my fate until I dozed off.

I couldn't see my watch to tell how much time had passed. I guessed it was late evening when the cellar door creaked open, waking me. A dark-skinned man holding a gas lantern descended the stairs, speaking to my captors. They opened the wire gate and raised the lantern so he and I could see each other.

"They say you claim you are American. Is that true?" the man asked. His English was fluent, but not American it was British, Australian, or possibly South African.

"I am. I'm not working with the Russians. I'm helping the Afghan resistance. I have a man who is gravely injured, about 40 kilometers from here. He needs medical attention right away. I need someone to help me get him."

I spoke with all the urgency and panic I had bottled up since being locked in the cage. I don't know if my words were even coherent. The man turned and shouted to the guards at the top of the stairs that their captive was, in fact, American not Russian.

Setting the lantern down between us, the man adjusted the light to its brightest level. The small cellar room was now fully illuminated. He removed a package of cigarettes from his jacket and offered me one. I declined, and he took one for himself and lit it.

"So, it is out of goodwill that you woke up one day and said, 'I think I will go help free the Afghanis'? From your reclining lounge chair in Idaho or Montana, or wherever it is you're from? That seems quite extraordinary."

"I'm not from Montana or Idaho. I'm from Arizona. And I'm guessing you already know why I'm here," I said.

The man took another drag of his cigarette and tapped the ash onto the ground.

"Well, there are two reasons Americans are in Afghanistan. One is because they're in the poppy business. It can be a very dangerous business, you know. The second is they're working with the CIA. There really are no tourists," the man said with a smile.

"But we don't need to discuss which business you're in. You don't look like a drug dealer. Let's move upstairs and see if we can get you something to eat. Then we can talk about this man you're so concerned about. My bet is he's dead by now anyway."

When we arrived upstairs, a table was set with vegetables, fruits, and roasted chicken. I hadn't eaten in thirty six hours and was famished. I attacked the food as the woman I'd met earlier in the day poured juice into a plastic glass at the table, smiling again with her tooth-challenged mouth.

"The Afghanis are remarkably hospitable. With so little, they'll offer a stranger a feast. It's part of their religion, part of their culture," the man said, waving his hand over the meal without touching the food.

"You won't join me?" I asked.

"I understand who needs the offerings more. You should eat. The rest won't be wasted, I promise."

"Where did you learn to speak English so well? Are you from Kabul?"

"No. I'm originally from Bombay, but I was raised in London. My father worked for the British government. He was moved to a post in Kabul when I was a young man. We lived here for eight years before I moved back to London. I'm not Afghani, nor am I Muslim. In fact, I'm Sikh. But I've grown to love this land and its people. It's a terrible thing the Russians are inflicting on the Afghans."

"So, I guess you're here out of goodwill too," I said, pausing my meal for a moment to offer a grin.

"I'm employed by a government as well. Not your government, but we can say we're on the same team. I make a point of stopping in several villages. I bring food, medicines, and the occasional bullet or two. That builds confidence and trust between me and the people. These relationships are quite valuable these days. I rarely come here more than once a month. Kind of a miracle that I showed up to save your ass."

The man paused as I returned to my food.

"So sorry, it just dawned on me that I failed to introduce myself. My name is Arjan Reid."

"Nice to meet you. I'm Jordan Rome. Your assumptions are correct. I'm working with the CIA to assist the Afghans, and I appreciate you saving my ass. I have a man, an Arab combatant who is badly injured. I think his back is broken. Two days ago, I left him alone in a cave with a dead comrade. He only had enough food for two days. I need a vehicle to go get him and my associate, and bring the injured man to Peshawar or Islamabad. I don't have any money with me, but I can get you compensated if you can provide a vehicle."

"Where is this cave?"

"If you have a map, I can show you the approximate location. As I said, it's about forty klicks from here. A couple of hours if we drive."

Arjan reached over and pulled a knapsack off the floor. From it, he withdrew a heavily worn map encased in two pieces of plastic. He located our position on the map, and after a moment, I pointed to the approximate location of Ibrahim.

"You made it on foot from this location to Asmar? Just the other night?" I nodded.

"Jordan, this is a very dangerous spot. We can't do this. I'm sorry. I understand your situation, but going back there now is essentially suicidal. There was a battle in Maravar recently. The Afghans ambushed a Russian company, and the Russians are seeking revenge. They're everywhere in this area. They may even come here. Come back with me. We can cross into Pakistan within an hour. Hope your wounded comrade can hold on for a few days. After that, we'll try again."

The weight of his words, combined with the food I'd consumed too quickly, left me with heartburn and a loss of appetite. I leaned back in the rickety chair and placed my hands flat on the table. Arjan and I locked eyes.

"I understand. It's not reasonable to ask you to risk your life for this man. But he'll be dead in two days. And you're right, he may already be dead. My station head in Islamabad can approve payment for a vehicle. You can call him. His name is Milton Beardon. Ask for double what the vehicle is worth. He'll give it to you."

Arjan laughed. "Like I give a crap how much the Yankees pay the Queen for a piece-of-shit vehicle. It'll be dark in an hour. You can take it then."

I sat in the chair and rested my head on the table. I must have dozed off again for a few minutes. When I awoke, my pack including the pistol sat on the table in front of me. Alongside it were some dates and a small paper bag full of nuts. Next to the pack were the keys to the truck I'd need to save my comrade.

I sought out my toothless hostess and offered my thanks. I took off my watch and handed it to her. She smiled, flashing her four teeth, and placed the $50 Casio on her wrist as if it were an exotic piece of jewelry, holding her arm out to admire her new gift.

When I climbed into the truck, Arjan was asleep in the passenger seat, his head resting against the window.

"Arjan, it's time to get up. I need to get going." He slowly raised his head and rubbed his eyes.

"There's no way you survive this trip on the road. The Russians will be everywhere. If I let you go alone, I might as well shoot you here in the truck. I might know another way in. We won't be able to get exactly there, but I think we can get within an hour's hike. We'll come in from the other side. Not really a road more like a path. If we go at night, right now, we might make it. Two trips back to the truck with your mates, and we could be back by morning. Then again, maybe we'll be dead by morning."

"Either way, we should know whether this is a good plan or not by tomorrow," he said, laughing.

The ride back to the cave was bone-crushing. The vehicle rocked back and forth over potholes and small boulders. I wondered out loud how this would be for Ibrahim in his condition. Arjan told me not to worry.

"He won't feel anything. If he's not dead, I've got something that'll make him think he is."

I watched him closely as he navigated the narrow road with limited light. The partially working dashboard cast a bluish-green glow on his face, giving him a monster-like appearance. We talked to pass the time and to make sure we stayed awake.

Arjan was about ten years older than me. He was stationed out of Islamabad but lived in London. He was married to an English girl. He took his wallet from his coat and showed me her photo. I looked at it under the one flickering overhead light. He guessed what I was thinking.

"Makes you wonder about her eyesight, aye?"

We exchanged smiles.

"Got a young son with her too. Sorry I don't have his picture. But he's a beautiful boy. He won't be a soldier. No sir. Maybe a barrister or a physician. She's really smart, and he's got her brains. A nurse, you know."

Just as he said that, we hit a massive hole that made the truck bottom out and groan.

"God damn, I need a different way to make a living," he said, laughing again.

About two hours into the drive, he stopped the truck.

"If you got it right on the map, we need to walk up this hill, then down, and we should be at the location."

I looked up the embankment we'd have to climb, and then descend twice, including the trip back carrying two men. I looked at him. He looked back.

"I never said it was going to be easy. I just said there was a way. Now, we can stand here and wait for these guys to walk to us, or we can go get them. My guess is the dead one's not walking anywhere, and the one with the broken back gives us about the same odds."

I nodded. We made the hike and struggled to find the cave. The orientation was different, and it took me about half an hour to relocate the spot. But we did. Ibrahim was unconscious. When I woke him, he smiled briefly but didn't speak. He had eaten all the food and water I'd left. Arjan handed me two white pills and some water, which I gave to Ibrahim.

"Let's take the other one first," he said, looking at Derek. "By the time we get back, your friend Ibrahim will be in a different place. It'll make the ride possible for him."

We drove the last two hours back to Asmar in the early daylight. Arjan white-knuckled it, constantly bobbing his head, scanning between the side window and the windshield. We continued past Asmar to the Pakistani border. At 8:30 in the morning, we crossed into Pakistan. At the gate, I called the Islamabad bureau, which arranged a helicopter lift for Ibrahim and Derek.

I thanked Arjan, climbed into the helo, and fell asleep in my seat as soon as we took off. It was the first time I'd gotten more than a couple of hours straight in nearly forty-eight.

Ibrahim survived, but it took two surgeries and four months before he was mobile again. His combat days were over, and he was going home. I spent most of my remaining time with the CIA at a desk in Islamabad, becoming something of an Afghan intelligence specialist. Struck me as crazy that I'd be the "go-to" guy on the status of the war. Only goes to show how little we actually knew.

I took the opportunity to visit Ibrahim multiple times. I was the only one who did. Though he would always see me as an infidel, I believe we had a genuine friendship. Before he returned home, he told me he had given my address to his bride-to-be. He said she wanted to write me a letter thanking me. I insisted it wasn't necessary but eventually relented.

Ibrahim's future wife actually did write me a lovely letter. No that's not an accurate description. Aaliyah wrote me a letter that brought tears to my eyes. It's true I had never received any kind of correspondence from anyone, let alone a lover. Still, I had never imagined one person could describe their love for another the way she did. I saved the letter. I wanted to write her back and tell her she deserved better than him. But of course, I didn't.

Arjan and I became close friends. As he was also stationed in Islamabad, we met every Friday for cocktails at one of the few places we could drink: the Hilton Hotel. Evidently, not all Sikhs abide by abstinence from alcohol. On two occasions, I traveled with him to London to visit his family. He also had a wife who deserved better, and I told her so at every opportunity. Arjan told her to ignore my advice, then kissed her hard on the mouth to prove his point.

By the late 1980s, the war the Soviets waged in Afghanistan was over. They didn't officially leave until 1989, but like a large water buffalo taken down by a pride of lions, it was over once the buffalo was on its side. There might still be some fight left, and the buffalo might still be dangerous, but it was dead just the same. That was the position of the Soviets in the late '80s. The resistance had the money and weaponry to make it impossible for the Russians to change the bloody stalemate. Fifteen thousand Soviets would lose their lives in the futile effort. Though it's hard to connect the dots in history, this marked the beginning of the Soviet Empire's collapse. The Eastern European countries would, one by one, extract themselves from the bear's grasp and declare independence. The Afghan puppet regime would remain in power but be largely confined to Kabul. By 1992, it was done. What followed was no better. The Taliban would ultimately become the victors, bringing their own brand of repression only to face the Americans again. That is another story, and fortunately, one I was not a part of.

In 1988, I returned to the States. My contract with the agency had expired, and I had had enough of the hypocrisy and violence it had to offer. Station Chief Milton Beardon provided an excellent reference letter and a list of contacts for future employment. This was helpful because I had no idea how I would make a living.

The flight out of Islamabad offers a spectacular view of the mountains stretching into Afghanistan. One's mind cannot reconcile such a beautiful country with its people being imprisoned by violence. Afghanistan would remain an unsolvable problem for decades. On my way back to the States, I stopped in London one last time to visit Arjan. His wife, as always, was a gracious hostess, and his son was growing into a young man. A soldier was what he wanted to be. Arjan immediately corrected him. The boy knew better than to argue with his father, but the determination was clear in his eyes.

As for Arjan, he was going back to Afghanistan. We joked about the danger, but both of us knew it was real. Arjan would take two more tours in-country. We embraced as brothers for the last time when he dropped me at Heathrow Airport for my flight to New York.

PART IX

REBECCA ROME

New York, New York
2018: 17 Years After

CHAPTER 29

I WOULD WAIT

I COULD FEEL HIS BREATH on my back. The gentle heave of his chest against my spine kept me in that sublime place between sleep and wakefulness. The room and the sheets smelled of body, sweat, and sex. I opened my eyes for a moment and closed them again. The shadows of early morning moving across the room remained in my vision even with my eyes closed. He moved the hand that was wrapped under my arm across my chest and gently ran it down my stomach, between my legs.

"Do you want coffee? I can go downstairs or make some up here." Though his voice offered coffee, I could feel from the press of his body that he had other thoughts taking higher priority.

"In a minute on that coffee," I said, taking his hand and pressing it further down until it reached the spot it needed to be.

Hart was an impulsive decision made in a moment of great weakness. After we went to see the performance in Cleveland, we stopped for a drink on the way home. This was going to be therapy sex, not romance. We were worlds apart, and he was a stranger. But the conversation was easy. He listened without judgment. We had familiarity far beyond the time spent.

I may have still been engaged; I didn't know for sure. I was assuming that Eric would call me one day, if for no other reason than to let me know we were calling it off. I was embarrassed that I hadn't initiated a call to provide the same clarity. Each time, I found a reason to postpone it. I didn't know if it was uncertainty in the decision or just ambivalence. Neither would be a good sign.

But Hart did all the dumb stuff that prince charming's are supposed to do. He sent me flowers the next day. He wrote a poem in the tiny card. It wasn't a poem really, more like an embarrassing limerick. But it made me smile all the same. He showed up not the next day, but the day after and waited in the lobby for me to come home. I didn't know how long he'd been there, but my doorman whispered, "An hour." Hart lied and said he was in the neighborhood and thought maybe we could get dinner. We did, and then had coffee the next morning.

So, as this love affair was seven days old, I was waiting for it to happen, the thing that makes you look at him differently. When you find out he's married, a misogynist, a drunk, irresponsible, or just fucking crazy. But it didn't happen. As time went on, he became more considerate, more attentive, more familiar. It snuck up on me. I was sitting at work Thursday afternoon and found myself daydreaming about him. I reprimanded myself. You're a schoolgirl with a crush. This is rebound romance. But the feeling crept in throughout the day. At five o'clock, I called Eric. He answered on the second ring.

"Hi. It's Becca. I can't go on like this. We need to talk. Can we meet somewhere, maybe in an hour?"

"I really can't tonight. But I can talk right now."

"Eric, I think this is important stuff. We should do this face to face. We need to clear the air."

"Becca, I don't think that's necessary. The air seems perfectly clear, and I think we can have the conversation right now."

I felt a shudder go through my chest and up the back of my neck. A switch had gone off. It was as if I had been driving through a downpour and suddenly reached the hard edge where it had ended. The sky in front was clear, and the landscape glistened, freshly washed by the storm that had passed through.

The man who hadn't called me in a week; the man I was supposed to marry had neither the time nor the good sense to know we should meet in person to decide the fate of what was meant to be a lifetime together. He did this either because that's who he was or because he simply didn't care enough about me to take the time. Clarity gave me strength.

"I've been thinking about what you said the last time we were together. I think you were right. We're not meant to be. We should meet with your parents so we can explain it to them. It wouldn't be right to end it without that conversation."

"So, you're thinking maybe a victory lap performance in front of my parents, where I can be humiliated to the fullest extent possible, would be entertaining? Should I do that in a clown costume or with my pants down? Because if we're going to reveal to the world that my fiancée has determined I'm not up to her standards, let's do it right. I've got it."

"No, just the opposite. I want to tell them that I can't do this. I want to tell them the only mistake their son has made is misreading how fragile I am right now. I want to tell them how lucky I would have been to be their daughter-in-law. This is not your screw-up. You're the same person I got engaged to. I'm just not the woman you asked to marry at least not now, and maybe not ever. And I'm so sorry about that."

"Go to hell, you crazy bitch. I never want to see you again." Click.

I spoke into the phone again to make sure I understood what had happened. Silence. I looked at the phone to confirm the call had ended. Of course it had. There it was, finished. Perfectly clear. I understood I would have to make all the nearly impossible phone calls to the guests, vendors, friends, the pastor. But the hard part was over, and there would be no turning back.

I didn't count on Hart returning. But there he was this time in the coffee shop, sitting and talking to Jack. He could see me as I entered the apartment building lobby. I smiled at both of them, and Hart strode out of the coffee shop, signaling for me to wait a moment.

"You know, I've seen the two of you in this coffee shop every day for the past week. Before that, I'd never seen you here. Why is that?" I asked.

"We're here on business. We'll be around for a while. The reason isn't that important, but I wanted to talk to you about how long we'll be here," he said.

"Hart, it's been a really hard day. This has nothing to do with you, but I think I really need to be alone," I said. He looked down at his shoes like a scolded schoolboy. I felt like I was reprimanding him for no good reason. I placed my hand on his cheek.

"I hope you understand."

He took my hand in his, holding it against his cheek. "Of course. I can come back later, or tomorrow. But I think sushi is in order. A little sake, a little sushi, then right back home. You'll be in bed in two hours. Alone, of course," he added with a grin and a glint in his eye.

He turned back and looked at Jack, pointing his finger like a gun to show he was headed in a different direction. Jackson smiled and nodded.

I don't think anyone's ever had just one sake. I know I haven't. And after two, conversation gets easier. So, I told him. I told him about Eric the engagement, how Eric reacted earlier that afternoon. I told him what a slut I was for sleeping with him while I was engaged to another man. He listened, as he always did.

"I would wait."

"What? You would wait? Wait for what?" I asked.

"If you asked me to wait for a month, six months, a year whatever it takes until you feel it's right I would wait."

I pushed back from the table and laughed. "You are the smoothest bullshitter I've ever met. It's that British thing. This is why they have you guys selling that cheap junk on infomercials late at night. Anything with an English accent sounds good."

He reached over and grabbed my hands first one, then the other. "No bullshit. I would wait. Wait for you."

As he said this, his phone rang. He looked at the screen, his smile dropped, and he asked for a moment of privacy. He stepped away from the table and returned a minute later.

"Becca, I'm afraid I have to go. An emergency of sorts. Do you mind if I drop you off now? We can talk tomorrow, if that's okay with you."

"Is there a problem? Did I scare you?"

"There's no problem. I just need to pick something up, and it's all the way in Jersey. Jackson asked me if I could do it tonight."

Hart didn't wait for the check. He walked up to the cashier, paid the bill, and walked me home. The Bentley was parked across the street, idling. Hart didn't think I noticed when he kissed me goodnight, but I did.

201

CHAPTER 30

BY THE NAME OF JORDAN ROME

I WAS TOLD THAT THERE were two men, two policemen, waiting in the lobby. Never a good sign. I went out, and the officers asked if there was a place we could speak in private. Cheryl, our receptionist, overheard the request and pointed to the conference room labeled Pacific. Each of the conference rooms carried the name of an ocean, indicating the global reach of the company. I thought it was a tad pretentious, but it wasn't my decision.

There were not two men. There was a woman in her thirties, athletically built with an immaculate short haircut. One didn't need a cocktail hour to guess her orientation. But her smile was professional, and her demeanor relaxed. Her partner, on the other hand, was a man in his mid-twenties, stuffed into a suit two sizes too small to leave any doubt about his gym time. They introduced themselves.

"Good morning, Miss Rome. I am Detective Banner, and this is Sergeant O'Grady." She would be doing the talking, I could tell. They both placed their wallet badges on the table for me to inspect. I picked up hers, wondering how I would even know what a fake badge looked like. I felt the metal for authenticity it was definitely not plastic.

I picked up the sergeant's badge as well. "O'Grady. Isn't that the name of every sergeant in every 1970s cop show?" Both officers couldn't help but smile.

"I get that a lot. But it's my real name. Three generations of Irish cops."

"Well, I'm assuming you're not here for actuarial consulting. And I think I'm caught up on parking tickets. So, if we could get to the point, I'd appreciate it. I've got a full day." When I finished my spiel, both officers sat down and asked me to do the same. I did.

"Miss Rome, we're here regarding the recent death of your mother. There has been a development in the case that you should be aware of. It also raised a number of questions we thought you might be able to help with," Detective Banner said.

It had been over a month since my mother was murdered. At first, there were daily phone calls and a couple of meetings at the station. There was even a moment when they said they thought they might know who it was. I asked how anyone could not know who did this; it was on video. You could see his face. But nothing ever came from those conversations. I surrendered to the well-documented truth that random killings and senseless violence rarely get resolved.

My body tensed; I could hardly catch my breath. What kind of development? Do you know who the man is? Do you know where he is? I would have kept going with the litany of questions that, until now, had seemed unanswerable. But the sergeant interrupted me.

"We think we've found the man. We hoped to identify him from the video, and now we're quite certain we know who he is."

Now it was my turn to interrupt. "Who is he? Do you have him? Did he confess? Did he say why he did this?"

The detective spoke again. "Miss Rome, I understand this may be a difficult question. Did your mother ever have any involvement with drugs or with people who used or sold drugs?"

I froze. I had never seen my mother with drugs, or with anyone who did drugs. But then there was the money. A large amount of it. And no one ever knew where it came from. Was I missing an entire part of my mother's life? I chose to respond by going on the offense.

"Are you fucking crazy? My mother never had anything to do with anyone or anything like that. She was one hundred percent against that sort of thing. Why is that even relevant here? The whole world saw the video a man came from behind a crowd and pushed her in front of a moving train. Where do you even get drugs from that?"

"And you, Miss Rome, are you 100% against drug use as well?" asked the sergeant. The detective and I locked eyes. I was sure they could feel the hate radiating from me after that comment.

"I've done drugs. Everyone in this office has done drugs. Everyone in my college class has done drugs. Are you trying to tell me that my past drug use is the reason a man pushed my mother in front of a train?" I was ready to keep going, but I didn't. I focused on controlling my breathing and calming my temper.

"No. We may have gotten off track. That's our mistake." The detective shot a dirty look at the sergeant, who lowered his head and stared at his folded hands on the table.

The detective started again. "I don't know if you saw this morning's news, but a man fell from one of the penthouse balconies at the Marriott Times Square." I nodded, indicating that I had. "The man didn't actually fall, nor was it suicide. He was forced off the balcony."

"Why would the news say he jumped or fell? And what does this have to do with my mother?"

"These large hotels have a lot of influence with City Hall and the press," Detective Banner replied. "Their public relations teams work hard to preserve their image of safety and security. But we are certain this man didn't jump."

"And how can you be so sure?"

Detective Banner suppressed a hint of a smile. "Because his hands and feet were zip-tied to the arms and legs of a dining room chair from the penthouse. Not exactly a position from which a man can climb over a balcony and throw himself onto the street below. We have strong reason to believe this was the same man who killed your mother. We suspected it at first, but the surveillance footage was such poor quality that the facial recognition software couldn't confirm it. The man who landed outside the hotel was Eduardo Diego a well-known gangster, brutally violent. He was also the only son of Cassandra Diego. Cassandra is one of the top cocaine traffickers in South Florida. She's not going to take this lightly. We may be looking at the beginning of a very rough storm. The coincidence of Eduardo's death and his appearance on that video is too unlikely to ignore."

I sat in shock. It simply wasn't possible that my mother had any connection to drug wars, dealers, or anything like that. I threw out the only explanations I could think of.

"Maybe he thought she was someone else. Maybe she accidentally bumped into him, and he wanted to teach her a lesson. You said he was psychotic."

"Miss Rome. Do you have any relatives by the name of Jordan Rome?" she asked a question she already knew the answer to. All I could think was how cruel it was to ask it.

"I think you know that I do. Or rather, did. My father's name was Jordan Rome. He died on September 11, 2001, in Tower One of the World Trade Center. I'm guessing he died around 9:00 that morning. He and 2,996 others, Detective."

"And there's no other Jordan Rome in your family?"

I stared at her. "I only know of the one. What would my dead father have to do with any of this?"

The detective folded her hands on the conference table, looked at them for a moment, then raised her head.

"I can't answer that. What I also can't explain is how a Jordan Rome could have checked into a penthouse at the Marriott fifteen days ago. And just as puzzling no one seems to remember anyone entering or exiting that room. Of course, we checked the security video. There's footage of Eduardo Diego and one other man entering the parking structure two hours before his death. That man left alone about ten minutes before Diego was killed. We then checked the footage from the hotel floor with the penthouse in question, but it looks like there was some kind of technical malfunction with the camera on that floor. Another coincidence, don't you think?"

CHAPTER 31

YOU NEED TO READ THIS

MY MOTHER LIVED IN A small co-op building on Park Avenue. It was built in the midcentury era and reflected that architectural vocabulary. Each time the lobby or entry needed refurbishing, a battle would break out among the twenty co-op owners over whether the building should be upgraded to today's style or restored to its original aesthetic. Fortunately, the residents who wished to maintain the original look won out. The lobby desk, metal details, elevators, and even the corridors all looked like a set from the Dick Van Dyke Show. It made me happy to visit.

At first, I had contemplated moving into her home. But the fact that Richard owned half of it made that impossible. He was anxious to list the property to liquidate it at its inflated value. I promised I would have it emptied of my mom's personal belongings by the end of the month. I was now down to my last week.

I had gone through the kitchen, the living room, and the guest bedroom. I had been putting off my mom's office and bedroom for last. In three days, Catholic Charities would stop by to pick up all the clothing, garments, and furnishings except for the few things I could not part with.

The idea of going through one's mother's possessions is impossible to describe. Each item is attached to a memory or a decision to intentionally bring something into her home. Some items describe a person better than words. These are intimate collections. Clothing reflects what made her feel good, the way she lived casually or formally. When I lifted a garment, I could recall the last time I saw my mother walk into a room wearing it.

Her kitchen and tableware were selected with such care. I would pick up a pan or a dish and remember watching her study all the options in each store before finally choosing the one that matched her tastes and needs. After each successful selection, she would smile her beautiful smile and pontificate about what an "extraordinary addition" this would be to our lives. There were pieces I didn't recognize, old pieces. I tried to recall when they entered our world. Were they her mother's? A gift from someone else? It really didn't matter; these would not be moving with me.

In her bedroom, in the top drawer of her right nightstand, was her jewelry still speaking of brilliant times and tender moments. My mother was not one to buy jewelry for herself, so each item was a gift expressing love for her. When I put a piece on my hand or wrist, it felt hot, almost as if the heat of her body was holding mine.

Many items I lifted and placed in the charity pile, only to move them back and forth between that and the precious few I would keep. It was as if time were ripping apart the embrace between my mother and me. At 4:00 in the afternoon, I found myself sitting on her bed, wearing her camel wrap coat and Jimmy Choo shoes, holding a half-empty glass of wine. This was the proper attire for going through the photo album of my father, my mother, and me as a youngster.

Bringing me out of this stupor was the ringing of my phone across the room. I dug through the clothes stacked on my mother's dresser to free my phone from captivity. It was Cat calling.

"How's it going?" she asked.

"I'm getting through it, but it's hard. Like in the middle of the sentence, she walked out of a room never to return. I keep expecting that when I open a door in a closet or a bathroom, she will be standing there screaming, 'Surprise!' It's a real mind fuck. Oh, and remind me before I die to throw everything out first. I don't want anyone to face going through it all."

"Becca, you shouldn't do this alone. I told you I would help you. It'll go faster, and it's more fun to cry with someone else." We both chuckled.

"You're right. I'm spinning my wheels here, big time. I do need someone to bring discipline to this moribund effort. Let me see how I do tonight, and we can talk tomorrow."

"I have a better idea. I'll pick up some really bad pizza the kind that can stop your heart. A cheap bottle of wine, and we can knock it out together tonight."

"Much appreciated, but I have wine here. In fact, I have wine here that is opened… in my hand. I'll see you when you get here."

The anticipation of Cat coming brought new urgency. When she arrived at 5:30, I was down in my mom's office. My mother had a desk, a credenza, a small console table, and bookshelves overstuffed with books. I turned on the music, playing my mom's old Fleetwood Mac collection. I thought it would be best for me to go through the desk and credenza in case there were any things of critical importance that I should see. Cat agreed to go through the books and console. Her task was more boxing up books for giveaway than anything else. Cat brought new energy to the task while singing along to Lindsey Buckingham.

At about 11:00, we were closing in on the finish line. Cat was going through my mom's console and pulled out a notepad. I was caught up on my mom's last filing cabinet when Cat walked over and turned off the music. She handed me a two-page letter on my mother's stationery. Her eyes were red. She stammered, "Becca, you need to read this. You need to read this now, and I can't stay in the room while you do. I'll be in the kitchen if you need me." She then dropped the paper in my lap and ran out of the room.

PART X

JORDAN ROME

New York, New York
1989: 12 Years Before

CHAPTER 32

DILLON-FREEPORT

I ARRIVED BACK IN NEW York City mid-winter. I had $15,000 in the bank, a 1982 Mustang convertible, and two passable suits for interviews. My skill set suited me for security guard or policeman, little else. Regardless, I was captivated by the allure of Wall Street and concluded if not now, never. In the four years I spent in Islamabad at the CIA bureau station, I had earned the respect and friendship of Station Head Beardon. He was kind enough to draft a recommendation letter and reach out to a handful of Wall Street contacts who had come through the military ranks. One such man was General McMillan, a Marine Corps general who was in charge of office management responsibilities at Dillon-Freeport. He was my final effort and the only interview from Beardon's contacts. It was not uncommon for a retired military officer to take on management tasks required to run finance or legal offices. A senior military officer would tolerate no nonsense and run the overhead aspects of a large organization professionally, without fear of reprisal. The military brass were among the few who could unflinchingly stand up to investment bankers, who often cleared nine figures a year.

Dillon-Freeport was a financial colossus involved in investment banking and money management, including mergers and acquisitions, debt placement, initial public offerings, and bond trading. They had offices in New York, San Francisco, and Dallas, as well as London, Frankfurt, and Dubai. The general had a big job in a big company. I met General McMillan in the New York headquarters on the 94th floor of the North Tower of the World Trade Center. When his assistant let me into his office, he rose and walked from behind his desk to shake my hand. His gait was that of a man past his prime who refused to let his body acknowledge the same. His smile was forced but genuine. This simply was not a man accustomed to smiling.

It is remarkable how sharp the details imprint at such a turning point in one's life. To this day, I could describe every piece of furniture in his oversized office. Not one piece of paper or pen was out of place. The chairs in the small segregated sitting area were perfectly aligned with each other and lined up exactly to the ends of the couch opposite them. The wood coffee table had a mirrored bright shine. Even the coffee settings on the tray were placed perfectly in line with the center of the table, with each cup centered with the coffee pot. General McMillan maintained the look of a general in civilian clothing. His haircut was high and cropped, his shirt immaculately pressed, and his tie set perfectly with the pinched crease under the center of the knot.

"Jordan, it is a pleasure to meet you. Please sit down. Would you like some coffee?"

"Thank you very much, General. I appreciate you seeing me," I said as I walked to the perfectly situated sitting area. When seated, I could see the furniture planning provided the optimal view from the 94th floor to the cityscape behind. "That's quite a view."

"Please, Jordan, call me David. No longer a general. And yes, it is quite a view. Money is never an issue when there's this much of it. These guys know nothing, if not how to make a bunch of money." He paused to fill the coffee cups. "But they're good to me, and they pretty much leave me alone." The General paused for a moment before sipping his coffee, allowing me to add something to the conversation. But all I could do was nod. "Now let's get down to you. I read the letter that Milton wrote. He called as well. He's written letters before, but I've never received a call. That will get you a meeting for sure. I'm assuming you're some kind of warrior for him to go that extra mile. You were deployed for six years. That's a long time to spend over there." The general took a moment and filled his cheeks with air before exhaling. "You guys sure waxed their ass, no question about that."

"I liked the work. I grew to love the people, the locals I mean. I imagine that from where we are, it looks like a backwards world… still fighting battles from centuries ago. It does take some getting used to. But it is also a place of great beauty and remarkable history." I took a moment to see how I could change gears to get back on the topic at hand. "But I have got to do something else now. I need to make a living, and I'd prefer a peacetime environment."

The general fiddled as he starred into his cup. "Being honest with you Jordan, these guys hire Ivy League MBA types. It is a very stuffy group. They wouldn't last an hour in the field of Afghanistan, but they can print money all right." He picked up a piece of paper I assumed to be my CV. "I see you got your high school GED, and I'm sure you're smarter than 95% of the guys here. But I'm not sure exactly where I could fit you in—I mean in a place where you would be not performing some menial tasks. So, as much as I would like to help you and Milton, I'm afraid we just aren't going to be able to do anything for you here." After he finished, we stared at each other for what must have been a minute. My gaze did more to tell my story than words would accomplish. This was a man who did not give in easily, or at all.

"I understand. But if it helps, I'd go to school while I'm working. The last couple of years, I spent less time reading up on history and more time on business. I know that's a long way from actually getting a degree, but I think this work comes to me pretty naturally." He gave me a look, and without speaking, I knew he was thinking that reading a book and getting an Ivy League degree are not the same thing. But he was polite and didn't say that kind of thing to a comrade in arms. Another awkward silence settled in the room.

"General, I mean David, I took a number of tests to get into the agency, and I think I did pretty well on those. I know they thought so. So, if you could see your way to finding any spot for me, I would make sure you don't regret it. I'm not afraid to start at the bottom and work my way up. But if you can't…" I did not finish the sentence.

"What kind of tests, Jordan?"

"I think they were aptitude or IQ tests. They said I performed at the higher end of these things. If it counts for anything, everyone at the agency also had advanced education, while I did not."

The general got up from where we were sitting, picked up the phone, and made a call. I could hear him inquiring about setting up an evaluation through human resources. He then hung up the phone and handed me a piece of paper from his pad.

"Tomorrow, I want you to go to this address. These are folks who do our evaluations for new hires — all sorts of tests. Plan to spend a couple of days with them. Let's see what happens next. If your results are as good as you say, well, maybe I can make something happen. But I am not making any promises."

I nodded. "I understand. Thank you, sir," I said and saluted. The general returned the same, casually, as a senior officer would do to a subordinate.

I took the tests and received a call the day after my second day of testing. It was the general. He put me on a three-party call with Jack Brown, head of research for Dillon-Freeport's bond department. I would start work on a trial basis starting Monday. My salary would be $55,000 a year — $10,000 more than I made risking my life in the CIA.

CHAPTER 33

I NEEDED MONEY

COMPANIES ARE FINANCED THROUGH DEBT and equity. These two major components are frequently divided into multiple layers called tranches. The highest-risk position is made up of various layers of equity by the stockholders. The lowest-risk positions are usually the bonds or debt; they have greater collateral and priority in the event of default or liquidation.

In the vast majority of small companies or partnerships, there is simply debt and equity. This is the same situation every homeowner faces with their house equity and a mortgage. But in massive corporations, debt can be issued in multiple forms: short-term lines of credit, collateralized bonds, and multiple bond levels or tranches, each with its own security, priority, and cost (interest rates). Corporate bonds are priced against the risk-free credit instrument benchmark, generally US Treasury bonds. Thus, if a 10-year Treasury bond is trading at 4 percent, a similar duration bond from a riskier corporation would trade at a premium (more than 4 percent) to the Treasury bond. That premium is set by the marketplace. The research department I worked in studied each bond for hundreds of companies and tried to price them, taking into account the strength of the company and the risk of the particular tranche of bonds. It was a blend of art and science. When dealing with hundreds of millions of dollars in bonds, missing the price by a few basis points (one basis point equals 0.01 percent) can make a large difference in valuation.

Bonds carry all types of risk from AAA-rated to unrated junk bonds. Rating agencies publish their opinions to rate the risk for each group. However, the rating agencies are paid by the very companies they are rating. This obviously creates a conflict of interest that must be accounted for. Thus, Dillon-Freeport had an independent, in-house research department. Not all risky bonds are bad. The higher the risk, the greater the return potential. A gentleman named Michael Milken became one of the country's wealthiest men trading high-risk junk bonds used for high leverage, high-risk debt. He also went to prison.

Milken's focus was the opposite of what the bond desk I was placed on did. We looked at rated, low-risk, high-quality corporate and government bonds. We referred to these as "widows and orphans investments." The goal was, first, to identify bonds we were highly confident would pay their principal and interest throughout their duration. Second, we aimed to identify companies or bonds with a good chance of improving their credit profile through management's efforts or potential improvements in their industry.

Another broad evaluation involved accounting for the duration of a bond and the potential movement of interest rates during that time. For example, if one believed interest rates would fall during the bond's duration, there was potential for that bond to increase in value. Conversely, if interest rates were expected to rise, holding a long-term bond could become quite risky if you needed to sell your position before maturity. Understanding the business climate and specific companies gave us a competitive edge in pricing and purchasing billions of dollars' worth of bonds on behalf of our clients.

There were five people on our research team. My direct report was a gentleman named Richard Anderson. He was a blueblood, born with a silver spoon in his mouth. Richard had all the buzzwords locked down. The combination of executive hair, expensive clothing, a Harvard degree, and the gift of gab enabled him to project capabilities he did not possess. There was a lot of that in this business. Richard chose to befriend me. At first, I thought it was genuine, but every aspect of Richard's life was transactional. He simply wanted access to my thoughts. I too was guilty of befriending him because I thought there was something in it for me in having my superior as a friend. Drinks and small talk after work became commonplace. Wall Street just worked that way.

Still, I loved the work. The more granular, the better. It was like reading a history book with numbers attached to it. We frequently had chief financial officers of companies come into our offices to pitch potential bond issuances. At the end of each pitch, there was a question and answer session. Sometimes I would know more about the CFO's company than he did. When questions were asked by our traders and the CFO was unable to answer, I would offer a hypothetical answer, knowing it was accurate. The CFO would then attach his perspective to my response as if it were his own. Richard was sure to chime in, making the same observation with a slightly different spin, again acting as if it were his own.

Jack Brown saw the way it really worked, and I was increasingly given more responsibility.

Big companies have layers, many layers. When bonuses or promotions are considered, the managing partners who, at best hardly know you, are reluctant to advance someone with a high school degree and no revenue stream attached to their work. This was where I found myself after two years at Dillon-Freeport. I pressed multiple times, in fact, but each time I met with the same year-end review from Jack Brown. "We think you're doing a good job here. Everyone who sees your work is pleased with it." That was followed by a raise at the higher end of the permitted spectrum and an annual bonus. In thirty years, I would be at the same job on the same plateau when they handed me the gold watch and showed me the door. This outcome was unacceptable.

In the meantime, Richard Anderson was promoted. He left the group and started on a track to become a trader. Being a bond trader with your own book was the path to making money. Richard, of course, was not capable of doing that job. He quickly moved to client relations. A promotion, he declared. Dillon-Freeport was about making money. The simple fact was Richard did not have the skill for that critical task.

There are people who are extraordinarily successful at one task while inept at others. Movie stars and athletes often take positions in business or politics, and the public concludes that their celebrity and success in one field will naturally translate to another. Not necessarily true. At the same time, almost anyone can obtain a basic level of expertise in just about anything. Every young boy can be taught to hit a baseball, and art teachers can instruct any student in how to draw a figure. Yet God has made certain people extraordinarily gifted at a task for no discernible reason. Mickey

Mantle, Lou Gehrig, and Babe Ruth could see and hit a baseball better than almost any of their peers. Two of the three could do it still drunk from the night before. Van Gogh, Rembrandt, and Chagall could create magic on canvas. There is no explanation for these one-in-100-million exceptions. But they exist.

Most people go through life with special skills but don't know it. As it turned out, I had a special skill. I could see market movements, industry movements, corporate balance sheets, and management aptitude, each overlaid, presenting themselves as rational when they were disjointed. That skill allowed me to identify inefficiencies in a marketplace where inefficiencies can't exist; they always get corrected. But if one could see them fast, in an instant, they could benefit by acting and richly. I just needed to figure out a way to put myself in a position of independence and trade from my own account.

I felt confident I could trade profitably day to day. So I set up a shadow account to test my theory. I programmed trade positions that I would have taken and the times I would have liquidated them. I kept track of my hypothetical gains and losses, despite the fact that no money would change hands. In my first full year, I returned 68 percent on my hypothetical investments. With real money, I could make an outsized gain like that real. For that, I would have to convince someone to provide that capital or acquire it myself. Neither was likely to occur at Dillon-Freeport.

CHAPTER 34

THE SONG IS OVER

IN JANUARY OF 1992, WE went out celebrating the receipt of our bonuses for the '91 calendar year. I received a $20,000 bonus, which was on top of my now $70,000 compensation. Earnings become relative quickly. What had seemed like an ungodly amount of money three years ago now seemed like scraps that had fallen off the table from the real earners at Dillon-Freeport. To blow off steam this Thursday night, we went to the meatpacking district north of Wall Street in Manhattan. The bars in this area had a more gristly feel. This would quickly change as high-end clubs replaced the original dives, maintaining only their nondescript facades.

Rosie O'Neill's was one of a handful of remaining original establishments. However, bikers and meatpacking laborers were now replaced with finance and entertainment clientele. The drinks were reasonably priced, the food was edible, and the live music was local. There were about a dozen or so of us who descended on the bar simultaneously. I cleaned off a rickety wooden chair and planted myself in the second row of tables from the stage, awaiting my beer. The band was in the middle of a set, rising above the constant background noise of bar service and chatter.

There is nothing unusual about a couple thinking they can identify the first moment they saw each other. I have also heard a number of people claim they knew as soon as they saw their mate, "that's the one." A more accurate assessment is when a man sees a beautiful woman; that thought enters his mind, even if for an instant. Should this one of 1,000 times actually turn out to be the future mate, they conclude they knew it all along. So, I might be wrong, but the first time I saw her, I knew.

Despite the winter air outside, the bar was crowded and warm. The five-piece band included a Black female singer, a keyboard player, a guitarist, and a drummer. The fifth player was a five-foot-five strawberry blonde playing the violin and keyboards. She wore cowboy boots, washed jeans, and a paisley sateen vest. The Black singer had striking good looks and a powerful voice. The song they were playing was a softer version of a new release Metallica's Nothing Else Matters. My tablemates were chatting amongst themselves as the vocalist's sultry voice emitted the lyrics until a break came when the violinist took center stage. I could hear what felt like a series of steps where the bar got quieter and quieter until it was silent as she made the instrument sing. I could not take my eyes off her. The spotlight refracted the drops of perspiration on her brow, neck, and chest. Every man at my table stared slack-jawed.

The song finished with her string solo. The bar maintained its momentary silence before returning to the prior clamor. I stood up, not certain why or with any reason to leave my seat. I just stood. She turned and looked at me and smiled. It was not a camera smile or a salesperson smile. Just a smile. A smile I would not know at that time I would see again and again for years to come. A smile that made me take a step forward from the table before I grasped that the signal offered was different from my perception. Because she turned right after she smiled at me and smiled at the singer the same way.

The band played two more sets that night. I was the only one left at the table as they packed their instruments. I worked up the nerve and approached her.

"I really enjoyed your music tonight. You are an excellent violinist."

She turned her head as she was packing up. She stopped for a moment and took some sort of rubber band out of her front pocket and tied her long hair back. Up close and without the stage lighting, I could see her gray eyes and porcelain skin. She smiled again, but this was a forced smile the kind of look one gets from a waiter when you are the last customer before closing. She was tired and wanted to go home. "Thank you. It's kind of you to say that. And I'm glad you enjoyed it."

"I'm not sure of the best way to do this. I am sure you get men coming onto you a lot. But I would like to take you out for a cup of coffee or maybe breakfast when you're done packing up."

She stopped rolling up the cord she was busy putting together. She stood with her hands on her hips and looked at me. This time she brought out the smile. That good smile.

"I see you were in with your friends tonight. Looks to be quite a prosperous group. I'd guess Wall Street, hedge fund, or something of the kind." She paused, lifting her chin and touching her lips with her finger. "So, what's going through that head of yours? Maybe you think that your 'boy next door' looks and a pile of money might get the hillbilly girl on her back with the offer of breakfast.

I'm sorry to disappoint, but I'd be looking for more foreplay than that," she said, tilting her head.

"Wow, that hurt. Coffee or breakfast just coffee or breakfast. Not looking for anything else."

"Okay, cowboy. Have a seat and let me think about it while I pack up. It'll only be a few minutes."

Ten minutes later, she laid her coat on top of her packed-up instruments and walked over to the sound equipment. She pressed a button, and music came over the speakers. Etta James's "At Last" filled the empty room. She pushed two of the front tables back and started to rock back and forth to the classic.

"Dance with me," she said.

I shook my head.

"It's not going to hurt, I promise."

"I really don't know how to dance."

"It's okay," she said. "Anyone can. I'll teach you a few steps."

I walked forward and stood in front of her, our faces six inches apart. She took my left hand and placed it on her waist just above her hip. I could still feel the perspiration that had dampened her vest. She took my right hand and interlocked fingers with our hands facing down. Then she instructed me: Move your right foot towards me. Now your left. Right; now left; now back. We continued the simple box step as Etta James and my dance partner's scent flooded my head. When the song ended, we stood facing each other, my hand still on her waist while holding her left hand in mine. I was staring into her eyes when she spoke.

"You're going to have to let go of my hand now." I looked down at our hands. "The song is over," she whispered.

I did. She backed up slowly and returned to the stage, put on her coat, and picked up her equipment and instruments. She then proceeded to walk backstage.

"Are we still going out for breakfast?" I asked.

"No. Sorry, it's late. Thank you for the dance though. See, you learned something tonight: there are different types of foreplay, and now you've learned one more."

"But I didn't even get your name."

She stopped and turned, facing me, still holding two armfuls of equipment. "If it's important, you'll figure it out. Good night, Jordan."

Before I could respond, she disappeared into the darkness of the rear of the building and the night.

CHAPTER 35

AND THIS ISN'T A FIRST DATE

OLIVIA DUMONT WAS BORN ON a farm just outside of Des Moines, Iowa, in February 1966. Her father, Arthur, worked the land he had inherited from his father, a Dutch immigrant. Her mother, Belle, taught school and gave music lessons thirty minutes from the farm at Rock Creek Middle School. Olivia grew up with an older brother and a host of pets she often brought home, much to her mother's displeasure. As a youngster, she was pasty and gangly, only growing into her beauty in her mid-teens. Her parents instilled in her the discipline required to work on a farm, empathy for the animals that provided their living, and a love for music that was a constant background in the home. Farm life left no room for excuses or braggart behavior. Each family member had tasks, and they relied on one another to complete them.

When Olivia graduated high school, her mother sent her to the University of Iowa in Iowa City to study music, despite her father's objections. In his mind, this attractive daughter would be an extraordinary catch for a young man with prospects. Her brother, Ian, chose a different path and enlisted in the Army after high school. In 1990, he made the ultimate sacrifice during Operation Desert Storm. Olivia's father died the following year on his tractor. Belle told Olivia he died of heartbreak; the doctor said it was coronary failure. Belle sold the farm and moved to Des Moines, where she continued to teach music. Olivia returned at first to look after her mother but soon left again to pursue her music career in New York.

She auditioned for the New York and Philadelphia symphonies. Her competition included hundreds of professionally trained musicians from the finest academies and universities in the country. Despite this, she managed to obtain a seat as an alternate in the Philadelphia Symphony. The pay barely covered her bills, so she supplemented her income by any means possible. That included part-time retail jobs, private music lessons, and various ensemble gigs for weddings, bars, or clubs. It was in one of these clubs where I saw the woman who would come to define my life.

She was right: if I truly wanted to find out her name, I would. I returned to Rosie O'Neill's the next night. A different band was playing. I asked when the band from last Thursday would be playing again, and the bartender informed me they performed on Thursday nights. It took twenty dollars to get him to tell me Olivia's first name. Even after I offered one hundred, he refused to divulge her last name.

The following Thursday, I was back at Rosie's. Olivia was in the same spot, playing the same instrument, this time wearing a black Abbey Road T-shirt tied at the waist, with the four Beatles walking across the street in white ink. When she saw me come in, she gave me her smile, that smile which I had now renamed Olivia's smile. I watched the entire set. As before, she walked off stage while packing up her equipment. I stood when she arrived at the table.

"Olivia, my name is Jordan Rome. I wanted to introduce myself properly."

"It's nice to meet you, Jordan. My name is Olivia Dumont; my friends call me Liv." A moment of awkward silence settled between us, thick with the unspoken charge of chemistry.

"I was thinking I could go for some breakfast. Are you available?" she asked.

At the corner of Washington Street and Little West 12th, there was an all-night diner. We took a booth—me carrying a box full of her equipment while she held her violin. I placed the small suitcase on the floor beside the booth, but she kept the violin wedged between the wall and her side. We picked up the menus and pretended to read them.

"Anything you want. My treat," I said.

"Anything? What if I wanted to box up a few meals for later? Is that okay too?"

"I'm not sure. Exactly how many are you thinking?"

She smiled. "I think I'm just going to get this one for now. But mind you, you're getting off easy."

We talked. I told her almost the whole truth that I was raised in Bisbee, worked in Miami, and did time overseas in the service. As I spoke, I wondered if I could ever tell the full story to anyone. Not likely, I decided.

She shared her story too. I learned about her upbringing in Iowa and the loss of her brother and father. She remained close to her mother, and they spoke every day. Like most people in New York City chasing the arts, she was fueled by passion. It's a long shot for an aspiring musician to find financial success in a town that costs a small fortune just to wake up in each day. But her youth and temperament allowed her to maintain a remarkable optimism.

We talked until daybreak. When I finally glanced at my watch, I sighed.

"I have to get going. I need to be at work in a couple of hours. Do you want me to help you get your stuff home?"

"I can do it. I do it all the time." She reached over and touched my hand. It was the first time we'd touched since we danced a week ago. "Jordan, I'm not sure if you're asking to carry my stuff or if you're asking to come over to my house for another reason, and I don't want to send the wrong signals. It would be okay for you to come over, but we should do that when we have more time. When you don't have to be at work in an hour."

She reached into her purse and wrote down an address. She lived on West 45th Street in a neighborhood that used to be called Hell's Kitchen but now went by the trendier name of Clinton.

"I can make us dinner on Saturday. I can afford the pasta if you can afford the chicken. How about seven o'clock?"

I stared at the address like it was a key to someplace else. It took me a moment to collect my thoughts.

"Sure. Seven is fine... Saturday."

We walked out of the diner and stood together for a moment. I kissed her gently on the mouth, both of her hands still full with her violin and gear. She leaned forward, and I cupped the back of her head, pressing a little harder. I felt her mouth turn up into a smile.

"Now that I think about it, you should probably bring the wine as well. I'll leave it to you quantity and quality."

"Chicken and wine. Got it," I said.

✱✱✱

I pushed the buzzer on the ground floor and got a response over the speaker.

"It doesn't work. Give it a good push with your shoulder, it'll open."

I gave it a push. Nothing happened.

"You have to hit it harder," came the voice again

I pushed it hard, and the door begrudgingly opened. I looked up the stairway and saw her peering down between the handrails.

"It's a bit of a climb, I'm afraid. But it makes it easy to go up on the roof after dinner," she yelled down.

Liv had a tiny 400-square-foot studio apartment on the fifth floor of a prewar walk-up. The building had been partitioned into a retail store with eight small residential units above. This was common—an easy way to maximize rent without much thought to the quality of life.

She was proud of how she'd decorated. Her bed doubled as her couch, and her desk served as her dining table. The one window faced a brick wall, part of a high-rise about twenty feet away. She'd obscured the non-view with hanging plants. The artwork in her home was her collection of musical instruments, thoughtfully spaced and hanging from hooks on the wall: a guitar, two violins, and a mandolin.

"Aren't you worried about security with the door downstairs?"

She looked at me like I'd just asked if she believed in Santa Claus.

"This building is owned by Joey Evangelista. In case you didn't know, he's the number two guy in the Concrete Laborers Union Local 6A. The good news is no one's going to bother anyone here. The bad news is, you don't want to miss your rent." She laughed to herself. "He really seems like a sweetheart, though."

"I'll bet. I got the chicken and a bottle of red and a bottle of white."

She stepped away from the stove and gave me a peck on the cheek.

"I'll grill the chicken breasts if you open the wine. Dinner should be ready in a jiffy."

We made it through dinner and the bottle of white by nine o'clock.

She rinsed the dishes and stacked them next to the sink. The conversation flowed as easily as the wine.

"Is it OK if I get a little serious for just a minute?" she asked as I was working on the red. I nodded without looking up.

"I don't date a lot of guys. And I don't date any Wall Street guys. As a rule, they're shallow and transactional. I'm not gay or frigid, but I am selective. I've come to terms with the fact that it's easy to be lonely in a city like New York, even when you're surrounded by people. And I'm okay with that." She paused, took a breath. "I don't need you to make up any stuff to..." She turned her head toward her couch-bed. "Well, you know. But if it's more than just a physical thing, I need some rules."

"What kind of rules are you thinking about, Liv?" I asked with my best playful grin.

"Well, we should be honest with each other and respect each other. If there's something on your mind, I'm good to hear it. If there's something on my mind, you can count on me to let you know. I'm okay with drinking, but if you have to do it every day, that's a problem. I don't mind a little weed once in a while, but I'm not okay with drugs. I think they're poison." She looked at the ceiling for a moment, then said, "I think that's about it."

I topped off our glasses with red, not bothering to rinse out the white.

"Is that pep talk a standard for you on first dates?"

Liv smiled that smile and took a long draw from her wine glass.

"Nope. This is the first time I've given it. And this isn't a first date. I think we both know that."

CHAPTER 36

THEY'RE HAVING A BABY!

ALEKSANDR SOLZHENITSYN HAD A FAMOUS quote regarding good and evil. To paraphrase: "The line separating good and evil passes not through states nor classes, but right through every human heart and through all human hearts." I had done some terrible things. I had killed my own father. I took up with the worst kind of people and immersed myself in the vanity, violence, and corruption that came with it. I fought a war against an enemy that had given me no grievance. Though I may have saved a number of lives, I took far more, without question.

Like all individuals, these experiences shaped the man I became. I didn't know I didn't have to be that man that I could become a better one. Liv showed me that.

She had characteristics I'd never encountered in another person. She woke up happy. If she could help a stranger, she did. She didn't keep score about who had the better deal between the two of us. When she was angry, she would leave the room. Her philosophy was that whatever conflict arose, it was best discussed with a cool head. She had firm rules for arguments: no personal attacks, stay focused, and don't bring up past disputes. She lived by those rules, and I was expected to do the same.

Our lovemaking was intense not because the act itself was extraordinary, but because of the connection between us. And Liv touched me all the time. This wasn't about sex. If I was working at the desk or dining room table, she would come by and kiss me on the neck. If I walked past her in the kitchen, she would turn and touch my shoulder, running her hand down my arm. If we were walking and I had my phone out reading emails, she would put her arm around me. When we slept, she rested a hand on me.

I asked her once why she did that all the time.

She said, "Because I want to. It's okay, isn't it?"

"Yes," I said. And I never asked again.

If being together was a foregone conclusion, then marriage seemed like a logical extension. It was never a chore to be with her, and it was unimaginable to be without her. I followed the rules. Some were excruciatingly painful.

Two months into our relationship, I was lying in bed, unable to sleep. I had wrestled with whether to share my past with Liv, weighing the potential damage against the unlikelihood of her discovering it on her own. That night I concluded I couldn't keep it from her. The notion sat in my head like an oven left on; it needed immediate attention.

I woke her. In the dark, I pulled the desk chair to her side of the bed. She sat up, elbows on her knees, rubbing her eyes.

"Liv, I need to tell you some things. Things about me, about my past. Things I've never told anyone else. I think I can tell you this now because the man who did these things is different from the man I am with you. And the reason he is different is you."

Over the next hour, I told her everything. I didn't know how she would respond. But she listened, straight-faced, and asked questions. Specific questions about my father, mother, and brother; about Gabriel, Miami, and the war.

"Jordan, thank you for telling me this. I can't fathom how hard it must have been to tell anybody these things."

Then she got out of bed and sat in my lap, her face pressed against mine, her legs straddled around my hips.

"I love you, Jordan," she whispered in my ear.

My body shuddered, and my eyes watered.

I proposed to Liv the day after Thanksgiving. In December 1993, Jordan Rome and Olivia Dumont were married in the Church of the Transfiguration, located on East 29th Street in New York. It was a beautiful, small Gothic structure built in 1849. The attendees were the bride and groom and Belle Dumont, both as a witness and the mother of the bride who gave her away.

We had discussed a larger wedding, but Liv, forever the rational girl, suggested we use the money to get a new apartment and furnish it. I had always seen my financial struggles as a need to make more money. If I could just earn more, I believed, I could adjust my lifestyle accordingly, and that would make me happy.

Liv saw it differently. After all, she woke up happy.

Our lifestyle, to her, was simply a matter of budgeting. She unabashedly asked what I made and told me what she made. A day later, she gave me a spreadsheet detailing how much money we had for each of our needs. This included saving for a home and going on dates.

She proudly presented her work over dinner, and the budget was accepted as law without debate.

Marriage has a trajectory. As newlyweds, each new acquisition and experience brought novelty and excitement. And for reasons unknown, they all culminated in lovemaking. We spent a year in this place, and I saw no need for change. I didn't know what to expect moving forward; my only point of reference was growing up in a home in a constant state of war.

In early spring, we went to the farmers market, a favorite weekend outing of Liv's, where we spent our budgeted allowance on our preferred fresh items. I wasn't aware of the budget and paid no attention to it. I was only told when we were done shopping. We bought coffee and split an apple fritter at a picnic table adjacent to the market.

"I know I'm supposed to tell you everything. So... I want you to know that I want to have your baby. And that last week, I stopped taking birth control."

My immediate thought was: Have we made love since then? A stupid question. I don't think there was ever a period of two days when we didn't.

"So do you think you're pregnant now?" I asked.

She laughed out loud, and a small piece of apple fritter shot out of her mouth onto my shirt, causing us both to pause the conversation while I located the partially ingested food particle. Liv just laughed harder, this time covering her mouth.

"You don't know that quickly. There's a timing issue. This is going to require a lot of work, and I'm counting on you to do your part."

I shrugged my shoulders and shook my arms like a boxer. "I'm ready, put me in, coach."

We went home and practiced. It turned out I was not well-versed in how this getting-pregnant thing actually worked. I assumed conception happened whether you wanted it to or not. But for whatever reason, we couldn't conceive.

This started a roller coaster of emotions and clinics and tests and clinics. And shots. And more clinics. Her body went through an endless ordeal to make it respond as nature intended. Then IVF. It was painful, exhausting, and expensive. The girl who woke up optimistically every day was visibly struggling, despite her refusal to acknowledge defeat.

After ten months, tens of thousands from our savings, and our most recent IVF failure, she locked herself in the bathroom. I could hear her sobbing and see her shadow leaning against the inside of the door.

I sat outside, my back separated from hers by the thin wood. After several minutes, I felt compelled to speak.

"I want you to know I'm okay, however this works out. You are enough to fill my life. If it happens, it happens. If it doesn't, I can be happy as we are. But I cannot be happy if you aren't happy. Liv, open the door so I can hold you. Liv, please open the door."

Another minute passed before she unlocked the door. We embraced. A week later, we agreed to look into adoption.

When you read books on economics, there's a notion called market elasticity. It refers to how much a price change for a given good change the demand for that good. The example they use for price inelasticity is natural children. They argue that your child is worth infinite dollars. This is the principle that makes kidnapping viable. People will pay almost any amount to get their child back.

We spent several days interviewing adoption agencies, both domestic and foreign. It was a daunting sea of bureaucracy. After our third interview, Liv asked if we could postpone the search. Her mind needed time to recover from all the attempts at fertility before embarking on this next effort. Her capitulation to the circumstances was heartbreaking to witness.

We agreed we needed a break from everything. The best thing to do was take a couple of weeks and rent a house at the Jersey Shore. It was early in the season, and though not in our budget, the prices seemed reasonable. The house was an adorable three-room cabin, and we spent our days reading, cooking, walking on the beach, and making love.

When we returned home, we settled back into the daily grind. My work was busy, and I spent more time at the office. I'm sure that sent the wrong signal, but Liv was not the kind of person who would ever call me on it.

Six weeks later, I walked into a candlelit dinner that Liv had prepared.

"Are you going to tell me something good or bad? Did I do something wrong?"

She tilted her head and smiled at me that smile.

"I think you did something right. I missed my period but thought it had to do with the remnants of everything I've been doing to myself. I went and saw the doctor. He told me I am with child."

I stood up at the table, arms raised, Rocky-style.

"Please don't get too excited. I'm trying to control myself, too. Early pregnancies often fail. Still, I'm definitely pregnant."

Though we didn't speak of our new addition outside the house, our whole world changed. We became hyper-conscious of what we were eating, made sure we exercised, and followed our doctors' orders to the letter.

Somewhere between eleven and thirteen weeks, the chances of carrying the child to term increase dramatically. At week thirteen, we felt confident enough to celebrate. Because we didn't have a budget for the celebration, it had to fit within our dating allowance. So we celebrated at the Olive Garden.

I snuck in a mini split of Moët Champagne, poured a sip into Liv's empty water glass, and poured the rest into mine. We made a toast to the Rome family. Our waitress overheard the conversation and made an impromptu announcement: "They're having a baby!"

A standing ovation from the various working-class families filled the room before we slinked out of the establishment.

CHAPTER 37

I AM 100% CERTAIN

WE WENT TO OUR CHECKUPS every month. Each visit felt like opening a new present. We were going to have a daughter we learned that in week 9. We saw appendages emerge in week 12. The ultrasound pictures became screensavers on Liv's computer, and the printouts were framed in an eight-box matted picture frame, showing the development of our child before she joined the outside world.

In week 18, we discussed names. It is one of man's illusions that this is his choice.

In our child's 20th week, we went to Mount Sinai Hospital for our monthly checkup. Dr. Schwartz was a man in his sixties who had delivered approximately 4,000 babies in his career. He was short, with horn-rimmed glasses and white hair, like someone cast for the role. Although many women were choosing female doctors for this journey, Liv had landed on Dr. Schwartz, and he seemed just as excited about the pregnancy as I was.

Like our previous visits, the mood was upbeat and optimistic. Dr. Schwartz asked if Liv had noticed any abnormalities in her breasts. She said she thought everything seemed normal. He asked if it would be okay for him to check, and she agreed. As he examined her, Liv shot me a dirty look, anticipating a snide remark from me.

Then Dr. Schwartz's face changed from his familiar smile to a serious expression.

"Liv, I want you to put your hand right where mine is. Do you feel that?"

Liv followed his instructions. Her face, too, shifted from joy to panic.

"Have you felt that before? For how long?" he asked.

"I haven't. This is the first time I've felt anything. My breasts have changed so much, and I didn't notice anything there."

She continued feeling the same spot on her breast, as if hoping that whatever she was feeling would vanish.

No one in the room dared say what everyone knew. There was a lump in Liv's breast.

"It may be nothing, but we should look at it while you're here. We'll do an ultrasound in that area. If we find something, we'll take a biopsy. I'd like to get this done before you leave today," Dr. Schwartz said. Liv began to tremble. He held her hand.

"I'm going to leave you two alone for a minute. I'll be back with the ultrasound schedule."

The ultrasound was positive, and we proceeded with the biopsy. Dr. Schwartz said he'd call that evening with the results. He did and asked us to come in the next morning.

Neither of us slept that night. We lay in bed in silence, perspiring, holding hands, tossing from side to side.

When we arrived at Dr. Schwartz's office, we were led into a small library with a conference table. There, we were introduced to Dr. Chadda, an oncologist specializing in breast cancer. There were perfunctory greetings and an offer of water. Liv and I both accepted.

Dr. Schwartz spoke first.

"Pregnancy has a number of side effects. One is an increased production of estrogen in a woman's system. That can trigger outcomes that feed on estrogen. Breast cancer is one of those. When this occurs, it's called gestational breast cancer. It happens in about one in 3,000 pregnancies. When it does, it's most prevalent in women between the ages of thirty-two and thirty-eight. At twenty-nine, you're a rare occurrence. Unfortunately, that doesn't change the facts. This diagnosis raises a series of very tough decisions, complicated by your pregnancy. I'm going to let Dr. Chadda speak more specifically to the challenges of breast cancer, and then we'll return to what it means for your pregnancy."

Dr. Chadda began, "I'm sure you know breast cancer is not uncommon. Caught early and treated properly, our five-year success rates are between 85 and 95 percent. From our perspective, that's considered curative. The good news is that we believe we've caught this early. That means it's important to act quickly.

"The next question is always: how quickly? The answer is now. Treatment would mean a mastectomy. In your case, a double mastectomy is probably the conservative option. After surgery, you'll undergo outpatient chemotherapy. The length of treatment will be determined by some additional tests we need to run. Once the process is complete, reconstructive surgery can create your desired cosmetic outcome.

"This treatment, which we've done thousands of times, is complicated by your pregnancy. I think Dr. Schwartz is best positioned to address those issues."

Liv's eyes began to spill over, tears sliding down her cheeks. She was squeezing my hand under the table so tightly it nearly cut off my circulation. I didn't dare point that out. Dr. Schwartz reached behind him to the credenza and placed a box of tissues on the conference table. Liv used her free hand to grab one and dab at her eyes.

Dr. Schwartz paused before continuing. "Your daughter is approximately at 20 weeks. Some would say that at 20 weeks, we can deliver a child, place her in the NICU, and have some chance of a positive outcome. I would tell you that the chance is extraordinarily remote. There are thresholds at which those odds improve. At 24 weeks, we believe the chances rise above fifty-fifty. At 27 weeks, they go above 90 percent.

"The reason this matters is that the timing of your treatment is critical, and it conflicts with the timing required for a successful outcome for your daughter. Under normal circumstances, I would recommend terminating the pregnancy to focus on your wellbeing, Liv. But I understand these are not normal circumstances."

Liv tried to talk but was unable to speak. She turned to me and whispered, "Can you please ask the right questions? I can't think." I nodded.

"Can we just start the treatment for Liv now and monitor the baby the best we can until it's safe to put her in the NICU?" I asked.

Both doctors stopped and looked at each other before Dr. Chadda began to speak. "It is possible to have the mastectomies now. Although this is really Dr. Schwartz's call, we would not be comfortable with chemotherapy and the child. The fact is, while the chemotherapy seeks to kill cancer cells, it will also harm the child. Mastectomies are helpful if the cancer is isolated. But if it is not, chemotherapy is the only way to address that circumstance and prevent the disease from becoming unmanageable. The sooner we implement the chemotherapy, the better the chances of success."

Liv let go of my hand and took two tissues, one to each eye. "If I understand this right, having my baby will most likely kill me. So, I need to kill her first so I can live. Is that about the long and short of it?"

Thirty seconds of silence passed before Dr. Schwartz responded. "There's a conflict between your treatment and carrying the child to term. That is accurate. Liv, I'm so sorry about this. I really am."

By now, Liv was nearly catatonic, somewhere between hysterics and total collapse. I interjected with another question. "Is it possible to perform the mastectomies now, wait to deliver the baby at 24 weeks, then undergo chemotherapy immediately afterward?"

Dr. Schwartz again looked at Dr. Chadda. Dr. Chadda responded. "It is my primary interest to save your life. Anything short of that is failure. The way to minimize that risk is to start the entire treatment now. If you ask me what an additional month means, it means there is more risk. More risk to you, my patient. If you are asking me to quantify how much more, being honest, I can't. I know there is history here. I understand these are difficult decisions."

A renewed silence took over the room. I caught Dr. Chadda turning off his phone, which was now vibrating every thirty seconds. I broke the silence. "We are overwhelmed with this information. Twenty-four hours ago, we were having a healthy baby. Now we wonder if we will have a child or worse, if we will lose everyone." I reached over and took Liv's hand. "We're going to think about it tonight. Dr. Schwartz, we will call you in the morning, if that's okay."

Dr. Chadda immediately excused himself, as there was clearly an emergency he had to attend to. Dr. Schwartz agreed that it was fine to wait until the morning. He took out a business card and wrote a number on the back. "This is my cell phone. If you need anything, anything call me. Otherwise, we will speak tomorrow."

The ride home was silent and painful. Every deformity in the road, every rattle in our car, seemed inordinately loud.

Liv spoke to me in a whisper. "Do you think God hates me? Why would He put me through this test? Why would He give me this baby and then ask me to kill it? It's like when God asked Abraham to kill Isaac. It's fucking biblical."

I did not answer. But I thought God knew what He was doing. He knew that I could become my father. That person should not have a child, and God was protecting my child from me. This is what I thought, but I dared not say it. Instead, I said, "I don't think this is God's work. No God would do this to a person like you."

We finished the ride in silence. At home, we finished dinner in silence. We lay in bed sleepless, staring at the blank ceiling. Liv then spoke. "What should we do?"

"This has to be your choice. I can't tell you what is best. But Liv, I really don't know if I can live without you. I thought we had a deal that I would die first so I didn't have to face that."

Liv chuckled. "We never had that deal. Now you're just making stuff up to get your way."

Ten minutes later, Liv got out of bed and went into the shower. I heard her standing under the water for half an hour. When she came out, the towel was wrapped around her hair, and she was up to her neck in her bathrobe. She turned all the lights on in the room. She was upbeat, completely different from when she walked into the shower. The transformation scared me a little. She sat on the bed, tapping it to call me next to her.

"Tomorrow morning, I'm going to call to schedule the surgery. I know that has to be hard for you to think about. But as a concession, I'll let you pick out the new ones. Just keep in mind that once you make that decision, we're living with those puppies forever, so try to be mature about it. Also, I'm going to keep our girl in the oven for another month. I will schedule the chemo right after the cesarean. Whatever it takes to deal with that, I will do it. In twenty weeks, I will be done with my chemotherapy, and we'll be taking our girl home. I am 100 percent certain this is going to work out. One hundred percent."

The next day we called Dr. Schwartz. The day after, Liv went into surgery, and twenty weeks later we brought Rebecca home. Six months after that, Liv had those perfect C cups implanted. After the night she came out of the shower, Liv never complained once in spite of the awful pain she endured for those months. On Rebecca's first birthday, I gave Liv South Sea pearls. She put them on, picked up Rebecca, and spoke to her.

"I know it's your birthday, so we will share these. I will wear them for the first twenty years, and then it will be your turn." She then looked up at me and smiled that smile. One hundred percent certain it will work out, I thought.

CHAPTER 38

YOU CAN'T FIND SOMETHING YOU NEVER LOST

LIFE WITH THE ADDITION OF Rebecca took on an entirely new perspective. Marriage is the consummation of an event that has already occurred. Two people fall in love and decide to spend their lives together. Wedding vows simply formalize that decision. Bringing my daughter into the world, however, was an entirely different experience. Here was a helpless being who couldn't care for herself, and we were responsible for her every need.

When we brought her home from the hospital, I openly questioned the nurse's decision to let me take this person home. After all, I was completely unprepared for parenthood. I knew absolutely nothing about it. Liv, on the other hand, acted as though she'd done it a thousand times. Despite her weakened condition from medical treatment, she was tireless.

Liv chose to call Rebecca "Becca" from the moment we brought her home, and we never used another name. From the beginning, Becca was comfortable in any environment. Liv took her everywhere: music lessons, practices, shopping. Mother and daughter were inseparable. I handled the fatherly duties of baths, roughhousing, and athletics. Even then, Liv would watch from a distance so she wouldn't miss any part of our child's life.

She read to Becca every night and worked on her letters, colors, and animals, as many mothers do. Becca spoke at a very early age and could read words by the time she was three. Liv seemed amazed, but I had no frame of reference. Of course, every parent thinks their child is gifted.

Though home life was flourishing, my work remained stagnant. I received the same raises and bonuses after the usual annual reviews. Jack Brown left the company, and the entire research group either got promoted or chose to move on. In their place came a new wave of young Ivy League men I now had to compete with.

Jack Brown's replacement, Dale Brite, at least had the courtesy to be candid about my prospects for a bond trading role.

"Look, Jordan, you're really good at what you do, and it's possible you'd be a good trader. But if you're wrong and lose a bet as every trader does, the first question will be, 'Who made the bad trade?' If the answer is a high school graduate, it'll reflect poorly on the firm. Heads would roll, including yours. My suggestion? Go back to school or take classes at night."

I had been at Dillon-Freeport for six years, and this was the first honest answer I'd received to that question. Sulking at my desk, I choked on the prospect of spending six more years in night school just to earn a college degree. Quitting work to attend full-time was not an option. I had a wife and child to support. The inability to advance gnawed at me like a cancer.

Just then, Richard Anderson poked his head over the partition. He needed to brag that he was being "promoted" to Compliance. It wasn't a real promotion, but Richard framed it as management giving him experience across departments because they were grooming him. No one believed it, but the move came with an invitation to take a few of us out for drinks. I called Liv and got a hall pass for the night.

Four of us headed to the bar at Cipriani, a high-end spot that caters to the finance crowd. We took a seat at a high-top near the bar. I had a couple of drinks, and at 8:00, I suggested I was ready to go home. Just as I was getting up from my seat, a lean man, approximately six feet tall with silver hair, approached the table.

"Good evening. My name is Jean Paul Dion."

The four of us turned as one and looked at the stranger.

"I am looking for Jordan Rome," he said in a French accent, making eye contact with each of us individually.

"I am Jordan Rome. How can I help you?"

"This is a most confidential conversation, Mr. Rome. I would prefer we conduct it in private. We have a room at the rear of the restaurant. My client is also in attendance, waiting for you there."

"Mr. Dion, I'm sure you can understand your request seems quite fishy. Perhaps you can contact me at my office in the morning. We can arrange a confidential conversation at that time."

"Thank you for the offer, Mr. Rome, but that would not be acceptable to my client. Their organization has substantial funds they're looking to place with Dillon-Freeport. We're hoping you can assist us with that effort. But if you cannot, we will certainly understand and look elsewhere to place our investments."

Richard couldn't help himself. He pulled out his business card still labeled "Investor Relations" and introduced himself. Mr. Dion reached forward with his left hand to take Richard's card. On this hand was a five-carat diamond ring, and on his wrist, a $300,000 Patek Philippe watch. No one at the table missed these items, nor were they supposed to.

"Thank you, Mr..." He squinted at Richard's card. "Anderson. However, my client is interested in dealing exclusively with Mr. Rome. So, Mr. Rome, do you have five minutes?"

My tablemates turned and looked at me as if I was crazy. Mr. Dion placed Richard's card in his suit pocket and began walking toward the back of the bar.

"Five minutes," I said, "but I'm not leaving the restaurant."

"Please follow me."

I followed Jean Paul Dion to the rear of Cipriani, which features a number of small private rooms where billion-dollar deals have been negotiated. He opened a massive wooden door, and I entered. The table inside was covered in seafood and steaks, all set on silver platters. Seated at the table were Casandra and Eduardo Diego. Standing at the rear of the room was Ricardo.

I froze, caught between the decision to sit or run. Mr. Dion moved from the door and took a seat at the end of the table opposite Casandra. The one remaining seat was across from Eduardo.

"My Jordan, haven't you aged well. I really didn't see you as the Wall Street type. But always ambitious, you have never ceased to surprise me. Please, have a seat. We've ordered far too much. You'd be doing us a favor by helping out."

She spoke casually, as if we had arranged this meeting months ago.

Casandra looked good, clearly the best work money could buy. The secret is always to make it look like you haven't had anything done, and in her case, it worked. In contrast, Eduardo looked awful.

Hard living was catching up to him. We locked eyes momentarily, and he nodded. I did not return the favor.

I thought for a moment about leaving but ended up taking the seat next to Casandra.

"I'd be lying if I said I wasn't surprised. How did you find me?" Casandra took a small bite of her steak.

"I don't know what they brag about. I think the food here is not so special."

Ricardo picked up her plate and placed a piece of fish on a separate dish, which he set in front of her.

"So, Jordan, I really didn't find you. You can't find something you've never lost. It's safe to say I've known where you've been and what you've been doing for the last, oh fifteen years. But relax, I'm here to help you. Of course, there's something in it for me as well. You met Mr. Dion. He assists me with investments. As you know, I'm in a business with substantial profitability. But like any businessperson, I look to diversify high-risk investments with lower-risk ones. Furthermore, those investments should be spread across a variety of places. You know too many eggs in one basket is never wise. Mr. Dion is a banker and helps me with this effort. But I think you can assist him in that role. Perhaps Mr. Dion could stop eating for a moment and explain exactly how you can help."

The banker instantly stopped chewing, swallowed, and wiped either side of his mouth.

"Mrs. Diego possesses a diverse investment portfolio through our bank in Zurich. A substantial portion of this portfolio is in high-quality bonds that carry low risk but provide an adequate coupon yield. Mrs. Diego's holding company is seeking to invest in the domestic bond market in the US. It's our understanding that Dillon-Freeport has a substantial bond desk that could accommodate our needs. We would like you to facilitate that. Of course, we would pay market rates for your services."

"How much are you looking to place?" I asked.

"These numbers change. Right now, let's say, on the order of 200 million. It should go into rated government or high-credit corporate securities. We don't need to make money, we just don't want to lose it. And if you're worried about pesky compliance issues, I can promise you these funds will look like they came from Mother Teresa herself," said Mr. Dion, before returning to his steak.

I turned to Casandra.

"You don't need me for this. Just send your banker in. We have an entire group that would be more than happy to take your money."

Casandra pushed her plate away after tasting a small piece of fish.

"I'm a little bit paranoid. But you already understand that. It's why I have to have people everywhere. Say some ambitious prosecutor from here or there starts tracking money from one place to the next and shows up asking questions. If I knew that in advance, the money could be moved and sent almost anywhere in an instant. Now, if I had a friend who was close to my money, he would know if such an inquiry had come up. That would be valuable to me. You could be such a friend."

"I don't know. This could be risky if compliance sends up a flag... Let me think about it."

"There's nothing to think about. Jordan, you've been stuck in the same place for years. Plus, now you have a number of mouths to feed. There is no risk to you. You bring Mr. Dion in, he provides whatever information your company needs to sleep at night, and we move forward. We've done this part many times. You invest our money cautiously, you let us know if anything bad happens, and you can take all the credit. It's a good-sized account, no?"

Casandra then signaled Ricardo to bring a lobster tail.

For the first time, Eduardo spoke.

"Jordan, you're a fucking grunt making a hundred grand a year. I spend that much on a bar tab. Wake the fuck up."

The man who killed Gabriel, the man I hated with every fiber of my being sat in judgment. He would inherit the hundreds of millions Casandra had accumulated. I picked up a steak knife off the table and toyed with the idea of sticking it in his neck. But I didn't. I sat in silence.

Casandra turned and chided her son.

"Eduardo, please. The adults are talking."

Eduardo took his napkin and tossed it onto his plate. He abruptly stood up and left the room.

"Okay, have your man come in tomorrow at 11. I will arrange for him to meet the right people. Casandra, I'm not sticking my neck out here. If something fishy shows up either in the initial due diligence or later, after we're up and running I will let you know. That's all I'm agreeing to."

Casandra broke into a huge smile. "Fabulous, just fabulous. Like old times."

As I turned to leave the room, Casandra called my name one more time. "Jordan, stay for a while. We'll have a drink, share a few laughs. It'll be fun."

"Good night, Casandra. I'm married now. Those days are over for me."

"Oh, that's right. Good for you, Jordan. Good night."

Ricardo opened the door and let me out of the room.

At 11:00 sharp the next morning, Jean Paul Dion arrived at our offices with three lawyers from the white-shoe firm of Lincoln, Solomon, and Pierpoint. In attendance from our side were two people from business development, two from the bond department, one from legal, and one from compliance. Although this was technically Richard's last day in client relations, he managed to insert himself into the meeting. It certainly wasn't by invitation.

The meeting was set in the lavishly furnished executive conference room. The traditional display of pastries, fruit, and coffee sat on the rear credenza.

Mr. Dion introduced himself, and all parties shook hands, exchanged false smiles, and real business cards. I noticed the large diamond on Dion's pinky finger was missing; it must be only for after-hours attire.

We sat at the table with our team on one side and Dion with his three attorneys each billing over $1,000 an hour on the other.

Dion began, "I represent a holding company based in the Cayman Islands. This company operates a number of business lines, including real estate, gas and oil, shipping, and sugar. The company has done business with our bank, Zurich Bancaire Privee, for the last twenty-five years. One of the founding family members served alongside Mr. Rome in the military. Unfortunately, this individual did not return from service. Before he passed, he spoke very highly of Mr. Rome's character. It is this connection that brings us to Dillon-Freeport. Though we have capital placed in multiple institutions, we would like to invest approximately $200 million with your bond desk. These funds should be placed in high-grade government and corporate bonds. Because of the aforementioned history with Mr. Rome, we would like him to serve as the direct contact for our investments."

The in-house group exchanged looks before Jack Davis, a managing partner who ran the bond desk, spoke. "Do you have parameters for this investment in terms of duration or anticipated yield?"

"We do not see a liquidity need. In fact, on the contrary, we anticipate this will be the first step in developing a larger portfolio with your organization. But as the saying goes, we should walk before we run. Regarding yield, we would benchmark it against like-kind investment portfolios. Certainly, you track those as well."

Jack Davis nodded. "We have a presentation to introduce the team we propose to manage your portfolio. My group will discuss objectives and prior performance. Compliance will address adherence to reporting requirements, and legal will answer any questions regarding the international tax aspects of the investment. We will also have to do our own due diligence on your group. I can email you that checklist, or we can discuss it today as well. We should be finished by noon, and I plan to have lunch brought in afterward."

Mr. Dion raised his right hand just above the table. "We appreciate the presentation, but it won't be necessary. We have done our due diligence as well, and we are confident this is an assignment Mr. Rome and your firm can undertake successfully."

The third and youngest lawyer picked up two expandable folios that appeared full of papers. The most senior lawyer then spoke. "I believe this will meet all your due diligence requirements. Inside the folios are hard copies, as well as two drives containing digital copies of the documents. In addition, I will email the information to you after this meeting. If you need anything else, please contact our firm, and we will get it for you."

The room went silent until Jack Davis spoke. "Well, very good then. Should I have lunch brought up early?"

Jean Paul Dion rose from his seat, buttoned his bespoke double-breasted suit, and adjusted the cuffs at each sleeve before speaking. "I'm afraid I will not be able to join you. I have additional business in town that I must attend to. Certainly, you gentlemen are welcome to partake at your discretion," he said, glancing at his lawyers and focusing on the most senior to his right.

Mr. Dion then left the room only minutes before the arrival of the elaborate lunch. Jack Davis excused himself with a small plate of food, while the remainder dined on the feast. This included the three lawyers, who undoubtedly continued billing their time as they enjoyed a free lunch.

After the meeting, I heard nothing, nor did I see any follow-up correspondence. Ten days later, I was copied on a wire receipt from Zurich Bancaire Privee for $200 million. I was now a revenue generator.

PART XI

IBRAHIM ASSAD

Ramallah City, The West Bank
2000: 1 Year Before

CHAPTER 39

I AM BEGGING YOU NOT TO GO

THIS MORNING, WE HELD A memorial for our son, Amir, whom we had buried one year ago. Nothing has been the same since. In an instant, our life shifted from bliss to tragedy. The love that once filled our household was replaced by a never-ending tension between two grieving parents. Aaliyah would never say it was my fault, but she thought it all the same. She did not have the capacity for hatred inside her being, but if she did, she would hate her husband.

It happened in an instant. Amir went from standing by my side to a boy crushed between the brick pavers and the ambulance's wheel. We were at a fruit stand, the same one we had visited a hundred times when a melon fell onto the street. Before I could react, the ambulance rounded the corner and struck our child as he tried to retrieve the fruit. Amir, our only child, was taken from us at the age of five, leaving the image of my mangled boy forever etched in my mind. Aaliyah was inconsolable. Whenever I tried to comfort her, I failed. I could not hold her; I could not speak to her. Meals became marathons of silence, where even forced conversation ended in hostility.

This was an abrupt change from the life we shared before Amir's death. After my return from Afghanistan, I immersed myself in my profession and family. I had a good job, as did Aaliyah. We enjoyed the comfortable life of young professionals, acquiring a two-bedroom flat and a Peugeot automobile. We presented ourselves as a smartly dressed young couple, embracing the cosmopolitan lifestyle and friendships available to us. I was enthralled by my secular life, a complete contrast to my hardened existence in Afghanistan. When Aaliyah shared that she was with child, we felt that Allah had granted our every wish. Aaliyah blossomed with the birth of our son. Each act, no matter how minor, was photographed and documented. The two were inseparable. I thanked Allah each day for the blessings He bestowed upon us.

After Amir's death, I returned to the only place where I found solace, the mosque. The men there understood my anger and offered comfort, camaraderie, and prayer. They shared that these tragedies happened all too frequently in our community. No one would be charged, and no one would be held accountable. A payment here, or a payment there, would wash away all accounts. This was the world of oppression I lived in a world controlled by the corrupt, created by the West, and financed by the Jews. The loss may have been erased for the ambulance company, but it did not go away for me. It did not go away for Aaliyah. Eight months after Amir's death, I had been fully transformed back to my prior self. My Western clothing was replaced with robes, head coverings, and a full beard. When my hostility toward my employer became untenable, I was asked to leave the engineering firm. I was unfazed by the event, as it allowed me to devote myself fully to the mosque and my community.

When the one-year memorial was complete, I walked home in silence with Aaliyah. At that moment, she did the unthinkable, she took my hand. We exchanged no words as we walked, still in silence, to our home. When we returned, Aaliyah prepared a light lunch for us. For the first time in a year, she spoke to me in the tone we shared before the loss of our son.

"Ibrahim, I want to tell you a story about something that happened to me at the hospital last Friday. A young boy, about the age of our Amir, had placed a toy soldier in his mouth and unintentionally swallowed it, causing him to choke. It was a toy that his grandfather had made for him. While his father was at work, the mother watched over the child as she did every day. It was during this time that the child ingested the toy. The mother ran with the boy in her arms for almost a mile to the emergency room at our hospital. The choking deprived the child of oxygen, and he was unconscious when we operated on him in the emergency room. We saved the child, but the oxygen deprivation caused irreparable brain damage. The extent will most likely not be known for some time, but it is certain that it is very bad. Within the hour, the father arrived at the hospital. The parents were very upset, as one might expect. Each was quick to blame the grandfather, the father, the mother, the hospital, Allah—really anyone who might have contributed to the terrible thing that happened to their child. The shouting was terrible to watch. Ibrahim, I don't think I was able to cry when Amir died, but I cried for this family that Friday."

Aaliyah now had tears streaming down her cheeks. "Sometimes terrible things happen for no reason. But one's mind won't accept that. I blamed you for Amir. I know if it had been me at the market that day instead of you, the exact outcome might have occurred. But you would have forgiven me. You would have forgiven me because you know how much I loved our son. I know as well how much you loved him. If we are to have a life together, I need to forgive you for me as well as for you. From this day forward, I will try my best to do that. In turn, I ask you to forgive me for the cruelty I put upon you. I know you too are grieving, and it was so unfair that I placed the additional burden of my grief upon your shoulders."

We slept together as husband and wife for the first time in a year. But our life did not return to the days of laughter and joy we enjoyed after my return from Afghanistan. How could it? One does not move on from the loss of a child. One only gets better at living with the pain. My medication for that pain remained my faith in Allah. I remained at the mosque, and we relied on the salary that Aaliyah earned to support our household. Though I'm certain there was resentment about her being the sole provider, not a word was ever spoken of it. She understood my obligation to a higher calling was now permanently cast to atone for my failure to protect my child.

***

I was working on fixing the water supply to the mosque restroom when the Imam said there was a man to see me. The visitor was dark-haired, in his thirties. He was clean-shaven and dressed in Western clothing. I recognized him; I had met him in Turkey on my way back from Afghanistan. He was an Egyptian, Western-educated, and a follower of the Saudi Osama bin Laden. I remembered this because I told him I had also read much about his teachings and found them inspiring. Though I recalled meeting the visitor, I could not remember his name.

Mohammed Mohammed Al Amir Awad el-Sayed Atta went by the abbreviated version of his name, Mohamed Atta. He was born in Kafr El Sheikh, Egypt, into affluence; his father was a lawyer, and his mother came from a wealthy merchant family. He studied architecture at Cairo University and then pursued graduate studies in Germany at Hamburg University of Technology. To all who met him, he appeared to be a secular Western professional. It was not until he was a young man in Germany that he saw his role as one to be carried out on behalf of Allah. He spoke four languages. When he introduced himself, he spoke to me in English.

"Ibrahim, we have met before, do you remember?" I nodded in agreement. "I am aware of your piety; bless you for it. I am also aware of the tragedy from the loss of your son." He put his arms around me and held me close before stepping back and looking around the modest mosque. "Your mosque is modest but well kept. Have you ever thought that perhaps Allah has something more important for you?"

I responded, "I am carrying on His work here. I teach the young people, I repair the building, I help those who are unable to help themselves. This is Allah's work."

"Maybe so. But maybe there is something far more important for you. When we met in Turkey years ago, I was very impressed. I remember you to this day. You had fought bravely. At that time, we shared our admiration for one of the great leaders of our generation." I continued listening but returned to my work on the sink. "I am working with him now on something very important. It was he who suggested I come to see you. We are working on a very bold plan, something that will bring the West to its knees. It will be a sword in their heart. It is a powerful and glorious plan. But we need people, people like you to carry it out. It would secure your place in heaven, a place such a great person, such a learned, pious person as you should obtain."

There was an immediate thrill at the thought of doing something important. Osama bin Laden had sent a messenger to see me personally! A calling from Allah to repay all those who had hurt myself and my people for generations. I felt a shudder run through my back and shoulders. I paused and stopped working as I stood before my visitor. Although I did not know what my new guest was suggesting, I was not naïve. It would be, at best, dangerous, and at worst, martyrdom. I responded to Atta, "I am a simple man living a simple life. I have a wife. Though we have lost our child, we hope to have another. I think you are asking more of the simple man than he can do."

Mohammed Atta replied almost in a shout, "There are no simple men; there are only men who think simply. That is not the man you are. You are destined to be etched in history. The West talks bravely when they sit inside their tanks or fly over, dropping bombs on the innocent. They are cowards, and we will show that to be the case. And when we do, all Muslim brothers will rise across Europe, North America, and throughout the Mideast. A caliphate of believers will return, and the oppressors will be subdued." I bowed my head in submission. He was right. I was afraid; afraid to live, afraid to act. I took refuge in the mosque to avoid facing the world I no longer wished to be in.

"What is it you are asking of me?" I asked. He responded with a smile, anticipating that he had made progress in persuading me.

"First, you must meet with our blessed leader. He will explain this plan to you, this enlightened plan. Ibrahim, we will learn to fly. The devil himself will teach us how. Then we will use the devil's tools to destroy itself."

I felt adrenaline surge. I wanted to shout praise to Allah aloud. But I did not. "I must think of this before I make any decisions," was my only answer.

"Very well. I will visit you here next week."

One week later, Mohammed Atta returned to the mosque. I agreed to meet our spiritual leader Osama bin Laden in Afghanistan. Atta had already purchased the plane ticket and placed it in my hand. I returned home that evening and told Aaliyah I would be taking a religious pilgrimage back to Afghanistan.

"Why? Why would you go to this foreign place and leave your wife, your home? How long will you be gone? What is the purpose of this sudden need to study in this foreign land?" She rapidly asked questions to which she knew there were no answers. She understood that the calling I was responding to did not have answers she would find rational.

"This is something I must do. A man does not have to explain to his wife, or anyone for that matter, his mission to fulfill his destiny and Allah's calling."

Aaliyah recoiled physically at my angry tone, leaning back in her chair. "Ibrahim, we were friends before we were husband and wife. You have been the love of my life since the first time we met as children. In all that time, you've never spoken to me in this manner. It is hurtful, very hurtful." She then stood up and walked around, placing her hands on my shoulders. "I have been given another offer to work in Europe, in a hospital in London. It could be a start for us, a fresh start. Please don't take this trip. There was a time when you thought it was Allah's will for us to raise a family in peace. I believe it still is. Once again, I am begging you not to go."

I took her hand from my shoulder and kissed it. Not another word was said. When my wife went to bed that night, I packed a small bag of necessities and left the house.

PART XII

Jordan Rome

New York, New York,
2000: 1 Year Before

CHAPTER 40

A LIGHT AT THE END OF THE TUNNEL

LIV AND BECCA DANCED IN circles around our new living room. Becca then curtseyed and asked me to dance, so I picked her up and held her close cheek to cheek with her toes three feet off the ground, waltzing around our new wood floors. Our concert was interrupted by the movers bringing the old furniture into our new home, a 2,500-square-foot, three-bedroom cottage in Roslyn, Long Island. Not a year after I had received a $200,000 bonus for generating new business for Dillon-Freeport, Liv showed me an online picture of the $750,000 home. That seemed like an extraordinary amount of money, even though it was at the lower end for Long Island. But it needed no work and had great schools. The one-two punch was that I could easily commute from the train station, and Becca would have her own normal-sized room.

When we saw the home, the entire family fell in love. The market was overheated, and there was an intense bidding war on the house. Liv took it upon herself to handwrite a letter to the sellers. Although she spared some of the worst details, she told them how she had struggled to create the family we now had, and how she had dreamed of a home like this since she was a little girl. The bidding stopped that day, and we closed on the house 45 days later. As a result, I had a $4,000-a-month mortgage, a fully depleted savings account, and Maximilian, a stray poodle mix Liv brought home to live with us. The idea of setting out on my own was set back another half dozen years. Concurrently, I received my annual 5 to 7 percent salary increase and a bonus in line with the business plan set forth by upper-level management for a department they knew little about. I did my best to remind management of the business I generated, now growing by over twenty million a year. But Dillon-Freeport made sure I did not gain control of this client. My role was finite. Once a month, I would have a conference call with Jean Paul Dion to review the portfolio expenses and income. The expenses were typical items for like-kind business accounts. When I received these invoices, I approved them, and we paid for them from Casandra's investment income. The call lasted fifteen minutes. Dion never asked a question about any of the details involved.

In the meantime, senior executives would jet to Zurich to meet with Dion, as well as provide junkets for him and his family to five-star resorts around the world. I was isolated and would remain so unless I appealed to Casandra directly. That was not going to happen. Eduardo's words "You are a fucking grunt... I spend that much on bar tabs" stewed like acid in my head.

It was then that the thought entered my head. For weeks, it would not leave. Eduardo could provide me would provide me with a portion of the inherited money that would be his. Although it escaped me at the time, I should have seen the good Jordan, Liv's Jordan, fatefully surrendering to this idea. I did not. Greed and vanity had become the master.

The idea could be tested easily. I sent an invoice to our office from a company based in Panama with an operating bank account in Albany. The name of that company was New York State Clearing Corp. The invoice was for clearing house services provided to Casandra's account. I approved the invoice, as I had done for all others, and had it processed for payment. The invoice was $10,000 and showed up in the monthly statement that I reviewed with Dion. Ten thousand dollars on an account which was now at $300 million meant nothing, and Dion never mentioned it. I got bolder. I increased the amount month by month until it was $50,000. At the end of each quarter, the money in the account was wired from Albany to Panama. The Panama account now had $1.1 million in it. In another fifteen months, it would have $2 million. At that time, I would offer my resignation to Dillon-Freeport. That would be the day that JR Trading would be founded. JR's capital source would be New York State Clearing. Corp.

With this scheme, my adrenaline surged, as if I was in Miami decades ago. I saw a light at the end of the tunnel and believed I could finally obtain the life we deserved. Liv and I would be in a great place. She had been clear of any potential cancer for five years. Our daughter, now six years old, would reach her potential. We concluded we could be happy with the small family we had; a family that would have all it could ever need.

***

In December 2000, I received a call from Milton Beardon, the station chief I'd worked under in Islamabad. The last time I spoke to him was eleven years earlier when I thanked him for the job reference for Dillon-Freeport. The request was unusual. There was a man he had known for a number of years who was responsible for the FBI counterterrorism group in New York. His name was John O'Neill. John had asked Milton to arrange a meeting. Beardon was not specific about the topic but would not accept no for an answer. We met in the cafeteria on the 88th floor of Dillon-Freeport.

John O'Neill did not look like an FBI agent. His dark, gelled hair was perfectly in place. He dressed like a high-priced lawyer. His pink silk tie and handkerchief matched and were impeccably placed. He wore Gucci loafers, something you didn't often see in law enforcement. He was alone at a four-person table at 3:30 in the afternoon. There was only a dozen people left in the cafeteria, as employees were cleaning up for the end of the day. O'Neill was staring out the window at the white smoke billowing in the cold, crisp air from the mechanical systems below straining to heat the buildings and their occupants.

I was given a physical description, so he was not hard to identify the man sitting alone. "John O'Neill? John, my name is Jordan Rome. It is nice to meet you."

"Thank you, Jordan. I do appreciate you meeting me. This is an incredible view you've got up here. Gives you a whole new perspective of the city."

I sat down opposite John. He held a to-go cup of coffee and pushed a second one in my direction. I nodded in appreciation. "So Beardon called and asked me to visit with you. Happy to do that. What can I help you with?"

"I don't know if Milton told you what I'm working on. I've been given the job to coordinate the FBI task force in New York for counterterrorism. The focus is on thwarting terrorism stateside before it happens. I'm sure you're familiar with what happened at the USS Cole in October, and I know you know what happened in '93 on the parking level in this building. These guys are here. We know it. And they're looking to do harm to us," he said, taking a sip of his coffee.

I took a moment, trying to size John O'Neill up. He dressed like he was out of Hollywood but had the passion of a warfighter. "Well, no argument there. They've got their own rule book and their own priorities... not possible for the Western mind to understand. Still, that doesn't explain what you want from me."

"Jordan, we have a problem. We've got half a dozen government silos, each with their own territory, their own budget, and their own objectives. The particular problem today is that the CIA and FBI aren't communicating. This rift is festering while the enemy plans and trains for carnage. The tension between the two groups is bad and needs to be mended quickly. I was hoping you could help us. Milton says you have more experience with these folks than anyone. Your reputation with the CIA still carries weight today. If you were on our side of the table, I think the conversation and cooperation would change overnight."

I took my turn to stare out the window

"Are you asking me to go to work for the FBI? Because if you are, it's out of the question. I have a job, I have a family. I can't drop that and go back to chasing bad guys. I'm a different man now. I wouldn't be good at it anyway."

"I'm not sure you understand what's happening. They have a shitload of people fanatics, well-financed, well-coordinated, staying up nights figuring out how to tear our civilization down to its foundations. They are in this country now. To these people, it's not a question of what carnage is acceptable; it's a question of what carnage is possible. If people like you don't step up to stop it, who will?"

O'Neill's tone seethed with frustration and urgency. I understood. I drew a deep breath to settle myself.

"John, you're wrong. I do understand. But you are not going to stop them. That's true with me or without me. You have three billion people who follow the faith. The vast, vast majority are good, peace-loving people who want nothing more than what we want: peace, prosperity, a family, a home. But even if half of one percent buy into the idea that they need to change the world through violence, that's still 15 million people. They take kids who are poor and hungry and feed them, then poison their minds in these Madrasa schools. These boys are isolated, never see women, and never hear anything but the incessant need to right a world of wrongs. It creates unimaginable problems both there and for the West. They are told there is a way out of all the injustice they see. Every problem they face would be gone if "Believers" replaced Western decadence and corruption. Whatever they need to do to get that outcome is sanctioned by the faithful. This includes killing themselves or others. In fact, the Muslim world is at much greater risk than the West. There is a modern interpretation in the faith referred to as Takfir. This edict allows killing innocents, including Muslims, if it's God's will. If innocents die, the Believers go to heaven as martyrs, and the infidels die by the sword of righteousness." I shook my head. As I went through this regurgitation of my thoughts ones I have carried for years I recoiled at my own cynicism.

"So, you think we give up? Is that what you're saying: we do nothing, just react?"

"You can reduce the damage, but you can't eliminate it. This war has gone on since Mohammed went to Medina. I do believe things can change. In many places they have. I believe it is possible for Western culture to live alongside a modern Muslim state. But there are entrenched forces at play. I'm afraid we're playing a whack-a-mole defense. It can get more effective with better intelligence gathering. Talk to the Jordanians, the Egyptians, the Israelis. They're good at this. And target the money, always the money. It is the lifeblood. As long as there's money to feed the hate, there will be danger to the West. The less money, the less potency." O'Neill looked at me like a beaten man. The sun was quickly setting, casting long shadows on the shortened day in Manhattan. "John, I'm sorry. I can't help you. Believe me, I understand what you're facing. I want to see a solution as much as anybody. If there was something else I could tell you that I thought would be helpful, I would."

John O'Neill said nothing. I did not speak to him again for twenty-one months. He stayed with the FBI for nine more months before resigning in 2001. There were a variety of rumors as to why he resigned, but the most common was that he failed to get promoted to a position where he thought he could be effective. He took a job as head of security in the same building in the World Trade Center where I worked. His office was on the 34th floor of the North Tower.

***

In December the three of us went out for dinner to celebrate our anniversary. Liv got unusually up dressed up for the evening in a form fitting black dress. Becca was wearing a complementary frilly black dress with a pink bow around her waist and light-colored lipstick that she had talked Liv into allowing for this evening. She also wore the pearls I had given Liv on Becca's first birthday. The two girls were talking, and a moment was frozen in time. As I looked at my girls, I thought, this is what a family could be. It could be defined by love, not a tornado fueled by alcohol and violence. I thought of my mother and wondered where she was. Could be anywhere. I hoped she was safe and taken care of, that she too could find peace in this lifetime. I should try again to locate her, I thought. I was interrupted from my trance.

"Jordan, are you going to rejoin us?" asked Liv with that smile.

"I was just lost in thought. I think I have everything I could ever wish for at this table."

"If I could have a wish, I would get a pony," Becca chimed in.

"Every little girl wants a pony," I said.

"I had a pony when I was younger," Liv added.

"See, Dad, Mom had a pony. Why can't I have one?"

"Your mom lived on a farm in Iowa. We live on Long Island in New York. It's not the same thing," I explained, pointing out the obvious.

"Maybe one day we could get a ranch. You know, somewhere where they make cowboy movies. It would be the three of us, and Maximilian, of course. We couldn't leave him behind," said my daughter with the optimistic naivete that only youth can offer.

"I'd love that, and I'm sure Maximilian would, too," said Liv. Then they ganged up on me and simultaneously offered the smile my wife had given our daughter.

"Let me think about it," I said.

When we left, we had the waitress take a picture of the three of us with Liv's phone; a photo that sat on my wife's nightstand from that day forward.

***

The monthly calls with Jean Pierre Dion happened on the thirtieth of every month. On December 30, I did not get a call. I thought it was possible the holiday postponed the meeting. I simply emailed the report with a note that I would be available if he wanted to discuss it. When I returned to work in January 2001, I received a call on January fifth.

"Mr. Rome, my name is Rudolph Erhard. I will be taking over Mr. Dion's responsibilities. I am calling because I am in town and would like to meet you." His accent was thick and German, but with an almost feminine sound to it. I sat silently, wondering what to say next. Did this man work for Casandra? Did he know who his client was? How do you replace someone with that level of confidence and access? Was this a setup by law enforcement? I took a deep breath and responded.

"I'm sorry to sound abrupt, but shouldn't Mr. Dion be making this introduction? I'm not comfortable discussing confidential business without some formal acknowledgment that you have the authority to do so."

"A perfectly reasonable concern, Mr. Rome. A registered letter will be delivered to you today. Your in-house counsel has been copied as well. The letter is from our legal counsel and provides authorization to change representatives for our investment group. I think you will recognize the firm and see that everything is in order. As to the rest of the issues, we can discuss those tomorrow.

I have a suite at the Waldorf. You can ask for my name at the front desk, and they will give you my room number. Noon tomorrow?"

"I would like to see the letter first. I will also need to discuss it in-house. But assuming all is in order, noon tomorrow is fine."

"Excellent, Mr. Rome. I'll see you tomorrow."

Though I had never stayed at the Waldorf, I was certain Mr. Erhard's suite was one of their finest. It had two distinct sleeping areas, a kitchenette, and a large living-dining space. A number of rooms at the hotel were known to be used for residential accommodation, and this was one. When I entered, we exchanged cards and shook hands. His hand was fleshy and moist with perspiration. He was a balding middle-aged man in frameless glasses. My guess was he was pushing 300 pounds, and I could hear him breathe with each motion he made. His clothes were impeccably tailored and expensive. The other remarkable characteristic of Rudolph Erhard was that, for lack of a better way to say it, he looked almost like a woman.

"Mr. Rome, I had lunch brought up to the room. I did not know what you prefer, so we have a little of everything." He pointed to the oversized spread that sat on the kitchen island. He then motioned to the table, which was set for two. I could see no one else in the room besides the host and myself.

"That's very thoughtful. Should we help ourselves and then sit to go through the business at hand? I brought a copy of the prior twelve months. You'll also find summaries for the last three years. I'm happy to go through those with you and answer any questions you might have."

Erhard made his way to the buffet and filled two nine-inch plates. He tucked his tie into his shirt and placed the napkin in his collar. Before I could make my way to the table, he was already taking in lunch with the tenacity of a woodchipper working through a fall cleanup. I packed a lighter plate and sat, doing my best not to stare at the feeding frenzy across from me. Twenty minutes later, he had consumed everything on both plates. He wiped his mouth and ingested half a glass of wine in a single gulp. I took that as a cue to place the financials on the table.

"Mr. Rome, that won't be necessary. I am really not here to review the performance of your organization. I have read through the financials since inception, and I am confident that your firm is more than capable. I simply thought it would be important to meet in person. I understand this client has unusually sensitive needs and requires the utmost discretion. I thought it would be important that I communicate these facts directly to you. There may come a time when special services or immediate action is required. Should that be the case, I want to make sure we both understand that I would be giving that kind of directive. Am I clear?"

I looked at the obese man for a moment, trying not to stare. Despite his best efforts, a small piece of food had landed on the forearm of his shirt, along with particles on each side of his mouth. "I understand. I am well aware of your client and their needs." What I didn't say was: by the end of this year, I will be done with all of you. That includes your client, her psychopathic son, and you, you fat slob. But I did have a question, so I asked it.

"What happened to Mr. Dion? I would guess this is the kind of job that pays generously not one you would leave easily."

Erhard rose from the table and brought back a third plate of food. But before he started eating, he offered an explanation for Mr. Dion's absence. "A most unfortunate accident, I'm afraid. Mr. Dion had rented a home in the Alps for him and his family over the holidays. In the middle of the night, there apparently was a gas leak which caused an explosion. Most grisly. If it would be okay, I will skip the details given we are in the middle of lunch."

"So, he was killed in the explosion?" I said as the blood drained from my face.

"Oh, quite so. The whole family, I'm afraid."

I sat for a moment in shock. Had Dion known about New York State Clearing Corp but failed to disclose it? Did this cost him his life, or did he have his own scheme and thought it would be better to keep quiet about mine? Was the fat man across the table about to pull a gun out and kill me? Or were men tasked with killing me waiting outside the door? I felt like I was going to throw up.

"I have to go now. I have a full schedule today. So, if there is nothing else you need, I will be heading back to the office."

Erhard looked up again, now his face fully engorged with the third plate. He stopped chewing long enough to talk, though his mouth was still full. "That's fine. I think we've accomplished everything we needed to get done here." He looked at his watch. "Nice to meet you. I, too, have another appointment. I'm sure you can see yourself out." He finished his wine in a single gulp and returned his face to the remains on his plate.

Without another word, I made my way to the elevator. Exiting the car were two flamboyantly dressed men chatting up a storm twenty decibels too loud. One wore visibly heavy eye makeup. I froze at the elevator, ensuring they meant no harm to me. I watched as they swished up the corridor, then knocked on Mr. Erhard's door. I took the next elevator down.

PART XIII

Ibrahim Assad, Rebecca Rome, Jordan Rome

New York, New York
September 11, 2001: The Day Of

CHAPTER 41

I Felt No Pain nor Heard a Sound

IBRAHIM ASSAD

I had been lying in bed staring at the ceiling of the run-down motor lodge since 4:00 a.m. The drone of the through-wall air conditioner unit would prohibit sleep even if one chose to try. Last night, after dinner, I shaved my body clean and then prayed before lying down. I had hardly slept since. Months of preparation were finally complete to deliver the ultimate blow to the Great Satan. And now I was having second thoughts or maybe I was just frightened, as any mortal would be.

When I returned to Afghanistan with Mohammad Atta, I met with Khalid Sheikh Mohammed, Osama bin Laden, and Abdul Aziz Al Omari. Their proposed plan was to hijack a plane and fly it into the World Trade Center. Osama bin Laden offered his expertise on how the fuel loaded in the plane would impact the structural integrity, causing the building to collapse upon itself. This seemed logical to my technical mind. My role would be to assist other martyrs in learning to fly. No harm would come to me because of my value to the future of the movement. Looking back, I am uncertain whether I ever believed that. The fact that I spoke English, was familiar with the West, and maintained a technical background made me a prime candidate for this critical task. Seeking martyrdom was something that needed to be instilled in my soul. This change could only happen through isolation and repetition. What the West would frame as the pejorative "brainwash," I saw as enlightenment. I knew this was why I was brought from my home back to the strange land, surrounded by those who lived through hate. It would be easy to claim I was manipulated. I was not.

I attended flight school with Atta at a private institution, Huffman Aviation, in Venice, Florida. In eight weeks, we learned to take off, land, and execute basic maneuvers for commercial flights. Although I had no direct communication with others outside my small group, I was aware that other individuals were learning to fly elsewhere in the United States. This was my first insight that the plan included more than a single flight. It also became clear that I was not to be an instructor—I would be the martyr. The communication was subtle. I was reminded how blessed I was to participate in an action that would change the course of mankind. It was not long after that , I prayed for that privilege.

Eight weeks ago, I returned home to visit Aailyah. I knew this would be the last time I would see my wife. I surprised her when I arrived and bestowed gifts from my travels. I did not share that I would leave five days later. I thought anger would be the emotion I would receive, but this woman did not have that in her being. She asked no questions, made no demands, and voiced no accusations. She welcomed me into our home and her bed. We slept together as man and wife for the five days I was home. On the fifth day, I spoke to her in the morning.

"Aailyah, I have come home to tell you that I have decided to give myself to Allah. This is not because I do not love you or because you have failed to be everything a man could ask for. It is my calling. It is what Allah has written for me. I wanted you to hear this from my lips."

For the first time in my life, Aailyah raised her voice at me. Her eyes flashed and her face reddened.

"Ibrahim! I do not accept this! You may not go. I will not let you. They will feed you to the flames for the glory of themselves, with no regard to the damage they do. They do not care about you; they do not care about the pain they will cause. They do not care that they will leave me without you. They simply want to pound their chests and claim might they are the arm of Allah. Where will they be when the widows and orphans mourn? It will not be their family. Ibrahim, listen to me! We can be as we were. We can live the dreams we had; they can be real dreams. We will leave this place this damned place of hate. We will build a house of love."

I stood and put my arms around my wife. For the first time, she pushed back, then struck me in the chest.

"You will not have my blessing to ease your conscience. I forbid you to do this. If you choose this path against my will, it will be for your selfish reasons, not because Allah, myself, nor any right-minded soul would ask you."

I tried again to embrace her. She pushed me away, then stood with her arms folded and her eyes gushing. I turned and walked out of my home for the last time.

***

At 4:30 a.m., I placed a call to her. It would be late morning at home.

"Aaliyah, it is Ibrahim," I whispered.

"Ibrahim, are you okay? Where are you?"

"I am fine. I had trouble sleeping and I wanted to hear your voice."

"I'm glad you called. I've missed you terribly. There's something very important I need to tell you."

Silence fell on the line for several moments.

"Though it is early, very early I am with child. It's from your last visit."

Almost a minute of silence followed, but I could hear her breathing into the phone with excitement.

"There's something else. I agreed to take the job in England. I will save lives."

I could not speak. My throat closed, and my heart ached.

"Ibrahim, did you hear me? We will have another baby. Come home please come home. Come with me to England. Start a new life with me. Our love is strong. We can overcome anything together. Anything."

"My love, it is too late. The lodestone of fate is upon my shoulders. I cannot change that. Know that I will always be with you, always love you. I never deserved you."

I covered the phone against my chest to breathe for a moment.

"Take care of our child. I know you can. You are strong stronger than I. You will be better on your own."

Aaliyah began to speak, but I interrupted her mid-sentence.

"I have to go... I have to go."

It was the last lie I would ever tell my wife. I didn't have to go. She had shown me that. I wanted to go.

I hung up the phone and wailed at the top of my lungs, alone in my room. Then I gathered myself and dressed in the new blue Western suit and white pressed shirt purchased for me.

At 5:45 a.m., three of us left the Portland, Maine, airport on the commuter flight to Boston's Logan International. When we arrived in Boston, we boarded American Airlines Flight 11 to Los Angeles, California. There were five of us in total on board, in addition to the seventy-six passengers and eleven crew members.

At 8:19, two comrades took two flight attendants hostage, allowing the three of us to enter the flight deck. Using the hostages to dissuade the pilots from resisting, we beat the crew unconscious, then murdered them by slicing their throats with box cutters. It was difficult to maneuver due to the blood filling the cockpit floor.

At 8:45, we saw the New York City skyline on the horizon. In that moment, a vision came to me. Aaliyah spoke to me, whispering at first, telling me to come back to her. Visions of my youth of our passion together seared through my mind. I spoke out loud to myself, willing the voice to go away. I prayed for the strength to finish the task. In spite of all efforts to remain focused, the whispers turned into a shout, then a scream.

I needed to go home.

I grabbed the yoke and turned the plane sharply to the left. Atta shouted to correct the course, and a struggle ensued as I tried to force him from the controls with my right hand.

289

"We must turn around!" I screamed.

As I begged Allah to help me, Abdul Aziz al-Omari rushed from behind, grabbing my neck. I tried to stand and face him, but I couldn't gain footing on the blood-slicked floor. I was pressed against the throttle controls as Omari sought to choke the life from me. The plane accelerated to its top speed of 560 miles per hour. Atta regained control in the pilot seat, returning the aircraft to its intended course at full speed, while I struggled with Omari for my life.

At 8:46, American Airlines Flight 11 crashed into the 91st floor of the North Tower. The plane arrived thirty seconds earlier than it would have, due to the increased speed. The Boeing 767-200ER was loaded with 20,000 gallons of jet fuel. The fuel exploded upon impact.

I felt no pain. I heard no sound.

CHAPTER 42

I Had Just Started Second Grade

Rebecca Rome

When I began therapy with Dr. Green, she suggested I participate in a group for children who had lost a parent during 9/11. I was one of the younger members. In September 2001, over 3,000 children lost a parent, more than the total number of people who died that day. These children ranged in age from infants to grown adults. My therapy group included thirty-two people, from seventeen to their early forties. We met once a month. Since I had joined late, everyone else already knew each other, but they welcomed me quickly. The conversation rarely focused on the day of the loss. Instead, it centered on how we were managing the everyday challenges of life in New York.

At my third meeting, that changed. Each person was given a minute to talk about the parent they lost and what they remembered about them on that day. Some spoke. Others did not. I was the fifteenth to be called, and I couldn't say a word. I couldn't remember my father. I wasn't even sure I could recall the day he didn't come home. I asked if I could speak next time. "Of course," came the unanimous response.

The following month, I made some notes and spoke.

"I had just started second grade. My mother would carpool me to school with two other friends. That day, she drove, and my friend Amanda's mother was scheduled to pick us up. Like so many others have said, I remember it was a beautiful day bright and clear. My father walked our dog, Maximilian, then drove to the station to catch his train. He always left before we did. I think he kissed my mother and me before leaving. He usually did. I've tried to remember, but I can't be sure he did that day. But he probably did.

Early in the school day, someone from the principal's office came into our room and whispered to our teacher. She whispered something back but didn't tell us what was happening in the city. Just before lunch, two students were removed from class. In total, five of us ended up in the principal's office, including me. Though we didn't know it at the time, we were the children whose parents were among the unaccounted-for at the World Trade Center.

Three of the students had no reason for concern their parents were simply out of the office or unreachable during the attack. A fifth-grade boy named Jamie Eisenman and I were not so lucky.

My mother picked me up and took me home. I remember seeing smoke on the horizon during the drive. At the house, she made me lunch and sat me in front of the television. The news was on every channel, so she tried to find something for children. That day, I watched Power Rangers, a show I didn't even like. My mom put the remote on top of the bookshelf so I couldn't change the channel. She spent the afternoon and evening calling my father, police stations, firehouses, hospitals anyone she thought might have information. At 10:00 that night, she put me to bed with her and our dog, Maximilian. I lay between them, still unaware of what had truly happened.

The next day, Wednesday, my mother began to panic. She cried throughout the day and kept calling the same people, hoping for new information. She slammed the phone down again and again after being placed on hold for hours. That was when I first realized something terrible had happened to my father.

On Thursday morning, my grandmother arrived from Iowa. She had driven through the night. That afternoon, the three of us took her car to the train station to retrieve my father's. The lot was empty except for five cars. My mother and I got into his car, and she started it. That's the moment I remember most clearly. She couldn't put the car in gear. She sat with her hands on the steering wheel and her head resting against them, sobbing uncontrollably. I took off my seat belt and put my arms around her. Then she said it.

'They've killed him. They killed your father. He's not coming home to us. Ever again.'

We cried together, holding each other until my grandmother knocked on the window. She came around and lifted both of us out of the car and back into hers. My mother and grandmother decided we would come back for the car another day. I don't remember when we finally did.

For the next few nights, my grandmother slept with her daughter and granddaughter in my parents' bed. When that week had passed, I returned to Des Moines with my mother and grandmother for what I believe was another week. When we came back home, my mother stood at the door. I said to her, "I keep thinking he'll be here if we come back enough times."

"Me too," she said. But he wouldn't be.

We later learned my father had arrived at his office in the North Tower just fifteen minutes before the airplane crashed into the 91st floor.

I try to separate my actual memories of my father from the ones I've fabricated based on photos or stories others have told me. I know he liked to play rough with me. We would wrestle or play bronco on his back until my mother scolded us, saying someone was bound to get hurt. We would play airplane, with him lying on his back and placing his feet on my rib cage. I'd fly with my back arched, arms wide open, as he twisted and turned to simulate flight.

He loved going out to breakfast and would rave as if Denny's were a gourmet feast. He always asked the waiters' names and addressed them personally. Though I may have been the most photographed child ever, we had few pictures of my dad and they never seemed to be good ones.

My mother had one picture from their ninth anniversary dinner, when the three of us went out somewhere fancy. I still remember the white tablecloths and silver place settings. The photo sat on her nightstand until she remarried, when she gave it to me. I bought a fancy silver frame for it.

When I opened the old frame to place the picture in the new one, I found a piece of paper tucked between the photo and the cardboard backing. I'm sure she had forgotten it was there. On it was a handwritten list.

I opened the picture I had of the list on my phone so I could read it to the group.

I will remember

1. *Told jokes poorly, often off-color, but thought he was the funniest man*
2. *Made an excellent breakfast, but even better at doing dishes*
3. *Loved to read, thought he should have been a history major*
4. *Never raised his voice to me*
5. *Brave, the bravest man I ever met*
6. *A devoted father, no task too large or too small, loved to play in the bath with Becca as a baby*
7. *Loved dogs, never passed one without stopping to talk to its owner and petting the pup*
8. *A handy repairman. Whenever he fixed something, he said he had" his guy" in*
9. *Ambitious to a fault*
10. *Not a day passed when he did not tell me he loved me, and I was beautiful, even if both were untrue that day*
11. *He held me for no reason at all*

He had a beautiful body, Was always in the mood.

The last comment was written in a different ink from the first eleven. I am guessing she added this at a later date. Certainly understandable.

So, I don't really think I knew the man. People who did know him spoke well of him. My mother ultimately remarried a man my father had worked with, but I don't think my stepfather really knew my father either. I simply can't imagine they were friends. I understand that 40% of the people who died on 9/11 never had their remains found. Their families could never have the closure of a burial. My father was on the 92nd floor of the North Tower. I'm not sure if he ever knew it happened.

Chapter 43

I Don't Know,
I Think a Plane

Jordan Rome

There wasn't a cloud in the sky. I kissed my family goodbye and promised to bring home Chinese food for dinner. My world was going according to plan. By the end of 2001, I would be in a position of independence. My worst fears regarding Jean Paul Dion had evaporated.

I used my parking trick, entering from the exit side of the lot. This allowed me to get the best spot possible, since traffic built from the entry side and those spaces were usually taken. When I pulled into my space, I reached into the back seat to grab my briefcase. As I turned around to open the car door, Ricardo was standing outside the driver's side. In my rearview mirror, a black SUV was parked directly behind my Volvo.

My heart dropped into my stomach. I rolled down the window. "Jordan, you're going to have to take a minute to talk to Casandra. She's waiting to speak to you now."

"Can this wait? I really have to get to work. We could meet somewhere afterwards."

Even Ricardo knew I was just trying to buy time. This meeting wouldn't be happening this way unless something serious was wrong and I was pretty sure I knew what the problem was.

"Not going to happen that way. We have a video link set up in our car. She's patched in right now. Jordan, don't make this harder than it has to be."

Ricardo opened the door, and I got out.

A man I didn't recognize sat in the driver's seat. Ricardo opened the front passenger door, and I climbed in, with him settling in behind me. The man in the driver's seat had a weapon resting on his lap. If I could just grab it, I thought, I might be able to turn the tables.

Leaning against the windshield on the dashboard was an iPad showing Casandra's face. For a moment, I saw Eduardo pass behind her. She was seated at a table, appearing to eat breakfast. The room could have been anywhere, but it was finished to a level that suggested one of her homes or a luxury hotel. When I came into view, Casandra dabbed the side of her mouth and placed a napkin on the table in front of her.

"Jordan. I don't know how to convey how disappointed I am to be having this conversation. But it's come to our attention that money is leaving our account and ending up in an account that appears to be yours. It seems the ambition I once admired in you will be your undoing."

These first sentences were spoken in a calm, disciplined tone. That demeanor escalated quickly.

"I trusted you. I offered you everything. When you refused, I let you go. No one has ever left my organization, but I made an exception for you. And then I helped you again. The goddamn house you're living in is the house I paid for. And what do I get in return? Theft. You stole my fucking money—from me. My money. No one does that."

She was shouting now. Then she took a deep breath, returned to her original tone, and sipped her coffee.

"I want my money back. And you will give it to me. All of it. But I will not be forgiving this time. You and your family will pay." She took a breath and stared into the camera for several moments. "You understood this the day you decided to steal from me. You're the one killing your family. You know that."

The driver pulled out his phone and showed me photos of my home and of Becca's school. The pictures were dated today. I felt sick. I needed air, but the windows were closed. My instinct was to grab the weapon on the driver's lap, but I knew Ricardo had a gun pointed at my back. If I made a move, I'd be dead and so would Becca and Liv.

"I'll get your money. I can wire it today. In fact, I can do it right now. There's no reason to hurt my wife and daughter. They've done nothing to you. They know nothing about this. They aren't a threat to you."

"Jordan, it's easy for a man to steal when he believes he's the only one at risk. When he risks more than that, he thinks twice. If I let your family go, I'll face the same situation with others who might take what's mine. It's a lesson you know well. Don't pretend you don't. You saw what just happened to Jean Paul. I had hoped you learned something from his demise."

I tried to think of some story to tell, some angle that might change Casandra's mind.

"If we're all dead, what difference does it make whether I give you the money or not?" I asked, stalling for time.

"Jordan, I'm not the monster you want me to be to ease your conscience. This is business. The three of you can die in an instant, or in ways that will eventually result in you transferring the money. But we both know you can't stand to watch your wife and daughter suffer for you to do the right thing. Return what's mine, and I promise they won't see or hear what hits them. That's my gift to you for old times' sake."

She took another sip of coffee.

"I have another idea. I'll wire the money right now. I have a safety deposit box at a bank two blocks from where I work. There's $50,000 in cash inside. You can drop me off there and I'll bring it anywhere you want. You'll have me and more money than you're owed. It's all I have and it's yours. Just let them live."

"You think $50,000 is enough to buy their lives? That seems like a real bargain." She paused. "I don't think so."

"I saved your son Eduardo's life twice and yours once. Think of it as two lives for three. There's no risk to you. You know that."

I heard Eduardo's voice in the background. Casandra raised her hand, and the sound stopped. Her expression shifted. If nothing else, Eduardo's perspective seemed to guide her on what not to do.

"I'll take your $50,000. I can use it to fuel the plane. Ricardo will drop you at the bank. I'll send two men to your office to wait. Make sure they can get in past security. If anything happens other than you bringing the money to your office and leaving with my men before 9:00, your coworkers, your family, and you will pay a steep price. You have fifteen minutes to wire the money you stole from me. Do we have an agreement?"

"I agree. But Casandra, how do I know you'll keep your end of the deal and not kill everyone anyway?"

"Jordan, what choice do you have but to believe me? Now wire the money before I change my mind."

I waited for the bank to open at 8:00. I fumbled through the process of entering the safety deposit vault. Inside was $50,000, along with my brother Jackson Martin's passport and a copy of a $250,000 life insurance policy listing Liv as the beneficiary. I had almost forgotten about it. I remembered there was another copy in my desk at home. I hoped she would remember it too. I took everything from the box.

I arrived back at the North Tower just after 8:30. I checked in at the security kiosk, which automatically recorded who I was and where I was going in the building. In the lobby, I received a call from the receptionist at the 92nd-floor desk. Two men were waiting for me. They said they had an appointment. She also added, in a hushed tone, some remarks suggesting they looked and acted strangely. I told her not to worry and to let them know I was in the lobby and would be up shortly. I ended the call and stood, squeezing my phone in my hand, staring at the ceiling, waiting to die.

I did my best to imagine a plan that would result in the three of us surviving—a plan that would allow me to take my family and run. My thoughts then turned to anger. How did she know? Which one of the two bankers had told her? It could be anybody. I was wasting my time thinking about it.

At twenty to nine, I pushed the elevator button. As I waited, a crowd gathered and filled the elevator. My feet felt like they were set in concrete. I let that elevator go and pressed another button. I waited for the next car to arrive. Still, I couldn't move. Entering the elevator felt like walking up the stairs of a gallows for my own execution. Despite having no choice, I couldn't bring myself to step forward. I stood frozen in place for several minutes.

And then it happened.

An explosion occurred somewhere nearby. The whole building shook. Alarms I had never heard before went off. Flashing lights for the hearing impaired blinked everywhere. Through the lobby windows, I saw debris falling onto the plaza. First, a few small pieces. Then, many large ones. The building groaned like a large ship. In moments, people scurried through the lobby, down the stairs, from everywhere, rapidly exiting the building like a concert or athletic event had just caught fire.

The security desk was flooded with phone calls and alerts as multiple alarms flared on their screens. I looked at my watch. It was ten minutes to nine.

At that moment, John O'Neill emerged from the stairwell. He ran to the security desk, shouting directions. I heard the first sirens approaching the building. I ran up to John.

"What's happening? What the fuck is going on?" I shouted over the security desk.

"I don't know. I think a plane. They say it could be an accident, but it was a big aircraft. I don't think it was an accident. I need to go back upstairs to help people get out. It's very bad somewhere around the 90th floor. It's a fucking inferno up there. Fire and rescue are on the way."

It struck me then the irony. This man, who had tried to prevent this very catastrophe, was now forced to live with the failure to do so. John O'Neill would do his best, but he would not survive the day.

"Is there anything I can do to help?" I asked, momentarily forgetting my own precarious position.

"The daycare center across the street. Five World Trade. They need help. The kids have to get out of there. Take the kids, help the staff. They're losing it," he said.

I nodded that I understood. He returned to barking into the phone in his ear.

I ran out of the North Tower and looked up. Black smoke poured from the structure. The entire top of the building was in flames. People ran in every direction. Onlookers stood frozen, staring at the structure. Large objects were falling from the top of the building, hitting the ground with awful thuds. I looked closer. This wasn't debris. These were people. They had chosen to jump rather than burn. Even for someone who had been in combat, it was a hard sight to bear.

I ran across the street to The Children's Discovery Center at 5 World Trade Center. The staff was in chaos, trying to organize the 140 children of all ages, including infants. We improvised with the rope they used to walk to the playground. Each student held on as we ushered them down the block. I ran back inside to ensure all the children were evacuated. The building was empty.

When I exited, I looked up just as the second plane struck the South Tower.

The scene was apocalyptic. Both towers were burning. Panicked people ran in all directions as first responders fought to enter against the flood of those fleeing. Bodies continued to fall. The sounds, the images, they were unbearable.

Even then, I knew. The world that would follow this day would be different from the one that came before. The fire, the smoke, the desperate screams. It felt like the end of days.

Suddenly, I was sick and disoriented. I bent over, hands on knees, struggling to breathe. I looked up at both towers aflame. The North Tower appeared to tilt. I ran. I ran for over twenty minutes, first south, then west. I heard the North Tower collapse behind me, debris and ash rushing through the streets like a tidal wave. I ducked into the nearest doorway, small steam-table restaurant. There, I cowered with forty other lost souls who couldn't grasp the nightmare unfolding around us.

Under a dining table, I huddled with a fifty-year-old Greek waitress, wiping ash from my eyes and mouth. It was at that moment that I had the idea.

PART XIV

JACKSON MARTIN

London, England
2017: 16 Years After

CHAPTER 44

I HAVE BEEN
THREATENED WITH
MUCH WORSE

THE ANGLO AFRICA MINING CORPORATION had offices around the world, but its headquarters moved from Amsterdam to London in 1984. It was a giant conglomerate with mining operations across the African continent. Anglo Africa was a corporate remnant of the era when Europeans dominated African resources, leveraging cheap labor and raw materials to fuel the Industrial Revolution.

On this Thursday, Anglo Africa requested that we bring our "team" to discuss our position in a much smaller mining company listed on the New York Stock Exchange, with field operations in South Africa. The company's original name was Belgium Mining, but they adopted the name International Mining Technologies (IMT) after a leveraged buyout in 2000. That LBO was again converted to a public company in 2004. Though the transaction stabilized IMT's balance sheet, it didn't change management's appetite for debt.

The folks at IMT were cobalt miners. By 2014, it was clear cobalt would be critical to the electrification of everything. IMT took on billions in debt to expand their capacity and began constructing the largest mine of its kind to extract cobalt. Expansion seemed like a no-lose proposition. Cobalt was priced at $20,000 per metric ton and projected to rise to $40,000. IMT could extract it, including capital costs, for $16,000.

What they failed to anticipate were the cost overruns, increased global supply, and an economic slowdown that left them in a precarious position. They were hemorrhaging cash just as several of their bond offerings were coming due. Their financial state made refinancing these bonds extraordinarily expensive, if not impossible and they still needed additional funding to cover expansion overruns.

If someone could fund the needed capital, and if someone believed cobalt prices would rise again, and if someone believed Western Europe, the United States, and Canada would push for electric vehicles, and if someone had the expertise to complete the ambitious mine expansion—well, then there was an opportunity to make money. A lot of money. But that was a long list of miracles that would have to occur in sequence.

IMT's bonds were badly beaten down. The senior bonds were trading at 90 cents on the dollar, but the subordinated bonds ranged from 24% to as low as 8% of face value. The total amount of bonds outstanding was $4.5 billion. The senior bonds accounted for $3.6 billion. Unsurprisingly, the stock had dropped to pennies. The market was betting on IMT's bankruptcy.

This was the position Alex Broad and I had evaluated six months earlier. It was my job to study IMT. Alex owned the firm I worked for. We had accumulated $500 million in subordinated bonds at a cost of $150 million. We had borrowed $75 million of that. As a result, we were the largest holder of subordinated bonds and controlled their decision-making. The holder of the senior bonds was Anglo Africa Mining Corporation. They had been acquiring that position through an offshore holding company for eight months. Their bet was that they could acquire IMT for a fraction of its value by leveraging their debt position.

What they didn't anticipate was that we would get in the way.

Our "team" consisted of Alex and me. Alex entered the boardroom first, dressed as always in a bespoke three-piece suit. He placed his alligator briefcase on the table and sat across from Anglo Africa's CEO. He sat upright, hands folded on the table. I sat beside him at one end of a boardroom table large enough to seat twenty-eight people. On the other side sat four lawyers, three executive vice presidents, the chief operating officer, and the CEO of Anglo Africa. Alex had asked me to speak on our behalf.

"It is my understanding that you would like to discuss our position in IMT. We are happy to hear what you have to say, but it is our intent to maintain ownership of these bonds. We believe there is value in IMT and that we will be able to extract it when the bonds come due, beginning next month," I said, keeping a straight face.

The most senior attorney responded. "The only reason you believe there's value in the company is because you think we'll save it. But if we don't, your bonds go to zero. Is that a loss you're ready to take?"

"We've had conversations with a number of alternative parties willing to step in and operate the business. They are prepared to fund the purchase of your bonds. Where there's value, the market will find it," I lied.

Everyone at the table knew the truth. The world believed cobalt prices would rebound, if not soon, then eventually. The mine needed to be completed, but doing so required a massive investment. Any capital injected into the business would be subordinate to our bonds. That would drive our bonds back to par. Our $150 million investment could become $500 million after just six months. Anglo Africa needed us to disappear and soon. If we forced IMT into bankruptcy, it could take months or even years to resolve. In the meantime, the mine project might be shut down. No one could predict what would happen to permits, the market, or any number of other variables. The fact was, Anglo Africa had more to lose than we did. They were committed and accountable to their board of directors. Our "team" answered to no one.

Marty Albright, the COO of Anglo Africa, had come up through the ranks. He was a stocky man with a thick neck, massive hands, and a flattop haircut. The tough Scotsman chimed in.

"You don't own all the bonds. We've talked to the minority holders. They want out, and they could sue your ass if the bonds go to zero. Your grandkids will be litigating this shitstorm. You've got a lot at stake yourself. And that doesn't even touch the $75 million you borrowed from Barclays for this mess. We bank with them too. Maybe we should give them a call. Long story short, if it comes to a fight, we've got the bigger cannons. We'll crush you like bugs."

I had to admit, he had a point. They probably could salvage a significant part of their position. Although they would lose more than we would, the impact would hurt us more. I glanced over at Alex. He looked unfazed. He waited a moment, then spoke.

"Mr. Albright, I'd like to address a couple of things. First, I have no children or grandchildren, so it's unlikely that my nonexistent heirs will be litigating anything. Second, and I'm sure this isn't intentional, but it almost sounds like you're trying to threaten me into taking an action that's not in my economic interest. I've been threatened before. I can tell you with great confidence, whatever you're thinking of doing, I've been threatened with worse."

Though I didn't mean to, I laughed out loud and immediately shut my mouth.

CHAPTER 45

11, 13, 17, 19, 23, AND 29

I MET ALEX BROAD IN December 2001.

I had arrived in London three weeks earlier. Between September 11th and December, I made my way south from New York, back to Miami. I had my passport updated and completed the transformation from Jordan Rome to my deceased brother, Jackson Martin. That process was more painful than I imagined. I abandoned the two things I loved most—the only things in my life that mattered—Liv and Becca. I had no illusion that it was anyone's fault but my own. Greed, ambition, and vanity destroyed everything dear to me. And now I had inflicted unknown pain on my family with the lie that I had perished in the North Tower.

I never discovered how Casandra learned of my theft. But I knew a secret is something only one person knows. If I were to tell my wife that I survived, she might take some small action, make a phone call, or tell our daughter. There were infinite scenarios. I faced the classic low-probability, high-consequence dilemma. The mere fact that my family was still alive affirmed that remaining silent was the best decision.

I fantasized about how this could end well. I would wait two years and hire a lawyer to tell them, or I would wait until Casandra died and then just show up at home. But the facts precluded these actions. Casandra was thriving, proving that crime does pay. Liv had found the life insurance policy, creating a potential fraud should Jordan Rome reappear. But the final, insurmountable hurdle came thirty months later when I read online that Liv had remarried. My wife had married my coworker, Richard Anderson. I now hated that prick more than ever, but it didn't change the fact that my family had moved on. This was as it should have been. Jordan Rome was dead, and that was my doing.

My meeting with Alex Broad took place after weeks of knocking on the doors of every financial institution I could find online. Finding a position with no history or experience in the business proved nearly impossible, a surprise to no one, including myself. Alex Broad's firm was simply named Broad Investments. His office was in a three-story townhouse in London's Primrose Hill. It had a pristine white marble front with lacquered black doors. Each door bore brass hardware and a kick plate. A simple brass plaque read Broad Investments. Above the plaque was an equally polished brass doorbell. I pressed it but received no response. As I was walking away, a delivery man opened the door to exit the building. I acted as if I had every right to enter and passed the delivery man as I walked in.

The townhouse, originally residential, had been renovated into elegant office space. The 100-year-old interior was updated with finishes of stone, glass, and carved wood, commensurate with much larger London financial institutions. What would have been the ground floor entryway had a small lobby with a red-haired woman in her mid-thirties sitting alone at a desk. I approached her.

"Good afternoon. I'm wondering if I could get a few moments of Mr. Broad's time," I said, wearing my best smile.

"I'm sorry, but Mr. Broad does not see anyone without an appointment." She returned my smile, showing no signs of relaxing her gatekeeping role.

"Well, is it possible for you to arrange an appointment?" I asked.

"I'm sorry again, but Mr. Broad also does not make appointments." With that, she returned to her work.

"Well, if I can't make an appointment but need one to see Mr. Broad, how does someone go about seeing him?"

"That would require a level of creativity." She set her pencil down, leaned back in her chair, and looked at me. "A creative man might take entry as a delivery is made, then simply sit in the lobby, waiting for Mr. Broad to leave. At that time, he could introduce himself. It's highly unlikely Mr. Broad would do more than exchange pleasantries. But if he should and that creative individual were able to convince him to continue the conversation that might lead to an appointment. But I am highly doubtful any of those events could occur."

"I think I'll sit here, if that's okay. Do you know what time Mr. Broad leaves?"

"Can't say I do. I've been here six years, and there's never been a day when I was here before Mr. Broad or stayed later than him. But if you could tell me what time he leaves, I'd be interested to know." This time she was almost grinning.

At 7:30 that evening, Alex Broad came down the ornate wooden stairs. He walked to the coatroom to turn off the lights and set the

314

alarm, but stopped when he noticed me still sitting in the chair. At that point, I had been there seven hours.

"May I help you?"

***

I'm not sure anyone but his wife, Esther, really knew Alex Broad. I worked with him longer than any other employee, just over sixteen years. He was a creature of hardline boundaries, perfectly mirroring a life defined by numbers. That's where he found comfort: in their clarity and certainty.

Numbers were the reason Alex Broad lived past the age of twelve. Numbers made him rich beyond calculation. Numbers, and Esther, gave him a reason to live.

Alex never worked, not in the way most people think of it. Each puzzle he solved was simply a game, one that kept his overactive mind at peace. The fact that it was attached to large financial transactions made little difference to him. The vast majority of his wealth would eventually be given away anyways.

He arrived at the office at 6:30 a.m. and left at 7:30 p.m. At noon each day, Esther brought lunch. They shared it alone at the conference table in his office. Lunch lasted exactly an hour and could not be disturbed under any circumstances. In my sixteen years, there was never an exception.

Alex worked every day except the Sabbath, though even that was a sleight of hand, because Alex's mind never stopped working.

I don't exactly know why we got along. But there was an immediate empathy in character, and a shared love of history and economic analysis.

It would be four years before I learned that Alex Broad was not an English gentleman, but a refugee from the Janowska concentration camp in Western Ukraine. Born Alexi Brodsky, he immigrated to England after World War II at the age of twelve. He was the only member of his family to survive the war.

During his journey to England, he met his wife, Esther, also a Holocaust survivor. In London, he went door to door as a kitchen utensil salesman, then moved on to financing home appliances, and later to buying distressed debt, first from banks, then from institutions. He became known in financial circles for his uncanny sense of timing and his steel nerves.

The couple donated vast sums to charities throughout England. This gave them access to the upper echelons of society, though neither Alex nor Esther had any interest in such status.

The first day I met Alex, he came down the stairs looking surprised that I was there. In fact, he'd received an email from his receptionist saying I'd been waiting since noon. He later told me he thought that level of persistence deserved a conversation.

He sat down and introduced himself. A few minutes in, he said, "I want to recite a series of numbers to you. Try to remember them."

The numbers were 11, 13, 17, 19, 23, and 29.

I said I'd try.

We spoke for over an hour on a wide range of business topics, including corporate structure and my understanding of the distressed debt market. I explained that my experience was mostly with high-rated corporate and government bonds, but that I had a great interest in distressed assets.

He shook my hand and said he had to go home to meet his wife for dinner. I asked if I could see him again to discuss a potential opportunity to work for him.

He asked if I could recite the numbers he'd given me a little over an hour earlier.

I said "Yes, 11, 13, 17, 19, 23, and 29."

He smiled. "How did you remember them?"

"I think you tried to give me an advantage. Those are the prime numbers from 11 to 29. I only needed to remember the number eleven."

"You can start work Monday. You'll need to dress appropriately if you're going to work in the office. We have a staff meeting to review work assignments on Wednesday mornings. Compensation is the same for everyone, including me. You'll make £50,000 per year, plus bonus."

I came into the office the next day and discussed logistics with the red-haired receptionist, who was now aware of my new employment and was kind enough to provide her name Sara. Although I didn't tell her I was down to my last $20,000, I asked if there was a reasonable place to rent housing.

"Mr. Broad said you could stay downstairs. We have a garden apartment there. I think you'll find it comfortable." She said this with a new upbeat, flirtatious attitude.

I never asked how he knew I would need a place to live. I never asked why he didn't inquire about references. I never asked how he had hired the other two research associates in the office. But everyone seemed to fit a mold. Lucy (not her real name) was a Chinese woman in her early thirties. No children or family. Peter (also not his real name) was an Iranian, twenty-eight, and also without family. Both were brilliant.

The meetings that occurred every Wednesday were held to review the portfolio each person had been given. The three of us tracked 200 companies in total. It was expected that you knew everything

317

there was to know about the companies in your portfolio. If you saw an opportunity, you presented it. The remaining three people would then question and challenge your assumptions. It was your job to address the open issues and reevaluate whether there was indeed an opportunity.

There was no limit to what could be done, including field visits to the company or hiring private investigators to look into the individual executives. You needed to know as much about your companies as they did. Although there was no fixed number of projects we would pursue, the expectation was to find between three and four opportunities per year, with the hope of being successful 75% of the time.

The work in the office was grueling, but it was also extraordinarily profitable. While the base salary was low, the bonuses could reach seven figures for each employee, including Sara, the receptionist. It was only a matter of time before someone would burn out, take their money, and move on to a lower-pressure life. Alex never questioned that decision. He gave each employee his blessing when they left, and then waited for the next gifted orphan to enter his office.

In my sixteen years, Lucy and Peter were each replaced three times always with similar types. Mistakes were made, but they lasted weeks, not months. Alex had no patience for anything but excellence and complete commitment to the task.

In my fourth year, Esther walked into my workspace on the second floor after her lunch with Alex one floor above.

"Mr. Martin. My name is Esther Broad. I am Alex's wife."

The introduction seemed ridiculous. This was the same woman, the only person to visit Alex every day for the last four years. Of course I knew who she was. All the same, I stood from behind my desk and walked around to shake her hand.

"Yes, I know. It's nice to meet you."

"Alex and I were discussing at lunch that we would like to have you over for Sabbath dinner tomorrow night. Are you available?"

"Yes, that would be nice. Thank you for the offer."

The fact of the matter was, I hadn't been out with company since I left New York four years ago. There were nights when I drank myself into a medicated state just to close my eyes without seeing my wife's face or hearing my daughter's voice. It often hurt to the point where my body ached. I thought I was having some sort of heart failure, but I wasn't.

This started a weekly event where I would dine with Alex and Esther. I learned the Jewish ritual for celebrating the Sabbath. Alex would often retire after the meal, leaving Esther and me to talk late into the evening. This is how I learned about their history. How Alex became the bookkeeper to track valuables and deaths so the Nazis could keep an accurate count of their "productivity." How Esther had been abused by her tormentors, abuse that left her unable to have children. Alex and Esther had only each other. When they met, he was twelve and she was thirteen. They hadn't spent a day apart since.

In 2013, Alex had a heart attack and crashed his Jaguar on the way from the office. He was hospitalized for a week. Esther stayed with him the entire time. Afterwards, she forbade him to drive or perform any work around the house.

I told Esther about a young man, Hart Reid, the son of a very close friend who had fallen victim to prescription drugs while recovering from a battle wound. I explained how far he had fallen, from SAS officer to drug addict and how hard the two of us had worked to get him back on his feet. I told her he might be a good fit to assist Alex but wanted to make sure she was aware of his darker history.

"Is this someone you would be comfortable with looking after your own father?" she asked.

I thought for a moment about what type of person I would let look after my father. I winced and smiled at the same time.

"No, I wouldn't do that to Hart. But I think you should meet him. If it works out, you can be confident that he'll do everything necessary to look after Alex."

Hart became part of Alex and Esther's life from their first meeting. He became the driver for the company's Bentley and lived above the garage at Esther's home. It was ironic how the only remaining people in my life ended up essentially under one roof.

CHAPTER 46

THE PUPIL HAS
SURPASSED THE TEACHER

WHEN I LAUGHED IN FRONT of the assembled team from Anglo Africa, Alex rose from his seat.

"Gentlemen, I believe our work is done here. We wish you the best in working out the acquisition of IMT. We believe it is an excellent company with a bright future."

This was Alex's way of stating the obvious. We would wait for Anglo Africa to make the next move. When our bonds went into default next month, the default interest of 15% would commence. This would be calculated on the face value of the bonds. Calculating that return on our basis of approximately 33% of the face value would yield a 45% annual return. This was in addition to the increase in value from our $150 million cost to the $500 million face value.

When Anglo Africa began acquiring the senior bonds, they assumed they would be able to purchase the subordinate bonds at the same discount we had secured. But as they bought the senior bonds, we quickly acquired the majority of the subordinate ones. They hadn't been minding their knitting, and now they were in a pickle. The only question was: how much would they have to pay to make us go away? The longer they waited, the greater our leverage. Their sole options were to let the company file for bankruptcy and try their luck in court, or buy us out.

We were waiting in the elevator lobby when the CEO, Ryan Hastings, approached us. He asked if he could speak to Alex alone. Alex surprised both of us.

"Ryan, you need to acquire these bonds. And we would be willing to sell them to you for a reasonable price. This will allow a vital company to survive its current bad management decisions. Jack here has done all the work on this deal. I'm going home for supper." He turned to me. "Jack, you have my proxy. Sell them at the price you think is fair. Or, if you cannot get a fair price, you don't have to sell them at all. Whatever you do, I will support your decision."

As he said that, the elevator car chimed. Alex stepped inside and nodded at me. When the doors closed, I stood alone with Ryan Hastings. He invited me back into the boardroom.

I paused for a moment, then turned to the CEO of a multibillion-dollar mining company.

"Mr. Hastings, I don't think it's in anyone's interest to play cat and mouse, especially given our time constraints. We will sell our $500 million worth of bonds for $400 million. This will be our one and only offer."

After making the offer, I pressed the elevator button.

"This offer expires when I get into the next elevator to arrive."

Moments later, the elevator chimed. As I stepped in, Ryan Hastings placed his hand between the doors, forcing them to open.

"You have a deal," he said.

With that, our $75 million equity earned a profit of $250 million. We had completed numerous transactions over the previous sixteen years. A few had even netted us over $100 million. But we had never executed a deal this profitable.

I rode the elevator to the ground floor but waited until I exited the building before calling Alex.

"That is good work. I don't think we've ever had a better day. You should join Esther and me for dinner."

There was no excitement in his voice. Another puzzle had been solved, only this time it had many zeros after it.

At dinner, Alex told Esther about the transaction we had completed that day. She smiled at me, then turned to Alex.

"My dear, it looks as if you've trained Jackson well. Maybe the pupil has surpassed the teacher," she said, teasing him.

But Alex didn't smile. He set down his knife and fork, took a sip of wine, and then raised his glass.

"Yes, indeed he has. A toast to Alex."

The following week, Alex informed me he would start working four days a week. That pace continued for six months. It soon became clear he was slowing down and visibly struggling. At one of our Friday evening dinners, he said the unthinkable. He thought we should unwind the company. If I chose to continue, he would contribute capital if needed. I was at a point where that wouldn't be necessary, but the vote of confidence was appreciated.

We had made a great deal of money, and Alex had been generous in allowing my participation. The banking relationships were now handled through me, and new opportunities were presented to the company with me as the point of contact.

"I think you should do whatever you want to do, Alex. If you want to close the doors, do it. If you want to work at any level, that's fine as well," I said.

"I am eighty-five. My time has passed. Esther and I are going to move to Tel Aviv, maybe at the end of the year. Think about what you'd like, Jack. For now, I'm going to bed. This will give you and Esther plenty of time to talk about me in my absence."

Alex stood up and kissed his wife on the top of her head. Esther and I talked, as we always did.

"I think this would be a good time for you to go home, Jack. Your real home, I mean," she said.

"That isn't possible, Esther. Jack doesn't have a home."

I stood and also kissed her on the head before returning to my flat.

That night, June 2nd, 2017. I received a call from Hart at four in the morning. Alex had died in his sleep.

I don't think anyone who knew Alex was surprised by his passing. Still, Esther took it very hard. She had not been apart from him in over seventy-two years.

We flew Alex's body to Israel, where the two of them had burial plots. Hart, Esther, and I were the only attendees, aside from the rabbi. This was at Alex's request.

Esther believed she might have cousins somewhere in Tel Aviv. I hired an investigator to try to find them, but he could not. Regardless, Esther decided not to return to London. She wished to move to Israel.

Together, we searched for and purchased a two-bedroom condominium on the shoreline. The entire process took five days. After closing, we went out onto the oversized patio overlooking the water. Esther and I sat on one of the benches left by the previous owner, staring out at the sea. She reached for my hand and wiped a tear from her eye.

"Jack, what is your real name?" she asked without looking at me.

I had to think. It had been sixteen years since I'd said it.

"Jordan. Jordan Rome," I replied, gently squeezing her hand.

"So now there are three people in the world who know that: Hart, you, and me."

Esther asked, "What awful thing would make you turn your life upside down and live alone in a foreign land?"

I sat quietly for a moment before answering. Then I answered honestly, and in full.

She did not flinch or say a word. After a long while, she spoke.

"When Alex and I met, we were to be deported separately. This was not a choice. We went wherever a country would accept us. He would go to Australia, and I to England. We would never see each other again. This was not acceptable to Alex. He hid in the attic rafters of the women's toilet room for two days in order to be deported with the same group as me. I snuck him scraps of food and water. This seemed like a small sacrifice for something so important after all we had been through. But he would have done anything, and so would have I. I don't know the risks you and your wife face, but I can tell you that the choice should not be yours alone to make. She should not be punished for what you have done. It is her life as well."

I listened but did not respond.

Hart and I returned to London alone. Esther would remain forever in Tel Aviv whether she found cousins or not.

"This is where Alex and I will rest together," She said.

I liquidated everything that Esther owned in London and sent it on to her. I agreed to rent the townhouse that we had our offices in for one more year as I decided what to do with the business and my life.

One week later I called her; I called my wife, Liv.

PART XV

REBECCA ROME

New York, New York
2018: 17 Years After

Chapter 47

Jack, The Whole Damn Letter

I READ THE LETTER MY mom had written six weeks ago—a letter that was never sent. She had been acting peculiar over the past several months, and I suspected she had met a man. She traveled more frequently and became unreachable for extended periods. This was unlike her.

The letter answered my questions and sent me into a rage.

I called the only number I had, but there was no answer. I called again and again—six times in the span of an hour. He finally called back.

"Becca, what is it? Are you okay?" said Hart, his voice urgent.

"Where the fuck are you? Where is he? Where is Jack?"

"We're at the airport. Just landed. We had to pick up some gear. What do you need?"

"Do not leave. I'm coming. I'll be there in forty minutes."

I hung up without waiting for a response.

I tipped the Uber driver an extra forty dollars to drive like a madman to the airport. When I arrived, it was just before 8 p.m. Jack and Hart were still on the plane, waiting. I walked up the lowered stairway, strode straight to Jack, who was seated, and tossed the letter into his lap.

"I want you to read this letter. It's from your wife, but she never sent it to her daughter," I said, trying my best to restrain myself.

Jack put on his glasses, opened the letter, and began to read.

"No, you don't. You don't get to read this to yourself. Read it out loud, so I can hear it, so Hart can hear it."

Jack adjusted himself in the seat and recentered his glasses. He swallowed, as if there were an olive pit stuck in his throat, then began to speak.

"*Dear Becca,*

I am writing you this letter because I did not have the courage to say these things to you. I have tried several times but could not make the words come out of my mouth. Seventeen years ago, when you were a young girl, the two of us shared an unimaginable loss. I had to live without the thing I loved most in this world; and you had to live without a father and with a mother who could not be whole. We have carried that pain and the additional wounds that came with it from that day forward."

Jack put the letter down and began to speak. I interrupted in a shout. "Finish the letter, Jack. The whole damn letter."

He cleared his throat and slowly started in again.

"*Any person who goes through this experience would hate those who placed them in that position. I have hated entire groups of people for as long as I can recall. I should also hate the man who did this to us.*"

But I don't. I love him and although I tried and I thought I could, I cannot live without him.

A few months ago, he called. Naturally, I did not believe it was him. I thought it was a cruel trick of some sort, but it was your father. I have learned your father made grave mistakes with the most dangerous people—people who would take the lives of his family as retribution. To save you and me, he utilized the events of 9/11 to create the appearance of his death. This was how he was able to provide safety for you and me. I cannot tell you that I will ever forgive him or that you should, because what he did is unforgivable. But forgiving something and moving past something are two different things.

Your father and I have now been meeting for the last couple of months, and I have decided I want to move with him to a place where we will be safe. I have told Richard I want a divorce, because I cannot live without your father. I understand that you may not want to, but I want you to come with us. I want you to see your father, and then make your own decisions; this should be your choice.

I love you. and as hard as it is to believe right now, so does he. Please call me after you read this. We should meet face to face and figure out what is best for you.

Love always, your Mom."

Jack pressed his fingers against the bridge of his nose and rested his thumbs beneath his chin. His eyes were squeezed tightly shut. He picked up the napkin from the tray table in front of him and wiped his eyes.

"You motherfucker." Jack winced as the words left my mouth.

"Okay, maybe that was a poor choice of words. But you are a despicable, awful human being. Who does this to people they love? You're self-centered and heartless. You didn't deserve her.

You never did. You should have never come back here. She's dead because of you. That man who killed her did it because of you."

I turned to Hart. "Did you kill that man at the Marriott? Did the two of you throw him off the terrace? Who even does that kind of thing, gangsters?"

Jack finally spoke. "Becca, you're right on all fronts. I shouldn't have come back, and I don't belong in your life. But right now, I need to fix some things. I need to make sure you're safe. And in this situation, there are only bad options. The man who killed your mother was the worst kind of man. He needed to die, and yes, we did that. You're safer now, and the world is better because of it.

"Becca, I have an important question. This letter suggests Richard knew I was alive. This is Richard Anderson, the man I worked with, and the man your mother married, correct?"

"Who else could it be? Of course it's him," I said.

"Hart, please make sure Becca gets home safely. I think it would be wise to walk through her house, just to be sure. We'll be leaving tomorrow afternoon."

The man I had only known as Jack, and now understood to be my father, stood up and reached out, as if to touch or hold me. I backed away, turned on my heel, and walked toward the front of the plane. Hart placed his hand gently on my back to guide me out of the jet.

I sneered at him. "Do not touch me."

CHAPTER 48

WE ARE GOING TO YOUR MOM'S HOUSE

THE FIRST TEN MINUTES OF the car ride back to my apartment were completely silent. Hart tried to speak, but I cut him off with a sharp reminder that I didn't want to hear anything from him. On his third attempt, he didn't oblige my insistence.

"I know you don't want to hear it. I understand you feel betrayed by me, by your father, maybe by everyone in the world. I know the story, and I'm not going to defend the decision to cross those people. It seems too dangerous to me. But Becca, he paid for that mistake. He paid with the things he valued most in the world. I know he'd turn back the clock if he could. Disappearing was the only way to save you and your mother. That decision wasn't the wrong one."

I turned away from Hart and stared out the window at the passing traffic before he continued.

"I know he looks like a bad guy to you. But your father has done some extraordinary things. I saw that firsthand when he pulled me out of the gutter, cleaned me of poison, and set me on a straight path. He was like a father when mine couldn't be. When my mum was dying, it was your father who paid whatever was needed to place her in the best facilities with the best doctors money could buy. When she was on her deathbed and I was too messed up to comfort her, he slept beside her. Becca, your father is a complex man, but he isn't a bad man. And as you might guess, I'd do anything for him."

"Including screwing his daughter? Deceiving her, lying to her? Would you do that for him too?" I recoiled as the words left my mouth. Even as I said them, I wanted them back.

"You don't believe that. I know you don't. It's true Jack asked me to look out for you, but everything else was honest and real. Every moment of it." As Hart said this, he reached over and took my hand from my lap. Our fingers interlocked.

"She couldn't send the letter, and she couldn't tell me. How awful for her." Hart looked at me and nodded. Not another word was spoken for the rest of the ride.

When we arrived, I turned the deadbolt and then the handle lock. The door was still locked. I put my key back in the deadbolt and turned it again. This time, the door opened. Hart noted that the deadbolt had been undone, leaving the door locked only at the handle. He took a firm hold of my upper arm and whispered in my ear to wait outside. Then he entered the apartment alone.

I stood in the hallway for several minutes, though it felt like an hour. The door was ajar, but there was complete silence inside. Then, that changed.

A loud crash erupted from my small living room. I pushed the door open. A giant of a man stood opposite Hart, swiping a knife at him. As I entered, Hart looked up briefly. The intruder lunged, slashing Hart's shirt with the blade. Hart quickly grabbed the man's right arm with his left, turned his body so his back was to the man, and smashed the wrist holding the knife over his knee. The blade clattered to the floor. Hart's shirt began to stain crimson where a deep cut had opened.

The giant countered, wrapping his arms around Hart in a crushing bear hug, holding him tight against his chest. Hart tried to turn and free his arms to strike, but he couldn't. The man ran full speed into my bedroom door, crashing through it with Hart's body as a battering ram. They both fell, the larger man landing on top.

Hart quickly rolled over, but the giant, much heavier, began to pummel his head. Hart raised his arms to shield himself as best he could while the man pounded on him. I screamed, but it had no effect. It was only a matter of time before a blow knocked Hart unconscious. That would be the end.

I spotted the bloody knife by the couch where Hart had knocked it loose. I picked it up, ran into the bedroom, and, using both hands, stabbed it into the man's back between his shoulder blades and neck. He howled, stood, and reached behind him to pull out the blade. He turned toward me, weapon in hand, cursing in Spanish. I stood frozen in fear. He was just two feet from me when he was knocked off balance, Hart had jumped on his back.

With his right arm locked around the man's neck and his right hand gripping his left elbow, Hart used his left hand to press against the back of the man's head. Scissoring his legs around the man's waist, he began to squeeze. The man thrashed, grabbing and punching at Hart's arm lodged beneath his chin. He staggered around the room, slamming into furniture and walls, trying to shake Hart loose. But he couldn't. Within minutes, the man dropped to his knees and took his last breath.

Hart rose to all fours, panting. His shirt was now completely red, blood soaking through from the gash just above his waist.

"Are you okay?" he asked.

"I think I'm fine. You're bleeding. Your side, your side is bleeding."

Hart looked down and pressed his right hand to the wound. "Close the door. The front door. Close it," he said, standing up and making his way to the kitchen sink. He removed his shirt, unrolled a handful of paper towels, ran them under water, and began cleaning the wound repeatedly.

"I need some peroxide and super glue. Do you have any?" he asked.

I ran to the linen closet and found an open package of super glue and a bottle of peroxide. He poured the peroxide directly into the wound. It bubbled. Although it wasn't my wound, I let out a yelp as it turned white. He opened the super glue and pinched the inch-long cut together with both hands.

"Squeeze the super glue over the cut. Hurry, before it starts to bleed again."

I dabbed the wound dry and quickly applied the glue. I patted it gently, then repeated the process. Within five minutes, the glue had sealed the wound. I ran back to the linen closet and brought out antiseptic gel and the few bandages I had. I carefully dressed the wound. Hart leaned against the counter, threw his head back, closed his eyes, and took a deep breath.

"Do you know who that was?" I asked.

"We met once before at the Marriott. I need to call your dad. Get me my phone."

Hart walked through the episode without emotion or exaggeration. Then he sat silently, listening for more than five minutes. His last remark was, "Okay, got it. We're on our way."

"Becca, you have to listen to me. Pack clothes for one week. Take all your jewelry. If you forget something, write it down. I'll try to come back later. You won't be coming back here. We're leaving in five minutes."

I was shaking. "Where are we going? What about him?" I asked, glancing at the dead man lying in my living room.

"Jack will take care of him. We need to leave your keys at the airport."

"The airport? Why are we going to the airport?"

"We're going to your mom's house. You need to pack. Come on, I'll explain later."

When we arrived at Teterboro, the plane's engines were already running. Hart and I carried my luggage on board, and the copilot immediately lifted the stairs. We hadn't even been on the plane for five minutes before it began to taxi.

Hart spoke. "Your mom has a place outside of Tucson. We'll be there in four and a half hours. You should rest. I'll fill you in when we land."

"My mom has a place in Tucson?" I shook my head, trying to absorb one more impossible event in a day already full of them. The fatigue was catching up with me. Moments after takeoff, I slipped into exhaustion.

The "place" turned out to be a 250-acre ranch northwest of Tucson. Out the expansive rear windows were the Catalina Mountains, the Tortolitas, and Mount Lemmon. Evidently, my father had bought the spread for my mother last year. Hart led me through the main house, a 4,000-square-foot adobe home built fifty years ago and recently renovated. It was beautiful and tasteful in every way. I was standing at the fireplace mantel, looking at old photos of my mother and me, when Emily and Roger Morgan introduced themselves.

Emily and Roger were the caretakers who lived on the property. They were a Black couple in their fifties, both retired from the military. With their children grown, they now cared for the land and livestock as part of their retirement. There was clearly history between my father and the couple—another mystery I'd have to unravel later.

Emily did most of the talking. "Welcome. Roger went shopping for you. He figured, you being from New York and all, you might have different tastes, so he bought you that organic stuff. If you need anything else, let me know. For now, I think it's best we go out together."

I had stepped into the world my parents had built for themselves to escape everything dark and dangerous. I thought back to the time I asked for a pony, saying we'd be better off on a ranch in one of those cowboy places. This was definitely a cowboy place, my mom's cowboy place.

"Becca, I have to go, just for a couple of days. You're safe with Emily and Roger. And don't listen to Roger, Emily was the tougher soldier." Hart gave Emily a hug and shook Roger's hand. Then he came over and hugged me. I wouldn't let go until he gently pushed me back.

"Becca, I really have to go. I'll be back. Two days, max."

"Promise?" I said, looking into his eyes and holding his arms.

"Promise."

I grabbed the back of his head and kissed his mouth. When he turned to go, I saw Roger wink at him.

PART XVI

JACKSON MARTIN

New York, New York
2018: 17 Years After

CHAPTER 49

THAT DIDN'T HURT

WHEN I CALLED THE OFFICE, I was told he had announced his retirement a month ago. His secretary believed he was moving to a villa he had purchased in Italy. Even though I said I was a friend, she was hesitant to provide more information than that.

Locating his home online wasn't difficult, so I took a drive out to Long Island. When I rang the bell, no one answered. Looking through the windows, I saw the house packed in boxes, ready for a move. I walked around back, gently removed one pane of glass with the butt of my pistol, and let myself in.

After waiting a little over an hour, I made myself a cup of coffee and took a seat at the kitchen table. He entered the room twenty minutes later with a bag of cleaning supplies.

"Hello, Richard. I hope you don't mind that I made myself a cup of coffee. I didn't know how long you'd be."

Richard Anderson placed the bag on the counter.

"Jordan, you've aged, but you've obviously been taking care of yourself," he said, sitting opposite me at the table.

Richard maintained his arrogant demeanor despite the discomfort of the situation. He used both hands to brush back his still-perfect executive hair.

"You don't look too surprised to see a dead man," I said.

"Liv said something to me. So no, I'm not that surprised."

"You told them, didn't you?"

"I don't know what you mean. I told who what?" he replied nervously.

"They hired you. Paid you something. Maybe made promises. You were supposed to keep an eye on me. So you started following the ledger. You told the French banker, then the German one too. But the Frenchman stayed quiet because he was stealing as well. The German took the information and passed it on."

Richard started fidgeting with his fingers on the tabletop.

"After I was gone, you became their contact. Maybe made a few hundred thousand dollars. Maybe got a promotion. And Liv, that was a bonus. On that particular topic, I can't blame you. She was irresistible. You couldn't believe your luck. I'm dead, along with thousands of others. You make a bunch of money and get the girl. At least for a while.

"But soon enough, she comes to her senses and kicks you to the curb. You're pissed off. The rejection hurts. Your overinflated ego takes a hit. How am I doing so far?"

Richard didn't say a word. I watched him look around the room, likely wondering what could be used as a weapon. Was he thinking about where he'd packed the kitchen knives? Were they still in the drawer?

"And then the real bombshell. She doesn't tell you outright, but she hints enough for you to realize I'm alive. Somehow, I'm alive. And she would rather have me, any version of me than ever be with you. So you get another idea. You call the German again. Tell him I'm alive after all. They've been duped.

"Maybe they'll act. Maybe they'll kill me. But they don't. They kill her. And that's on you. Now you're scared. Scared of me, or scared of them, or maybe both. So you pack up and plan to move as far away as possible. Take your guilt, if you feel any, with you.

"You tell the office you're moving to Italy, but that's just to throw everyone off. You're going somewhere completely different. Maybe South America. Maybe Portugal. Doesn't matter, as long as no one knows. Honestly, I think that's a good idea. A smart move. You don't want to be around those people if they ever turn on you."

Richard's head dropped. Then he looked up, clearly angry.

"How did you know?"

"I didn't until I sat in this kitchen with you and you confirmed it just now. I suspected. Now I know."

"I swear, I didn't know they would hurt her. I loved her, you know. I even loved her when she wouldn't love me. She wasted that on you. On the man who would throw everything away for his own greed. Like that was going to give you anything more important than what you already had."

He was so enraged that spit flew from his mouth as he spoke.

"It's what you did that got her killed. What you did separated me from everything I loved."

"But none of that could've happened without you making it possible. So now what? Are you here to shame me? To hurt me? What are you going to do, Jordan, beat me up?"

He seemed to finally find his backbone and sat up, staring me straight in the eye.

"No, Richard. I'm not going to hurt you," I said, leaning back in the chair.

Richard straightened and smiled with his perfect, veneered teeth. Again, he brushed back his perfect hair with his right hand.

"Australia. That's where I'm going. Tomorrow, in fact. Now that you've said your piece, I think it's time for you to go."

"Yes. It is time to go."

I pulled the nine-millimeter from my pocket and shot him in the center of his forehead. He blinked once before collapsing on the table.

"I told you it wouldn't hurt."

I got up from the table, wiped down everything I'd touched in the room, and walked out the same back door I'd come through.

CHAPTER 50

WHY AM I NOT SURPRISED

HART AND I LOADED THE Challenger 300 as we waited for the plane to be refueled and for the new flight crew to arrive. Certain cargo must be loaded personally. This cargo met those criteria. In two and a half hours, we would be landing at Ocala International Airport. I had arranged for the rental vehicle in Florida, as well as all the necessary cleanup in New York. This included the man in Becca's apartment and the visit to Richard Anderson this morning. It had been three days since Eduardo volunteered the location of his mother as his last words. Those were not exactly his last words; I believe his actual last words had something to do with carving my heart out. But Eduardo was never heroic, and it was certain he would say whatever was required to save his own skin. And he did just that before he went off the 51st floor.

We were both exhausted, having gone nonstop for close to forty-eight hours. Hart assured me that Becca was safe in the Tucson home, and Roger Morgan confirmed the same. My body hurt as I attempted to get comfortable in the seat. I closed my eyes and tried to steady my breathing. I thought of lying next to Liv and waking up beside her in the mornings. I heard her whisper, "Be careful," before I was finally embraced by sleep. The sudden jolt of the wheels hitting the tarmac jarred me awake.

The pilots took an Uber to the hotel. We would be wheels up tomorrow at 8 a.m., and they would be ready. The rented Sprinter van waited in the parking lot. It looked perfectly normal, except for the articulating arm and basket that rose from the roof. We drove the vehicle onto the tarmac and loaded our cargo into it.

Our equipment included four DJI Max photographic drones, each with a five-pound payload capacity. Four pieces of 3.8-pound C4 explosive, individually wrapped and prewired with detonators tied to cell phone receivers. One AI AXSR sniper rifle with suppressor and night scope. A Polish-made RPG-40 (a six-shot revolver type), a forty-millimeter grenade launcher, two Sig Sauer handguns, and one Special Forces MK-16 5.56 carbine rifle. Lastly, a BNVD Pinnacle night vision headset for my entry to the compound. These were not items one would pick up at the local hardware store. But between the two of us, we had enough contacts from my CIA and Hart's SAS days. One has to know where to shop, and as always, anything can be purchased for the right price. We finished loading the van before commandeering plates from a truck parked in the extended lot. It was 11 p.m., and we were fifty minutes from Cassandra's ranch. We planned to park the van and capture a few more hours of sleep before heading out.

The odds of killing someone increase if you are willing to die in the process. That is why suicide bombers are so effective. Our plan was simple—more blunt force than precision. At 3:45 a.m., we would cut through the fence on the south perimeter of the property and move the van into position. With the lift arm fully extended, a clear view of the front doors from approximately 200 yards was possible. Hart would remain in the basket and raise it to its full height after the fireworks started. At 4 a.m., the first of the four drones would explode on the roof of the mansion. Hart would then press the three remaining speed dial numbers, one after the other, for each drone stationed on a different wing of the home. This would ignite four explosions of 3.8 pounds of C4. I hoped the C4 would kill Cassandra as she slept. Regardless, I would immediately launch six grenades through the windows of the home, starting on the east side, moving to the north, and then to the west. The garage to the west of the house housed the vehicles, including the armored car. Hart was to watch the front door on the south side, targeting anyone who left. At 200 yards, using a night vision scope, he would see them, but they would not see him. At that range, he would not miss. The explosions would be overwhelming. The intent was to have Cassandra and her men conclude that a competitor was staging a larger attack on the compound, causing the occupants to flee. Our assault would last less than five minutes. The closest police station was at best fifteen minutes away. We estimated the fastest law enforcement could become aware and respond would be twenty minutes. Hart had strict instructions to leave in fifteen. If I was not there, he was to leave without me and return to Tucson.

If Cassandra survived the drone explosions, the grenade blasts, and the sniper rounds, she would retreat through the basement tunnel to the armored car in the garage to the west of the home. She would drive the car through the front gates and onto the highway as fast as the vehicle could move—the same way we left the Mutiny Hotel over three decades ago. Once that occurred, it would be impossible to catch her, and law enforcement would swarm the site in minutes. That was why I would wait for her there, at the car.

Success in combat comes from the ability to respond to the fluid nature of the battlefield because plans and field conditions are never the same. At 3:45, we opened the fence half a mile from the main entry of the compound. We entered the compound within a pasture and parked the van 200 yards from the house. We checked our cell phone headsets, then I removed the four drones from the van. One drone at a time, I armed each, then flew them from the pasture, attempting to land them on the roof. The remote vision was poor in the darkness, and I was uncertain that I had positioned any of them on the house itself. I only hoped they were somewhere near the structure.

Using my night vision headset, I proceeded toward the home, armed with the RPG-40, the MK-16, and the Sig. At exactly 4:00 a.m., the first drone detonated, exploding the entire backyard furniture collection but missing the house completely. Lights all over the house went on immediately, along with lights in a small outbuilding 100 yards to the west. I saw movement in both the house and the outbuilding. Drones two, three, and four did better. The second blew a hole in the backside of the home the size of an automobile. Three and four landed on opposite wings of the house. In an instant, the structure was ablaze as the roof caught fire. From fifty yards out, I fired two grenades into the east windows. I saw the shadows behind the curtains fall with each explosion.

I shifted to the north and fired two more rounds into the hole created by the second drone. When I moved to the west, I saw half a dozen men running toward the home from the outbuilding. I fired the last two grenade rounds into the bedroom wing where I had stayed a lifetime ago.

I checked my MK-16 and lay flat, awaiting men running toward the home. Then one dropped, then another, and the remaining four men scrambled for cover in the grass and behind a parked pickup truck. Hart had pinned them down, but it would only be a matter of time before they triangulated his position. Men now rushed from the house and the front gate toward Hart. I rounded the south end of the house and took aim at the men coming outside. Three were positioned behind the oversized columns trying to locate Hart. I took out two in rapid succession as the third returned to the burning home. The remaining four men from the outbuilding took advantage of the activity at the entry and advanced toward the house. I scrambled toward the east wall of the garage. The door was locked, no surprise. I took the Sig and fired into the lockset.

I heard it but didn't see it, a blazing hot streak on the back of my shoulder. I had been hit. Immediately, I fell to the ground, the Sig still in my hand, taking aim at my assailant who was now rushing toward me.

Two shots to the chest, and he collapsed to the ground. Gunfire erupted from two directions. For the first time this evening, I heard Hart speak to me over my headset.

"There are still three hostiles about fifty yards west of you. I think there are two more inside the house. The two from the front gate are parked in the Escalade halfway up the drive. I got a round into the front tire and the passenger seat. I'm not sure what they're going to do; my bet is they're trying to figure that out themselves.

I can keep the three outside at bay." I heard a thud on the phone. "Scratch that, two left west of you."

I responded to Hart, "I'm in the garage. She's either dead or coming here. The house is in flames—there's no staying inside. I want you to leave now. You've done good work. I can handle it from here. I'll take one of her cars. I'll contact you when I'm out."

"I'll give you five more minutes, then pack up shop. I may get one or two more."

"Hart, I got it. Go look after her. Get the fuck out of here."

"I heard you. I said five minutes. Five minutes, and I'm going." I heard another thud. "Correction: one man left on the west," he added.

I was bleeding badly from my wound. I could feel the blood dripping down my back into my pants. I couldn't see it, but I guessed it went in and out. If it had punctured my body cavity, I'd be in much worse shape or already dead.

I steadied myself against the wall adjacent to the door that opened to the basement passageway below. That was where she would exit. Two minutes later, he walked out the door. His hair, now gray, was tied back in a ponytail.

"Ricardo, don't move." He casually turned and looked at me. He was older, the man I'd met in his twenties was now over sixty. He was still big, but not as massive as I remembered. He nodded and slowly reached into his coat pocket, pulling out a pack of cigarettes with a silver lighter stuck in the cellophane. He showed them to me and lit one.

"Jordan, I told you to aim and shoot, no thinking. If you don't, you'll end up dead. I should be lying on that ground right now. I thought I taught you better," he said, glancing down at the blood behind me.

"There's no need for you to die tonight. I'd prefer you didn't. But I need to end it with her."

He sighed and snapped the silver lighter closed. "Hmm, I think I've lived a cat's life, and this may be my ninth." He took a deep drag on his cigarette before exhaling. "You know, I think she would have left it alone. She's old and tired too, like you and me. But her kid, the psycho fucking kid, couldn't leave it. Always had it out for you, you know. Some sort of perverted jealousy thing with you and Casandra, I think." He took another drag. "And no matter how fucked up, she always let him do what he wanted. She just could never say no to him." He puffed again and flicked the ash off the end. "It was his crew up there, not hers. Personally, I never liked him. Really fucked up what he did to your girl in Florida. A nice girl... can't remember her name." He pulled a small piece of tobacco off his tongue. "Oh yeah, Gabriel, that's it. A real good-looking girl too. You know, I'm glad you killed him, he deserved it."

"Ricardo, is she coming here?" I thought for a moment. "Stupid question: you wouldn't be here if she wasn't. Where is she?" I fought to stay conscious without lowering the gun a millimeter.

Ricardo took a moment and looked at the ash at the end of his cigarette. Then he stared into my eyes. He could tell I wouldn't last long. "Jesus Christ, look what you guys did here tonight. I think I've always underestimated you. But she didn't. She thought you could run the whole show." As he said this, his eyes darted toward the door as it slowly opened.

She stepped out. Badly wounded by the fireworks, her arm was wrapped with a bathroom towel, blood seeping through the fabric. She followed Ricardo's eyes, turned, and looked at me. I aimed my gun at her. Casandra looked more like a grandmother than the Latin beauty of thirty-eight years ago. Her face and hair were blackened with soot from the fire. She wore blue jeans, fleece Ugg slippers, a T-shirt, and a quilted vest.

Our eyes locked. She smiled and shook her head. "Why am I not surprised? Always too ambitious." Those were the last words I heard Casandra speak before she pulled the tiny Walther from her vest pocket. I remembered hearing three shots fired, mine being the first.

PART XVII

REBECCA ROME

Tucson, Arizona
2019: 18 Years After

CHAPTER 51

LET'S TALK ABOUT THAT TOMORROW

SMALL THINGS WE DO EVERY day create both rhythm and comfort. I looked to my right, and he was brushing his teeth—something we did together daily. Not a big thing, but an intimate one. You can't look beautiful with a mouthful of toothpaste and spit. There's simply nothing sexy about it. But when I looked at him, he smiled, toothpaste smeared across his lips and teeth.

When we arrived at the house, there were two toothbrush holders on the sink. On the left was a pink one; on the right, a blue one. The pink one still sits in the same spot it did the day I arrived. It was her toothbrush, and it would stay. She had left other things in the house—clothes, some photos, and a few pieces of jewelry. I use as many of these items as I can. I'm not sure she ever truly felt like it was her house. Maybe she dreamed it would be one day. That it would be our house. That the three of us would live together again, as we had two decades ago.

My mind drifted as I paused my brushing. It dawned on me that she must have looked over at him the way I'm looking at Hart now. She probably remembered dreaming about brushing their teeth together until they were old and gray. How good it must have felt to brush their teeth together again, after thinking he was lost. I looked at Hart again and hoped that we could brush our teeth together until we died.

"What? Why are you staring at me?" he asked after spitting out the last of his toothpaste and leaning over to stick his mouth under the faucet to rinse. An act I could never understand. There was a cup right in front of him on the counter, but he refused to use it, as if in protest. Pick your battles, I thought.

"I wasn't really staring. Just thinking. I was thinking how lucky we are to have each other and Billy."

After I said it, Hart came over and kissed my cheek just as I turned my face away. He had been aiming for my mouth, despite the fact that we both still had toothpaste in ours. I picked up the washcloth and wiped my cheek, rolling my eyes. I accused him of being a child, something I meant as an insult, but which he took as praise, as if it were one of his more charming traits.

Like clockwork, the alarm went off. Billy crying was the alarm.

"It is definitely your turn," I said. "I got up, changed her, and fed her last night. I also took the five o'clock shift this morning. So, it's your turn."

"I'll handle it," he said. "But I want to point out that you're the only one who can feed her at night. That puts me at a serious disadvantage in these daytime negotiations. That should be acknowledged somehow."

"Well, I have an idea. Grow a pair of boobs, and then you can nurse her at night too," I said, finishing up my brushing.

"See, this is what I love most about you. Not only are you beautiful, but you come up with real problem-solving solutions." He smiled and blew me a kiss.

Billy's crying stopped, a sign she was enjoying the milk he had warmed up for her. With the minor crisis handled, I allowed myself the luxury of solitude and took time to prepare for the day.

When I came downstairs, I was greeted with scrambled eggs, toast, and a self-proclaimed "husband of the day."

I felt most at ease in our kitchen. At first, I thought we'd sell the house. I had no attachment to it, and it was worth a substantial amount. Then I discovered that my mom had set up a trust fund to take care of the house and its expenses. She had also created one to take care of me. Evidently, my mom had come into quite a bit of money. I didn't have to wonder how.

Once we learned that Billy was on the way, we decided to stay until the baby was born. Now the house felt like home. It's ironic that my mother once envisioned it as a home for her family of three—and now it was. Hart and I had no trouble deciding this would be where we'd raise Billy, and, if we were lucky, her siblings too.

I'm not sure where my father is. At first, I thought he had died. I followed the press coverage about what happened in Ocala. It made national news, with video clips showing the house in flames and experts speculating about the ongoing drug war in Florida. When Hart returned the next day, I asked if he knew what had happened to Jack. He said he didn't. He was telling the truth then, because Hart would never lie to me.

I've avoided asking if he has heard from my father since. My guess is that if my father were alive but didn't want me to know, he would have told Hart to keep it quiet. Asking Hart would force him to either lie to me or break my father's trust. I've chosen not to put him in that position.

My office called to tell me they'd heard from the two police officers who came to speak with me about the man pushed off a balcony. Detective Banner and Sergeant O'Grady told me that my stepfather had been executed at his kitchen table. Apparently, he was planning to leave the country. The police now believe he was involved in some kind of illegal activity, which is why they believe my mother was drawn into it. I didn't correct their theory.

I've spoken with Dr. Green several times about my father. We still have biweekly calls. She recommends that if I ever decide I want to speak to him, I should tell my husband first. If it's meant to happen, the rest will fall into place. I've come close to bringing it up a few times. Maybe soon.

We live a relaxed life. I explained it to Cat once—it's like Christmas break in college. There are no pressures, no timelines. Our days are filled with whatever we choose to do. Cat has visited twice since Billy was born.

I've started taking piano lessons. I'm strict about practicing ninety minutes a day, just as my mother used to. I'm not good yet, but I'm improving. Hart has converted one of the barns into a workshop and has become a proficient woodworker. He found a local retailer in Phoenix to represent him, and now he makes custom furniture pieces. It seems to give him purpose and makes him happy, which makes me happy.

We both love the three horses that came with the house, but neither of us is brave enough to ride them. Our caretaker, Roger Morgan, who grew up in inner-city Pittsburgh—is now a cowboy.

We're still dogless, but not for long. As soon as Billy is out of diapers, I'm getting a puppy.

Every day feels like a Saturday, except for Sundays during football season. Then Sunday becomes football day. Hart isn't really a fan, but he understands the family obligation to spend the day in front of the screen. So that's what we were doing that Sunday, watching my beloved Jets get crushed by the Bills, when Hart's phone rang. He muted the television, earning a dirty look from me.

"Do we know a Dr. Isaac Kravitz in Phoenix?" he asked as the phone continued to chime.

I paused, staring into space as if flipping through a mental phone book. "No, I don't think so."

Hart turned the sound back on and walked toward the kitchen. I could still hear him on the phone.

"Yes, this is him," he said, followed by about thirty seconds of silence while he listened. Curiosity got the best of me, so I got off the couch to find out what was going on. Why would a doctor be calling us on a Sunday?

Hart was standing with the phone to his ear, staring at the floor. Then he said, "Okay, one moment and I'll see if she's available."

He covered the receiver with his hand. "There's a woman on the line. She thinks she might know you. She sounds elderly. I asked if I could help, but she said she only wants to speak to you. I told her I'd see if I could find you. She clearly knows I'm asking you now."

I held out my hand. Instead, Hart put the phone on speaker and set it on the kitchen island.

"Yes, this is Rebecca Rome. How can I help you?"

An elderly woman's voice came through, soft and feminine despite her age. "My name is Carmen Kravitz. Last Friday I was contacted by an attorney from New York. He was asking about my life before I moved to Phoenix." She paused to clear her throat. "Before I married Isaac, I was married once before. The attorney asked if my name from my first marriage was Rome. He also asked if I had two sons in Bisbee, Arizona. I told him I did. Then he asked if their names were Jordan Rome and Jackson Martin. I said they were. He emailed me this phone number and said I could reach my granddaughter here. At first, I thought it was some cruel trick, but I couldn't sleep after reading the email. Isaac insisted I call. If I'm bothering you, I'm sorry. But are you related to Jordan or Jackson?"

It felt like I'd been broadsided at an intersection. I couldn't speak. My eyes filled with tears, and my nose began to run. Fortunately, Hart stepped in.

"Carmen, this is Becca's husband again. She's unable to talk at the moment, but if you give her a few seconds, I'm sure she'll be okay. And yes, we both knew Jordan Rome. I'm afraid we don't know Jackson. Jordan is Becca's father."

There was silence on the line for nearly a minute before a man began to speak.

"Good afternoon. I'm Isaac Kravitz. Carmen and I have worked together for ten years and have been married for thirty more. She has spoken of her sons countless times. I think she's a bit overwhelmed. Maybe we can plan to meet. You have a New York number, is that where you live?"

I finally gathered myself enough to respond. "No, we live west of the 10, outside Tucson. If you're in Phoenix, we're probably an hour and a half away."

Carmen spoke again, her voice bubbling with disbelief. "You're an hour and a half from Phoenix? I have a granddaughter an hour and a half from here?"

"Yes, you do. And a grandson-in-law, and a great-granddaughter."

"A great-granddaughter? I have a great-granddaughter?" she exclaimed.

Isaac chimed in. "We can come down to you if that's easier, or we can meet closer to us. I can make a reservation for tomorrow night, if that works. Will that be okay for the little one?"

"She's very young. Like a centerpiece on the table, no problem at all. But we should plan for something early," I said.

Isaac laughed. "Rebecca, we're in our eighties. The only time we eat is early. How about five?"

Carmen jumped back in, her voice full of joy. "Excellent! I'm so thrilled. Isaac will text you the restaurant."

"Me too," I said. "Me too."

Just as we were about to hang up, Carmen spoke again. "Do you know where he is? Is he still alive? Jordan, I mean. Is my son Jordan still alive?"

Hart looked down. I stared at him, but he wouldn't meet my eyes. After a long moment, he finally looked up and our eyes locked.

"Let's talk about that tomorrow. Yes, I think tomorrow is a good time to fill you in on all that," Hart said as he walked behind me, wrapped his arms around my back, and pressed his face into my neck.

PART XVIII

JACKSON MARTIN

London, England
2019: 18 Years After

CHAPTER 52

THERE IS NOTHING MORE VALUABLE THAN OUR CHILDREN

WHEN I CAME BACK TO consciousness, the seat had a sticky, slick feel of blood beneath my head. The T-shirt wrapped around it had completely soaked through. My first sight was the flashing lights and sirens of passing emergency vehicles, their glow reflecting off the Suburban's headliner. Through the glass passenger window at my feet, I saw dawn creeping over the horizon. I tried to sit up but couldn't. I closed my eyes again, anticipating the worst.

Ricardo and another man dragged me from the car and stood me on my feet. I looked toward the rear of the Suburban. She was lying there, lifeless, eyes wide open, two bullet holes visible in her vest.

"Is she dead?" I asked. Neither of them answered. Even in my semi-conscious state, I questioned the second round. This is the end, I thought. I closed my eyes and relaxed, relieved that at least she was gone.

"You're going to need money to pay this man, lots of it. If you're savable, this man will save you. Do you have a card you can give him?" Ricardo asked.

I nodded, blood still pouring onto the ground from the wound in my head.

"Then this is goodbye, Jordan," Ricardo said, leaving me leaning on the other man. He returned to the Suburban and drove out of the parking lot.

My place of repair was a strip mall surgery center. I had a wound that entered my back and exited beneath my arm. A second wound had scraped my skull on the right side of my face, just above my eye, leaving a nasty gash along the side of my head. That one had knocked me unconscious and caused the heavy bleeding. The surgeon closed both wounds, leaving scars on my back, forehead, and beneath the hairline on the right side of my head. I recuperated on excellent medication, for two weeks in a second-rate memory care center located thirty minutes outside Ocala. The day I left the center, I texted Hart to tell him I was okay. No soldier should carry the guilt of leaving a fallen comrade. That was my last contact with him.

The man who survived is not the same person. This one is slower, older. But I was still alive after Ocala, and I often thought about those last moments of consciousness. The only answer was that Ricardo had decided to retire from his career. The only way to do that was to retire Casandra.

I returned to London to finish closing the office. I phoned Esther and informed her of the proceeds. Her instructions were to donate her monies to the Great Ormond Street Hospital for Children in London. The gift was to be made anonymously.

She asked how things had gone with Liv. I told her the whole truth. There was silence on the other end of the line before she spoke.

"Oh, Jack, I am so sorry about that. You should come here. You should come here and stay with me. I will look after you."

I thought of the irony, a woman in her eighties offering to care for someone else.

"Thank you, Esther. I'll visit, but just to visit. The last thing you need is to care for a boy who will only bring you problems."

She laughed. "Jack, I'm going to hold you to your word. You must come see me, and soon. No one lives forever, you know."

"I promise."

I had a cashier's check drawn for the generous gift to the hospital. I phoned the Development Group and arranged to drop it off. Greeting me were the CEO, the CFO, and the Chief Development Officer. They asked if we could organize some sort of celebratory dinner. I explained that the donor was not one for such occasions. The act of making the gift was all they sought.

When we finished, I walked out of the hospital and into the coffee shop across the street. I placed my order for tea. Seated throughout the small venue were employees in scrubs and lab coats. I waited in queue for my drink. A young man stood in front of me, and they called his name.

"Abraham, large coffee with oat milk. Abraham?" the young woman behind the counter called out. The man received his coffee and turned around to face me. It was him.

Ibrahim Assad, reincarnated. The young man looked exactly like him. Of course, it wasn't him. He would be over sixty now, and this man was young. But this Abraham looked just like Ibrahim Assad. I stared. I couldn't take my eyes off him. He looked back at me.

"Excuse me, sir. May I help you?" he asked in a distinct British accent.

He made me aware that I was staring and blocking his path. "I'm sorry. It's just... I knew someone who looked exactly like you. His name was Ibrahim. Yours is Abraham. His last name was Assad. Perhaps you're related?" He shrugged. "I'm so sorry to bother you," I said.

"No worries. Have a good day," he said, then walked over to a woman who appeared to be his mother and whispered something to her. They both turned their heads to look at me. Her hair was black with gray streaks, tied in a ponytail. Her face was framed by large horn-rimmed glasses. Though not a young woman, she was certainly a beautiful one. Her son kissed her cheek and left the shop. As I walked past her, she stood and asked if I would join her for a moment.

The name embroidered in red on her white lab coat was Dr. Aaliyah Ash, Pediatric Surgeon.

"My son says you knew a man named Ibrahim. You said this man resembled him," she said nervously, folding her hands in her lap.

"It was a lifetime ago. I was working overseas, and there was a man I worked with named Ibrahim Assad. He looked very much like your son. Ash, Assad, a remarkable coincidence," I replied.

Her eyes seemed to grow larger. "Do you know what became of this man, Ibrahim?" she asked, looking down at her tea.

I thought for a moment, silently. The whole world knew what had happened to Ibrahim Assad. He became one of the infamous participants in the worst disaster in modern American history.

"I do," I said.

"Then you know no one should carry that burden. Especially not a child. And no man should learn such things from a newspaper. Wouldn't you agree?" she said, her eyes welling with tears.

It was impossible not to feel her pain. A thick air of silence settled between us.

"He wasn't always that man. There was much good in him. It isn't as simple as good or bad. Do you believe that?"

"I have good reason to. I knew him as a man who loved his God and loved his future wife. He loved you, Aaliyah," I said. She flinched at the sound of her name.

"I'm guessing you must be Jordan." I nodded. "Mr. Rome, did you get my letter?"

I smiled. "It was beautiful. I believe I still have it."

She looked out the window and down the street where her son had walked. "He doesn't know. Abraham doesn't know about his father. He was born here in London, after his father died. He knows he's dead but nothing more. He's a good boy and will make a fine man." I nodded again.

"Do you have children?" she asked.

"I do. A daughter."

"So you know the love a parent has for their child."

"I do, but we're not close. It's a complicated circumstance." We sat in silence again. I began to rise, but before I could, she interrupted my movement.

Aaliyah reached over and cupped my hand in both of hers. Our eyes met.

"Jordan, you can fix that. You must fix it, for her, more than for yourself. There's nothing more valuable than our children, and people aren't meant to be alone. I know you understand," she said, then smiled, squeezed my hand, and stood. As she turned to the door, I looked down and found her business card in my hand. I read the number before slipping it into my pocket.

I looked at my watch. It was 2:30. That meant 7:30 a.m. in Tucson. I dialed the phone and waited for an answer.

"Hart, this is Jordan... is Becca with you?"

www.ingramcontent.com/pod-product-compliance
Lightning Source LLC
Chambersburg PA
CBHW020418030726
47495CB00006B/1566